the

UNNATURAL

the

UNNATURAL

a novel

DAVID PRILL

St. Martin's Press • New York

THE UNNATURAL. Copyright © 1995 by David Prill. All rights reserved. Printed in the United States of America. No part of this book may be used or reproduced in any manner whatsoever without written permission except in the case of brief quotations embodied in critical articles or reviews. For information, address St. Martin's Press, 175 Fifth Avenue, New York, N.Y. 10010.

Production Editor: David Stanford Burr

Design: Junie Lee

Library of Congress Cataloging-in-Publication Data

Prill, David.
    The unnatural / David Prill.
        p.   cm.
    ISBN 0-312-11910-0 (hardcover)
    I. Title.
    PS3566.R568U56   1995
    813'.54—dc20   94-45090
                                                                CIP

First Edition: March 1995

10 9 8 7 6 5 4 3 2 1

This book is respectfully dedicated
to the
funeral directors of America.

about the record

In 1942 Janus P. Mordecai achieved immortality by embalming 1,215 victims of the Good War. This total, added to the 554 customers he had embalmed previously that year, gave him 1,769 for the season, breaking the old record of 1,616 set by Thomas H. Holmes in 1863 at the height of the Civil War. Although Holmes's record had been eclipsed, his legendary status in the annals of undertaking remained assured due to the fact that his work during the war marked the first widespread use of embalming, turning it into the publicly acceptable art form it is today and placing funeral directors into the advance guard of civilization. In more primitive times, loved ones had been preserved in so-called "corpse coolers" until burial.

Mordecai's status after he broke the record was less certain. In 1955—his glory days long since behind him—Mordecai was given his unconditional release by Sunnyside Funeral Homes. Although *Shroud* magazine reported that Mordecai had a substance abuse problem, Griff Grimes, award-winning journalist at *Embalmer's Weekly*, wrote the following in his column, "Behind the Headstones":

Yes, Janus Mordecai was bedeviled by the demon schnapps. Yet I believe his real problem lies much deeper. Here was a man who found spectacular success very early in his career. After breaking Holmes's record, what was he to do for an encore? Look at the record book. His productivity in the years following his record-breaking season declined steadily; this "sophomore jinx" turned into a shortened career. Of course, events conspired against him as well; world wars don't happen every day. The fact that he hung on so long is a tribute to the loyalty of P. T. Sunnyside. It's a sad story. We fear what the future holds for Janus Mordecai.

preface

There were many voices, many temptations at the first day of the Minnesota State Fair: The Bee Man, giving demonstrations six times daily behind a screened wall in the Horticulture Building, honey bees covering his hand like a mitten, his body jerking at the occasional sting; beauty queens in butter; Arlo, the world's biggest sow—enough to sidetrack most visitors, to cause them to forget the sights and shows they had marked in their souvenir programs.

One visitor, however, did not forget why he had come to the fair. One visitor was striding with single-minded purpose down Commonwealth Avenue through the heart of the fairgrounds in the breezy late August heat, his pale face stern and his dark eyes set straight ahead, clutching a small paper bag. He did not pause for cotton candy or the snake zoo or the wonders of Machinery Hill.

His name was Andy Archway. He was nine years old.

Andy lived on a farm near Golbyville in the southwestern corner of the state. He had talked his parents into coming to the fair on the very first day, then persuaded them to let him run off as soon as they entered the gates. Actually, Dad didn't go for much of it. Oh, Machinery Hill was fine, and the Sheep Barn had its good points, he would say, but the rest was a load of humbug. He didn't think much of Andy's hobby, either. So Andy won over his mom first, then they double-teamed Pop.

Now Andy saw the ornate arch leading into the Midway. People in straw hats lugging shopping bags jammed the street. Andy dodged around them. A natural-gas-fueled train carrying weary fairgoers rounded the corner, clanging its bell, and Andy leaped out to beat it across the avenue.

"Watch it, kid!"

He felt hot metal brush his flank, but he did not look back. He hurried his pace, almost running past the Tilt-a-Whirl, the Haunt of Fear, Over and Under the Sea.

Then he heard the barker.

". . . breaking the old record of 1,616 set by Mr. Thomas Holmes in 1863! He has handled more *dead bodies* than any human alive on the face of the earth! He knows *death* by name! See him embalm an *actual corpse* before your very eyes! Secrets *never before* revealed!"

Andy had made it. He passed by a curtain of lurid paintings, showing a tattooed woman with tiny words spiraling over her skin, a glass case with a giant red question mark in its center and . . . was it him? Sure didn't look like him. The third painting showed a man in a long black coat inserting tubes into a naked, bluish, eye-bulging body, with blood streaming onto the floor.

". . . most incredible!" continued the barker, a man with an egg-shell head, wearing a black vest with gold buttons and waving a cane. "What is it? Where did it come from? It's all a mystery, my friends! But I guarantee you will be astounded and frightened by this amazing display of nature! We call it the *THING!*

"Three unique exhibits for the price of one! All witnessed by the crowned princes of Europe! All for the very modest sum of fifty cents! Step up, my friends, step up!"

Andy was not sure who the man was talking to, since there was no one else around. He dug into his pocket for the money his pop had given him and stepped up. The barker lit a cigarette and blew a smoke ring that looked like a ghost.

"Here's my fifty cents," said Andy, holding it up for the man to take.

"Beat it, kid," the barker said, not looking at him. "This show is strictly for grown-ups. Naked girls, gore—not for you. There's a nice merry-go-round right back where you came into the Midway. Try us again when you're sixteen."

"Mordecai. I want to see Mordecai."

The barker looked at Andy for a moment, watery eyes squinting. "What does a squirt like you know about Mordecai?"

"He broke Holmes's record in 'forty-two. Gosh, everybody knows that, mister. He's the greatest ever." Andy removed his beat-up old copy of *Embalmer's Weekly* from the bag, the special issue featuring Mordecai on the cover, and showed it to the barker. "I want his autograph."

The barker snorted a laugh, then leaned over his stand and said, "Look kid, Mordecai is pretty, uh, sick these days. He . . ."

"Please."

"I can get in big trouble letting you in, you know. The cops . . ."

"I'll tell them I snuck in. I promise."

The barker scratched his ear, quickly scanned the area, then held out his hand, palm up.

"Fifty cents. Don't sit in a chair. Stay in the back corner in the shadows. If you see someone who looks like a cop, under the flaps you go and never come around here again. If you get me into trouble, don't worry about finding a career, you'll be the show's fourth attraction: the headless boy. Now get out of sight." The man grabbed the coins, and Andy scooted between the tent flaps.

Only a handful of people, three older teenage boys and a pair of sunburned men in overalls, had paid their way in and were seated on wooden folding chairs, their red paint chipped and faded. Andy crouched in the back corner, setting his sacred magazine close by, digging his sneakers in the dirt, trying to be patient.

Finally the barker appeared on the small stage, which was dimly lit by a string of bare light bulbs that swayed slightly as the wind buffeted the tent.

"Ladies and gentlemen," the barker began. He smiled. "Or should I say, gentlemen. You are about to witness three of the most amazing and educational exhibits ever presented at any exposition in this country. The beautiful, the unusual, the mysterious. Something for every taste. Now, I present to you, for the first time on this continent . . . the Amazing Margo, the Woman Whose Body Is a Book!"

From behind the curtains came a large woman with a blonde ponytail, wearing glasses and little else. She stepped to the front of the stage and began dancing, moving slowly, as tiny classical music came over the loudspeaker.

Her nakedness fascinated Andy. *I wonder how much embalming fluid it would take to fill 'er up?* he thought.

"What perverse desire caused this woman to disfigure her body so? But no, perhaps this is not disfigurement but art! For you see, my friends, she had Shakespeare's *Hamlet* in its entirety burned into her skin by a world-renowned tattoo artist. Why? Was it love or insanity? You *are* familiar with *Hamlet,* are you not? *To be or not to be,* and so forth? You there." The barker pointed at one of the farmers. "You seem to be amused by this, and perhaps skeptical. Please step onto the stage."

The man shook his head, laughing. "Naw, she looks like too much of a woman for me."

"Go on, chickenshit," said his friend, dragging him out of his chair.

The barker grabbed the man by his elbow and led him onto the stage beside the tattooed woman, who was still swaying to the music. Taking the man's hand, he guided the index finger to a spot on the woman's body just below her shoulder blades.

"Read, please, starting here."

"Uh, sure, uh, 'how all, er, occasions do inform against me and sp' . . . hey, get her to stand still! . . . uh, 'spur my dull revenge! What is a man, if his, uh, chief good and market of his time, uh, be but to, uh, sleep and feed.' "

"Thank you, my friend. You may be seated. That was from Act four, Scene four. You can look it . . ."

Suddenly a look of panic crossed the barker's face. He seemed to be staring at something. Andy followed his gaze to the back of the tent, where a husky man with a badge stood, hands on hips. "Nude dancing again, eh? I thought we straightened this out last year, Benny."

"It's not nude dancing, it's art!" protested the Amazing Margo.

The barker shot Andy a glance, but it was not necessary. At that moment he was scrambling underneath the tent. Once outside, he picked himself up and headed around to the front of the tent; then, seeing the flaps open and a large black boot step outside, he turned back and raced down the dusty corridor between the tent and a long trailer into the area behind the Midway.

Andy dashed between another set of smaller trailers, hooking around the corner and dropping down by the trailer steps. Breathing hard, he suddenly realized that he had left his copy of *Embalmer's Weekly* in the tent. Gosh. He knew he could not go back in there, and he feared that the barker would be less than friendly after his brush with the law.

Andy hung his head. Just when things were going so well . . .

The trailer door creaked open and a large shadow fell over Andy.

"This is no place for you to be, little stranger."

Andy slowly lifted his head. He held his hand in front of his eyes to block the sun, but could not see the man's face. *Little stranger.* He remembered reading about the term "little stranger" in one of the magazines. Was it in *Progression?* Parents in early America called their children that because kids often died very young and it was painful to become too attached to them.

That could mean only one thing . . .

"I know you."

The man raised a bottle to his mouth, gulped down a mouthful, and coughed painfully.

"You're Mordecai."

"What do you want, little stranger? I'm running a little late." He did a slow, haggard tap dance with one foot, as if it took great effort, then coughed again and laughed. "It's almost show time."

Andy hesitated. He had wanted his hero's autograph, but now the magazine was in the tent and he had nothing else for him to sign.

"I—I—"

"Gotta get going." The man weaved around Andy, heading toward the tent.

"I'm going to break your record!" Andy blurted out.

The man looked back, nodded, and said, "The way the world's going, little stranger, I shan't be surprised."

THE BIRD DOG

one

IT WAS A great day for a funeral.

Wallace "Wake" Wakefield tooled into the parking lot at Carrots Funeral Home in Houdin, Minnesota, population 2,257, early on a July afternoon. He was bird-dogging a hot prospect, name Dan Slade, a real stud according to Wake's contact down at the filling station. A follow-up call to the director confirmed the report.

A sense of excitement jumped through Wake as he grabbed his notebook and headed up the steps to the home. Behind those doors could be the next Tom Holmes. Or a real dead body. You just never knew. This feeling of anticipation, of the possibilities, was what had kept Wake going the past three-plus decades, made up for all the bad meals and crummy motels.

Putting on his best visitation face, Wake smoothed back his thinning gray hair, stuck his notebook in the back pocket of his corduroys, and stepped inside.

My good friend has died, Wake thought, as he entered the visitation room. How very sad for the family, he mused, walking reverently, head bowed, up to the casket. Sure was a swell guy, he contemplated, and at the same time expertly surveyed the boy's work, lingering perhaps a little too long, gazing at the corpse a little too carefully.

A slight frown creased the corners of Wake's mouth. Goddammit, he thought.

Wake broke off and sat down at the back of the room. He pulled out his notebook and began filling in the boxes and making check marks on a piece of paper that had the words SCOUTING FORM at the top.

Name: Dan Slade. Location: Carrots Funeral Home, Houdin. He skipped down to the grading area. Complexion: 3. Dress: 2. Placement of body: 2. Placement of hands: 1.

To the amateur, the corpse no doubt appeared to be in tip-top shape. But to the trained eye of a veteran scout like Wake Wakefield, it was an entirely different memory picture. Take hand placement, for instance, that underrated yet vital category. Now, everybody knows that the hands should be cupped slightly, using standard rubber positioning blocks, giving the appearance that the corpse had just laid down for a nap. But the hands on this fellow were flat on his stomach, as if he had just eaten a chili pepper. Not natural at all. Amateur stuff. No sense of the art whatsoever.

And the clothes! The boy had dressed the corpse in a suit so big that it looked like he expected him to gain weight.

Terrible body placement, too. Much too low. You had to strike a delicate balance. Too upright and it was a little frightening, as if the corpse was ready to climb out of the casket and join the party. Too low and he looked overly dead, not with the bereaved at all. Too low and the bereaved almost felt like they were intruding on the dead's personal space, like voyeurs. The corpse must have a welcoming posture, a posture that is neither threatening nor reserved. The corpse must try to be a good host.

In the comments section on the scouting form, Wake simply wrote, *"Forget it!"*

Wake completed the form, signed and dated it, and stuck the notebook back into his pocket. Have to make nice with the director, he thought glumly, even though he doesn't know talent from a hole in the ground. Never know, he might come up with something worthwhile someday. Wake got up and left the visitation room.

❈   ❈   ❈

"... rough around the edges, but with a few more years experience, he could be a very respectable member of the profession."

"Danny's just an intern, you understand," said Mr. Carrots. "I see some real potential in the lad. Comes from a fine family. Very well respected in the community." He grinned. "May be a future Sunnysider, eh?"

"You never know," Wake replied with as much noncommittal inflection as he could muster.

"Why, there he is now. Come in, Danny, there's someone I want you to meet."

The boy who came into the office surprised Wake. Judging by his work, Wake expected Slade to be a dead body, a real lounge embalmer. But no, this tanned kid with the slick black hair and muscular build did have an impressive personal bearing.

Without waiting for introductions, Slade came over and gave Wake a knuckle-cracking handshake. "Mr. Wakefield, it is a genuine pleasure to meet you. I've admired your work for many years." He reached into the vest pocket of his European-cut suit. "Here's my card. Let's do lunch sometime."

Correction, Wake thought dourly, an ass-kisser with no talent. *Management* type.

"I was telling Mr. Wakefield that you are interning with us this summer," said Mr. Carrots.

"Where are you going to school, kid?"

"Holmes U. My parents wanted to send me to a private embalming school, but I wanted to get the real college experience, not be locked away in some ivory vault. That's why I'm interning at Houdin. I have always believed in the community funeral home. I believe it takes planning and awareness of the community in order to serve the town with all the local funeral-related services, something the big funeral homes cannot provide with their vast coverage area. I have always believed that the community funeral home is in partnership with the community that it serves. It's local people informing you who's recently passed on. It's community funeral directing."

"Interesting." What a load of gibberish, Wake thought, giving the exit a longing glance.

"Say, do you have any job openings?"

"Well, not on the community level. It's not really our area of interest."

Slade grinned. "I'm flexible."

"Why don't you finish school first, then send us a resume."

"Things are really going well here," said Slade. "We're burying Strum and Dang Funeral Home. We stole that guy in there from them, almost right off the slab."

"Local competitor," Mr. Carrots chimed in.

Wake said, "Yes, I'm familiar with them." He glanced at his watch. "Well, gentlemen, I need to run. I have an appointment in Bald Lake at four. Thank you, Mr. Carrots . . . Mr. Slade."

Management type, Wake thought as he pulled out of the funeral home. Lord help me if I ever have to work for someone like him.

two

ON HIS WAY out of Houdin, Wake gobbled down a piece of meat loaf at the Anytime Café. Now running very late, Wake took off down gravel county roads to make up lost time. It was part of his job to know all the back roads and interstates and where the funeral homes were located. But when he reached Seven-Mile Corner he stopped, debated for a moment, then took a left instead of a right. After a few more miles and a few more uncertain turns he realized he was in unfamiliar territory. All the farms, all the crops merged into an indistinguishable mass. The dusty road shimmered in the heat. He thought: I'm long gone lost.

So Wake decided to try to retrace his steps. He slowed as he reached the next driveway, planning to turn around. Then he saw the sign at the head of the driveway. It was a hand-carved American flag, painted the usual colors, but instead of a field of stars there was the following advertisement: EGGS — SHEEP SHEARING — EMBALMING.

A full-service stop, Wake thought with a grin. Odds were that this was just a sign leftover from a bygone era. Home embalming went out with corpse coolers. But you never knew. It was every scout's ultimate dream, a once-in-a-lifetime vision, to discover that "embalmer behind the barn." The raw-boned, talented natural unseen by any other scout. This was becoming a rare event in this modern era of the funeral business. Everything these days was so regimented, so high tech, so predictable. Youngsters were shunted into youth embalming programs almost as soon as they could say the words "injection pump." From then on, they were studied keenly by parents, scouts, and funeral directors. Certainly, the modern embalmer was arriving at school better trained and better equipped than his predecessor, but what was lost in the process? Sometimes kids just needed to go out in the backyard and play with the trocar without any adult supervision. That way, they learned to be creative and think on their own. They learned the *joy* of the funeral business, the thrill of the corpse.

Wake drove down the long driveway and circled the farmyard. There did not appear to be anyone around, so he parked by the barn and got out. An orange tabby cat raced into a hole in the corner of the barn. Wake heard a crashing noise coming from out in the grove behind the chicken coop, so he headed over there.

Stepping through the tall weeds and over a circle of rusty barbed wire, Wake found a young man rummaging through a junk pile. The boy had disheveled black hair and horn-rimmed glasses. He was wearing a black T-shirt, work gloves, a pair of olive Bermuda shorts, black socks, and sandals.

"Excuse me," said Wake. "I was trying to get to Bald Lake and got lost. I was wondering if you could get me on the right track."

"You're a long way off," the fellow said, continuing to dig through the pile. He picked out an old alarm clock, inspected it on all sides, then tossed it high up onto the pile where it shattered a bottle.

"Ever been to Bald Lake?" Wake asked him. "The fishing there is amazing. I caught a northern there once the size of Duluth. Great little cafe right on the lake, too. Mexican place. Serves the best enchiladas in the county."

"I don't travel much. Why don't you ask my pop how to get there. He's probably in the barn."

"Thanks, I'll do that." Wake turned to leave, then paused. "Say, I've got plenty of eggs, and don't own any sheep, uh . . . who does the embalming around here? Did your grandfather used to be in the business?"

"I've done some," said the young man, standing up. He slapped at a mosquito on his leg. "Look, mister, I'm really busy. My pop would be glad to help you out. If you can't find him in the barn, my mom is down in the garden by the hog house. Okay?"

"What's your favorite drainage point?"

The fellow stared at him, then said, quietly, "Jugular vein."

"What do you do with the mouth?"

"Sew it up."

"What kind of embalming fluid do you use?"

"My own recipe. I sort of do these color effects."

Wake stepped forward and extended his hand. "My name is Wallace Wakefield. I'm a scout for P. T. Sunnyside Funeral Center. I'd like to see your setup."

The boy shook his hand, staring at him in disbelief. "You're *Wake Wakefield?*"

"You know me?"

"Gosh, yes. I mean, you discovered Mordecai!"

"Boy, that was a few brain cells ago. You follow this stuff pretty closely, then."

"Yes, oh yes. Gosh, I'm sorry I didn't recognize you, Mr. Wakefield. I've just been so busy with Uncle Ned."

"What's your name, son?"

"Andy Archway."

"What are you looking for in all this junk?"

Andy smiled. He snatched up a canvas bag propped up against a nearby tree and said, "Come on, I'll show you."

Wake followed the boy through the grove to a derelict dirt-floor garage. Inside were shelves lined with muddy, multicolored bottles and a variety of ancient-looking surgical instruments, a plank resting on a pair of oil drums, a stack of sheets, several buckets, and a can of bug spray. At the back of the garage was a small area that had been shielded by a shower curtain. Andy set the bag down carefully by the curtain and raised his hands, shrugging. "Well, this is it."

Nodding, Wake strolled through the garage, running a finger along the plank, inspecting a jury-rigged trocar, holding the bottles up to the light. "Very interesting." He gestured at the row of bottles. "How do you get the colors?"

"It's food dye."

"I see. But what's wrong with flesh color?"

"Nothing, I guess. I just like to experiment. Take Uncle Ned, here." Andy tugged the shower curtain aside.

Wake stood there stunned for a moment. He searched for the words, and all he could come up with was "funeral diorama." It was the damndest thing he'd ever seen. "Uncle Ned" was fishing among the clouds. He sat reclined in a motor boat, hands locked behind his head, fishing pole on his lap, a very peaceful smile on his sewn mouth. He was dressed in a T-shirt that read GONE FISHIN', along with swimming trunks and beach thongs. The clouds appeared to be made out of cotton matting. Hovering in the clouds was a baby doll dressed like an angel, complete with wings and halo.

"See, he's been sitting out in the sun, and Ned always sunburned easily, so he's red like he's sunburned, see?"

"That makes sense."

"You have to stay away from blues. They showed us a movie in health class once about a guy who got electrocuted and went unconscious. He turned blue. I don't want anybody to look like that."

"So Ned liked to fish, I take it."

"Yeah, he loved to fish. Didn't like to clean them, though. That's why I show him not trying too hard to catch anything. I think he liked being out on the water more than anything." Andy knelt down and opened the bag, removing a big red-and-white bobber and a beer can. Fingering the bobber, he said, "It feels like it's cracked. I can use it, though." He attached it to the line, then sunk it into a cotton cloud. "What do you think about the beer can?"

"Uh, I'm afraid you've put me at a loss, Andy. How did he die?"

"Heart attack at fifty, just like his pop. You know, he raised three kid sisters all by himself? A good ol' guy, that Ned." He set the can on the boat seat beside Ned, then stood back, tilting his head from side to side. He sighed. "Not an easy call," he said deliberately. "Guess I'll sleep on it. You know, it's these little touches that make or break you."

"So what are you doing now?" Wake asked. "Have you finished high school?"

"Just graduated last month."

"Have you ever thought about doing this type of thing professionally?"

The kid's voice dropped low. "I don't know . . ."

Wake moved in front of him, not saying a word until the boy raised his head. "Let me tell it to you straight, kid. You're the oddest duck I've come across in my thirty-odd years in the scouting game. This diorama shit, this designer embalming fluid shit won't fly in the world, not yet anyway, but it shows you've got real imagination. And you've already got the basics down. The business, the art, will wither if it doesn't keep moving forward. Some of us were put here to do business as usual, and others were put here to take the next step, to advance the art. You can be that person if you don't lose yourself and let someone bully you to their way of thinking. But the question is, kid, you're doing this for someone you care about, your uncle. Can you put the same devotion into a stranger?"

Andy looked puzzled, then said, "I'm sorry, Mr. Wakefield, I didn't mean to confuse you."

"What do you mean?"

The kid pointed at the body in the boat. "He's not *my* uncle."

        ❖   ❖   ❖

Wake had Andy round up his parents, and while he was waiting he tried to devise his signing strategy, even though his brain was bouncing off its container. Stick to the basics. Pay special attention to the mother, reassure her; it means losing her boy, after all. Let them know who you are and who you've signed in the past. Tone down the enthusiasm, don't want to break the bank here. Maybe he just looked good after seeing that Slade punk. Maybe I'm losing my instincts, Wake thought. It's not supposed to happen like this. It's been so long. Was Mordecai like this? Was anyone ever like this?

Shortly, Andy returned with his folks. Mrs. Archway looked fit and outgoing, her gray-threaded black hair tied up like a sweet roll. Her husband was a short man in a straw hat who looked like he had better things to do.

After the introductions, Wake began his spiel. "Your son has real talent," he began. "Unique talent. I've worked with a lot of outstanding individuals in my time, many of them from good homes just like yours, people like John J. Fallingwater, Tris Tine, Galvin Blockmore—I imagine you've heard of them. No? Well, believe me they were, and are, all highly respected professionals who have established very distinguished careers for themselves. The funeral business isn't what it used to be in our youth. It's one of the most vital callings of humanity."

"Can Andrew stay at home and do this?" asked Mrs. Archway.

"I'm afraid not, ma'am. But we're a family-oriented organization, and we make sure our kids are well taken care of, both in school and when they join our organization. For example, every incoming student is assigned an upperclassman to act as a 'buddy.' We also demand our kids get home at least once a month. You have to care about people to be in this business. That's why I got into this profession in the first place. I grew up on a farm much like this one outside a little town named Atlantis, South Dakota. It's in the Black Hills. Every summer I helped cart out the bodies of tourists who got lost in the Mystery Spot. It gave me an early lesson in how crucial proper treatment of the deceased can be."

"How much will this cost us?" Mr. Archway asked, wiping his nose with a red kerchief.

"Cost you? Cost *you?*" Wake grinned. "Why, sir, it will not cost you a dime. In fact, we will *pay* your son to sign with us."

"How much?"

"I'm sure we can work that out later."

"Nope. Nothing will be signed until we agree on a figure."

"Now, Herman, don't be hardheaded."

Wake shot a look at Andy; he looked a little rattled. "That's quite all right, ma'am. Your mate is a good horse trader. I agree to your terms."

"Where would he go to school?"

"Thomas Holmes University of Embalming and Funerary Practices. It's up in the Cities, not far at all. It's a two-year program, including a fully paid internship in the summer. By the time your son graduates and receives his certificate he will be qualified to practice his profession anywhere in the country."

Mr. Archway nodded, more in a gesture of understanding than agreement. "Well, nothing is going to be decided today," he said. "Do you have any literature on your outfit? And a sample contract?"

"Sure do." Wake got them a packet of information from his trunk, thanked them for their time, and departed, whispering to Andy as they passed each other, "You're gonna be great, kid. I'll be in touch." Wake proceeded directly to the Linger Longer Motor Hotel in Golbyville, paid for a week's stay, and placed a call to Sunnyside headquarters in Rancho Norman Rockwell, California.

"This is Wake calling, Elsie. Is the big fella in? Well, when he gets back tell him I'm going to be in Golbyville, Minnesota, for the next few days. I'll give you the number in a minute. Tell him . . . wait a sec, be right back." Wake held the receiver against his chest and listened. Footsteps scraping across the gravel, just outside his room. Probably the housekeeper. A low cough, definitely male. Wake set down the phone on the bed and slipped stealthily over to the window. He nudged up a section of the Venetian blind with his index finger.

Shit. It was that overweight chucklehead with pop-bottle eyeglasses, Bing Daniels, superscout for Sunnyside's biggest rival, the Drabford brothers, those goddamn midgets. In his excitement, Wake had forgotten one of scouting's basic rules: Never leave your car sitting in full view in a motel parking lot. If another scout sees it, he knows you're birddogging a prospect in the vicinity. And if someone asks at the desk how long my good buddy Wake Wakefield is going to be in town, my best friend whom I haven't seen in fifteen years, and the clerk says he's checked in for a week, then the enemy knows something big is up. Wake knew the scam; in fact was pretty sure he invented it.

Wake moved back to the phone and said softly, "Gotta run, Else. Call you back later." Popping open his suitcase, Wake crammed his belongings inside and went into the bathroom, locking the door behind him. Gettin' too old for this, the old scout thought as he propped up the small window over the toilet. He fiddled with the screen catch for a moment, yanked it up. His suitcase went out the window, then he climbed up on the pot and awkwardly forced his body out. Landing with a bump, Wake searched for an escape route. A stand of birch trees lined the back of the motel's property, cornfields beyond.

A pounding came from inside, followed by a hoarse voice yelling, "Open up, Wakefield, I know you're in there! Who's the boy, Wake? Don't worry, ol' Bing won't tell a soul. Come on, pal, give me a fair shot, it's the American way!"

Wake started running. He puffed along, and when he reached the birches a voice cried out, "There you are!" Wake pulled up, his chest heaving, and looked back. Daniels was trotting toward him. Wake waved and smiled, friendlylike, as if he was going to wait for him, but when Daniels slowed to a walk, Wake turned abruptly and dashed into the corn.

Knowing he would not be able to stay ahead of the younger man for very long, Wake ran in about a dozen rows, the rough stalks scraping his face, tripping over clods of dirt, then broke off and headed to his left, going directly parallel to the motel's property line. When he heard a crunching noise as his rival reached the field, Wake pulled up and waited.

After a minute or so Wake carefully trod back toward the daylight. He came out of the field at the edge of the motel parking lot. Quickly, he hopped into his car and took off. That was too close, he thought. Have to get this boy wrapped up in a hurry.

So Wake slept in his station wagon that night, parked behind an abandoned schoolhouse, and returned to the Archway farm in the morning. I'll get him for $40,000, no less, no more, he told himself.

As he came down the driveway, Mrs. Archway, who was hosing down the sidewalk, peered at him, then smiled warmly and waved. He parked at the bottom of the sidewalk and got out of the car. "Morning, ma'am," he said jovially. "Hope I haven't come at a bad time. I planned to call ahead, but things got sort of, uh, hectic at the last minute." Fine drops of water spattered Wake's cheeks.

"That's quite all right," she replied, turning the nozzle to stop the flow of water. "Andy and his dad aren't here right now. They went into town to pick up some feed. Should be back before too long, though. You're welcome to stay for coffee."

"It'd be a pleasure."

Over a load of special Lewisville Blend java at her polka-dot bovine-deco table, Mrs. Archway exchanged a few pleasantries with Wake before the conversation shifted to Andy. "Did you folks get a chance to talk about my offer last night?" Wake asked.

"Yes, we did. I know this is something Andy really wants. His father isn't so sure, I'm afraid."

"What's the problem?"

"Oh, I don't know."

"Has anyone else been here to talk to you about this?"

"Oh, no, it's just that it's something new, and we were hoping Andy would take over the farm from us someday. But the boy has absolutely no knack for farming. He doesn't know the difference between silk balling and yellow hopperburn. You would think he would have inherited some of those genes from us, but I guess God gave him gifts in other areas."

"He is very gifted, Mrs. Archway. With the right guidance he could be a big star someday. Tell me, how did he ever get involved in embalming? Was it in the family?"

She sipped her coffee. "You know, I was thinking about that after you left yesterday, and I really haven't been able to figure it out. We certainly never encouraged him, although we have tried to be supportive. He was just born that way, I guess. It's all he talks about anymore. Did he show you his shed?"

"Yes. His equipment is crude, but he seems to be very resourceful. He could do wonders with . . ."

"No, no," she broke in. "I don't mean his workshop, I mean his *collection*."

"His collection?"

"You won't believe it."

They went out back by the grove to a small shed, which appeared to be a brooder house for chicks, that was nestled between a snow fence and a box elder tree. Mrs. Archway lifted the latch and swung open the door. A musty odor poured forth.

Holy horse-drawn hearse, Wake thought, stepping up into the doorway. Magazines, pamphlets, prints, and books were stacked on shelves and piled waist-high on the floor. Early copies of the *Western Undertaker, Shroud, Progression, Embalmer's Weekly*. Even pulp magazines like *Undisturbed* and *Respectful Casket Tales*. Rolled-up posters were piled like cordwood in the corners. There were photographs, newspapers, trinkets. The image of Mordecai was everywhere. It was by far the largest collection of funeral-related material he had ever seen. It was a shrine.

So this is where the kid learned his licks, Wake mused. A self-taught embalmer, how absolutely perfect. This burned away any lingering doubt Wake had concerning the kid's dedication to the art. Wait till P.T. hears about this one.

"He used to keep the stuff in the house," Mrs. Archway said, "but his room got too full and those old magazines smelled so bad that I didn't want them all over the the place."

"You're a fine woman, Mrs. Archway," Wake told her as he stepped down and she latched the door again. "My mother threw out all my old embalming magazines when I went away to school."

On the way back to the house an old green four-door

sedan circled the farmyard, pulling into the garage between the corn crib and granary. "There they are now," Mrs. Archway said. She headed down to the sidewalk, Wake trailing, and waited there for the pair to approach.

Before Wake had a chance to say anything, Mr. Archway looked squarely at him and said, "I've had a talk with my boy. Let's get down to business." He told the missus and Andy to stay outside, then led Wake into the house, pulling out a chair for him at the kitchen table.

As negotiations began, the scout laid back, allowing Mr. Archway to take an aggressive lead. Wake now listened to a recitation of all of Andrew's fine qualities, was told that they would be making a great sacrifice by allowing their only son to leave, and was reminded of his own phrase from the day before, "unique talent."

Wake nodded throughout all this, then removed a pad and black felt tip pen from his pocket. He began writing a number using big figures with curlicues, and held it up to Mr. Archway.

He shook his head. "I talked to the funeral director when we were in town. Thirty thousand dollars is the average figure for rookies, not for someone with"—and here he drew out the words—"unique talent."

"Can I use your phone?"

"Sure."

Wake went over to the phone on the far wall of the kitchen, pulled out a card from his wallet, punched in a seven-digit number, and waited.

"When you're in Rancho Norman Rockwell, be sure to stop in at Six Flags Over Rover, the world's only amusement park for..."

"Mr. Sunnyside, Wallace Wakefield here, sir. Fine, sir. How are you? Good."

"Open only on federal holidays or other days the postman is off..."

"It's the Andrew Archway signing, sir. We've run into a

snag in negotiations. I'd like permission to increase our offer. I know, sir, but he's really a top-notch kid. I don't think we should let him get away . . ."

"The time is 7:33 A.M. The temperature is ninety-nine."

Now Wake looked back over his shoulder at Mr. Archway and whispered, "I think he'll let me go to $40,000. Is that acceptable?" The father nodded approvingly. "My guess is that it will take $40,000," Wake said. "His father is handling the negotiations and he's really taking me to the preparation room."

"When you're in Rancho Norman Rockwell . . ."

"Yes?" Wake grinned at Mr. Archway, giving him the A-OK sign. "Thank you, sir. Thank you very much. Yes, indeed. Good-bye, sir."

Locked up, Wake thought with relief as he hung up the phone. Mother and son returned and were told the news. Andy hopped involuntarily, while Mrs. Archway embraced him, saying, "Oh, Andy, I'm so proud of you." After they signed the contract, Wake looped his arms around both of them and beamed. "This is the best decision you'll ever make in your life," he said. "There's grand adventure waiting for you out there, son. We'll be behind you every step of the way, you can count on it. Just make sure you report to school by August 28. We'll be sending out a letter reminding you of that fact, plus all the essentials you'll need to know before embarking on your college career." He shook the boy's hand. "Mordecai would be proud of you, son."

Andy smiled self-consciously. "Gosh, Mr. Wakefield, this is so neat. I promise I'll try my best."

"Just be yourself, bud. Just be yourself."

Wake left the Archways in their happiness. He bounded to his car and zoomed off, whistling that old favorite, "Song of the Coffin Drummer."

Passing through Golbyville's main drag, Wake met Bing Daniels coming in the opposite direction. Wake pounded on his horn and stuck the contract out the window, waving it maniacally and hooting.

"Take that, you chucklehead!" he roared and sped out of town.

COLLEGE DAYS

three

IT HAD BEEN a long, glum bus trip up from Golbyville for Andy. He had been so excited the week before he left, trying to decide which copies of *Shroud* to bring and how many bottles of his home-brewed embalming fluid to pack. But once he stepped onto the bus outside Prone's Bible and Bait Shop and waved good-bye to his folks through the dirty bus window, he felt a great big hole inside, like someone had shoved a trocar into his abdomen and pumped out all his entrails. He had never really been away from home before, apart from the summer several years ago when he went to embalming camp. And then he had gotten homesick after the second day and called his parents to take him home. So that didn't really count. This time, though, he was older and determined to stick it out no matter what happened.

His expectations almost made him dizzy. *The Thomas Holmes University of Embalming and Funerary Practices.* Think of it! The words spun through his mind like honey. Giants must roam the campus. Geniuses. All the wisdom and truth in that place must give off a glow at night that could be seen for miles around. Hallowed halls, nothing—those must be heavenly halls.

As the bus wheezed to a stop outside the gates of Holmes U, Andy gaped in awe at what he saw. The stately white buildings were more beautiful, more immense than he ever imagined. What great things were occurring behind those walls? The lawns were greener than any cemetery could be, and it was not just the tinted bus window. And there, just beyond the entrance, stood a huge statue. Could it be?

"C'mon, buddy, this is the end of the line. Get your stuff off."

"Uh, right." Andy pulled out his canvas pack from under his seat and moved to the front of the now-empty bus. He stepped down into the sunshine, stretching his cramped back. Taking his duffel bag and beat-up suitcase from the driver, he stood on the sidewalk, grinning. Then he slung his duffel bag over his shoulder, grabbed his suitcase, and headed directly to the statue.

It was him, all right. Thomas Holmes himself, as big as a barn. Andy craned his neck at the figure, who stood regally, head held high, left hand on his hip, right hand raising a bottle of embalming fluid to the heavens. Andy bent down and read the plaque: THOMAS H. HOLMES, 1810–1870, PIONEER EMBALMER, SAGE, POET. Andy wiped away a tear. Someday they'll erect a statue to Mordecai, he thought.

Andy found the main office without too much trouble, having studied the campus map every night since it arrived back home. He picked up his room key and started for dorm row. The letter said he was staying in Inominata Hall, room 121. Walking down the shady sidewalk, he clicked off the names in his head. Lychwake. Upholder. There it is. Inominata.

Going down the hallway to his room, Andy passed another student, a dark-haired fellow swinging a tennis racket at phantom balls. "Hiya, pal," said the stranger.

"Hi!" Andy said happily. He fumbled with the key in the lock, and pushed open the door. A perfumed scent washed over him. He stayed on the threshold for a moment, just taking in what was going to be his home for the next two years. Tiny bed. Orange plastic chair. One shelf. The desk was mostly hidden by a floral tribute: daffodils and carnations, even a rose or two. How thoughtful, Andy said to himself.

"Say, pal, are you in room one-twenty-one?" came a voice from the other end of the hall.

Andy turned. The stranger again. "Yes, I am."

"You wouldn't happen to be Andy Archway, would you?"

"That's me."

The fellow sauntered down the hallway. "I've been waiting for you," he said brightly. He gave Andy a rock-hard handshake and said ceremoniously, "In keeping with a long-standing tradition here at the Thomas H. Holmes University of Embalming and Funerary Practices, every incoming student is assigned a 'buddy,' an older, more experienced student, to help guide him through the sometimes difficult road that is college life. As part of that tradition, the university has assigned me the honor of being your official buddy."

"Oh, yes, I remember reading about that. I didn't catch your name, though."

"Daniel J. Slade." He slung a chummy arm around Andy's shoulder. "We're going to be spending a great deal of time together over the next year, Andrew."

✳ ✳ ✳

Going to his first day of classes the following morning, Andy was glad to know that he had already made a friend. An official friend, but a friend nonetheless. Truth be told, Andy found a great deal to admire and even envy in Slade; he wished he could be so outgoing, so quick on his feet, so popular. Fortunately, the upperclassman had promised to take Andy under his big, outgoing, popular wing and straighten him out. Slade had even hinted that he would try to dig up some girls for them, no easy trick at an institution top-heavy with males. Andy nervously told him not to go to any trouble, but the possibilities still intrigued him.

So Andy was feeling pretty good, not hardly homesick at all, as he found a seat in the classroom on the third floor of Blockmore Hall, site of his first class of the day, Consolation Literature 101. Before long the room filled up, the bell trilled, and a red-haired woman wearing wire-rimmed glasses and a fringed black dress walked through the doorway at the front of the room. She placed a sheaf of papers and a book on a small open space on the desk, which was otherwise inundated by a variety of fragrant and colorful flowers.

How thoughtful, Andy said to himself. He opened his black spiral notebook and held his pen poised, ready to write.

"Good morning," she said. "This is Consolation Literature 101. My name is Professor Emma Budge. Check your schedules if this doesn't sound correct to you. It's the first day, so there's bound to be some confusion for both you and me."

Andy was sure he was in the right place. He had memorized his schedule all last week, then to make double-certain, he had looked at it again when he got out of bed this morning and once more when he was coming down the hall five minutes ago.

"Now," she continued, "what is consolation literature? Well, as your syllabus states, consolation literature is literally that literature whose purpose is to comfort the bereaved. This would include actual mourners' manuals, prayer manuals, poetry, hymns, fiction, and biographies. This is genre writing, much like westerns or science fiction, so the writing is generally of a low standard. Many of the authors wrote for the pulp funerary magazines, such as *Respectful Casket Tales* and *Undis-*

turbed, which often paid less than a penny a word and sometimes not at all. So these writers had to produce reams of material in a short time just to keep food on the table. The lot of the consolation writer has improved somewhat in the last twenty years, but not as much as you might imagine. I see a question there."

"Will the tests be multiple choice?"

"I want you to learn the material, and let the tests take care of themselves. But no, the tests will be of the essay breed. Now, some of the writers whom we will be paying special attention to this quarter include Elizabeth Stuart Phelps and her ground-breaking fictionalized mourners' manual, *The Gates Ajar,* and a book of poems, *Songs of the Silent World;* Elizabeth Prentiss and her classic, *Stepping Heavenward;* and the Rev. Theodore Cuyler and his opus, *Agnes and the Key of Her Little Coffin.* We will also be looking at American hymnology as well as taking a short side trip into millennial literature. Another question?"

"Can we leave if you're more than fifteen minutes late?"

* * *

The first day puttered along smoothly for Andy. He had an 11:00 A.M. class, Introduction to Embalming, which he enjoyed, then he broke for lunch and finished up the day with Beginning Casketing. Afterward, he stopped at the bookstore to buy his assigned texts and returned to the dorm.

Struggling down the hallway with the load of books in his knapsack, he noticed some of the fellows were engaged in a vigorous conversation in the lounge. His friend Dan Slade was there, and when he saw Andy he smiled fraternally and waved him inside. "You haven't met these guys yet, have you Andy? Fellas, this is Andy Archway, freshman from Golbyville. Andy, this is Jimbo Hinn, Francis P. Pitifore, Dirk Deane. We were discussing the relative merits of Holmes versus Mordecai. Why don't you join in?"

"Thanks," said Andy, letting his books drop to the floor

with a thud. He pulled up a seat at the edge of the semicircle.

"Jimbo, I think you had the floor."

"Asterisk," said Jimbo, a scholarly looking type with thick glasses. He wore a black T-shirt that read GOD IS DEAD AND I WANT TO EMBALM HIM. "Gotta be an asterisk after Mordecai's name in the record book. You can't compare the two, not the same record no how. Mordecai had all the advantages. His equipment was better, faster. He could fly around to all these different death sites. Most of all, embalming was an everyday practice when Mordecai broke the record, while in Holmes's day some people thought an embalmed body might not get to heaven."

Andy's heart pounded hard. A thousand objections burned in his mind's sky.

"Hmmm. You've got some good points there, Jimbo," said Slade.

"N-No!" Andy blurted, much too forcefully.

"Go ahead, buddy," Slade said with a friendly grin. "That's what these bull sessions are all about."

Inhaling deeply, Andy said, "Yes, Mordecai had some advantages. Many advantages, okay. But he also had some other stuff that Holmes didn't have. When he was getting close to the record he began to get hate mail, even death threats. I mean, the pressure that people put on him was unbearable, the press following him around, asking him every five seconds when he thought he would break the record. He got ulcers and started drinking, and it wasn't because he was all that bad of a guy, it was because of the record." Andy sat back slowly, self-consciously.

"But an asterisk just says there were special circumstances involved with the record," countered Jimbo. "Holmes set the record during a war between some states, but Mordecai had the whole *world* to embalm."

"A record is a record," Andy insisted.

"Do any of you guys think the record will be broken

again?" asked Slade. A few mumbles. "Why not? In fact, why can't it be one of us?"

"You're nuts, Danny," said Dirk Deane.

"But why not? This is one of the most prestigious, best-connected schools in the country. We've got the talent. All we need is a colossal catastrophe. It's a dangerous world, guys. Wars, earthquakes, famine, pestilence, plague. Holmes and Mordecai were great, but they were also in the right place at the right time. Maybe one of us will find that place, that time."

Slade stood up and looked imploringly at his classmates. *"Why not?"*

four

ANDY'S FIRST BIG challenge at Holmes U was an assignment in his casketing class to design a model casketing tableau. He had been making good progress on the setup of the visitation room, staying close to the instructions in the text, and now he was ready to move on to the deceased. Picking up his system disk from the archive librarian, Andy sat down at a terminal in the computer lab. He booted up the program, waited for the casket lid on the screen to pop open and the words "Body English" to float zigzagging upwards, and opened his file.

Professor Tute had provided surprisingly few details about the deceased, just technicalities like height, weight, skin tone, and a name, of sorts, "Mr. X." — and nothing about his hobbies or personality. So Andy made a few assumptions. Mr. X. Anonymous became Mr. X., World-Famous Butterfly Collector. Andy began painting a butterfly, a man-sized swallowtail in midflight. On its back he placed the once-prone Mr. X., butterfly net in hand, his face bearing a happy countenance, dressed in khakis and a pith helmet. Andy was uncertain, though, how Mr. X. should be positioned. Flat on his stomach? Straddling the creature like he was riding a horse?

Or standing upright, like the Master of the Butterflies? His teacher would probably be able to shed some light on this dilemma; he probably had run across the same situation many times before.

Andy stored what he had worked on, and dialed up Professor Tute.

"Hi, Professor Tute, this is Andy Archway from your casketing class. . . . I'm fine, thank you. I have a question about my project; I'm sort of stuck. . . . Okay, I'm using a butterfly motif for Mr. X., because you sort of left that up to us, so I made him a world-famous butterfly collector. So this giant swallowtail butterfly is taking him to heaven, he's riding on its back, see, because he loved butterflies and so now he's being taken to the other world by this butterfly, and he's feeling very happy and peaceful because he's still with the butterflies, and maybe the swallowtail is taking him to a whole land of butterflies, thousands of different kinds that Mr. X. has never seen before, and he'll be happy there, so the question is should he be riding, laying down, straddling like a horse or standing upright? . . . Yes, I think I understood the assignment. . . . Okay, I'll do that. Thanks, professor."

Andy doubted if he had expressed his dilemma very well. The professor hadn't seemed to understand the problem at all, but he reminded Andy to bring in his project tomorrow because the class was going to be doing some preliminary critiquing. That's good, thought Andy, maybe my classmates will have some useful ideas.

At casketing class the following day, as the students came in, they handed their works-in-progress to a teaching assistant, who took them off to be copied. Meanwhile, Professor Tute began a discussion on the proper footwear for the deceased, and when the assistant returned, the class moved their desks into a circle and passed around the papers.

"Okay, let's begin," said the professor. "We'll start critiquing at my left with Mr. Glasband, going counterclockwise. Try to keep your comments short and to the point. First victim is Roger Clap."

As Andy leafed through the papers, looking for the one with Roger's name on it, he began to notice something odd, something that made him feel very anxious. The designs on the students' papers were all virtually identical. They had all placed Mr. X. in a box at the front of the room.

Plagiarism! Andy thought. Boy, is the professor going to be steamed now.

"Good basic design," said Glasband. "Good fundamentals. You forgot the flowers, though."

"It was P.O.," Clap replied, and everyone roared with laughter. Andy whispered to the fellow sitting next to him, "What's P.O.?"

"Please Omit. They say that in the newspapers when they don't want flowers."

"Oh."

As the critiquing moved around the circle, Andy become increasingly nervous. Everyone, without exception, had positive comments about Clap's design. Should I repeat what they're saying and not cause trouble? Andy wondered. Or . . .

"Mr. Archway, you're up."

Andy shifted apprehensively in his seat. "Um, I . . . I guess I liked it a little less than everybody else. I mean, I don't really understand it. He dressed Mr. X. in a suit and put him in a box. Now, if he was in suit, then shouldn't he be going someplace, like to the office or a movie? And if he is laying down to take a nap, shouldn't he be dressed more comfortably? Gosh, I know undertakers did this way back when they didn't know any better. I mean, this was probably hot stuff during the Civil War, but why do it now? Unless it's a tribute to our pioneers, of course. That I can understand. Maybe that's what it was . . .?"

An uncomfortable silence filled the classroom. Finally,

Professor Tute said, "Well, Mr. Archway you certainly do have some interesting ideas. Perhaps if I explain to you what I perceive to be my mission here at Holmes U, things will become clearer to you." He folded his hands on his desk. "When all of you fine gentlemen leave this school after two years, I want you to be fully prepared for the real world of the business of the dead. Professionals do things a certain way, and you need to learn those ways and speak their language if you are to succeed. This isn't art: You can't make up your own rules; you can't change the realities of the business field you have chosen. It would be counterproductive of me as your instructor to encourage such behavior. You need to go by the book; that's why we have them. And, Mr. Archway, you seem to have read the book, so none of this should be a surprise to you. Now let's move on."

Andy sank into his chair as the critiques continued. When they reached Man and Butterfly, Andy shut his eyes.

"I thought the design was extremely well hidden."

"Unreliable design. Unreliable designer."

"I don't think it's a design at all."

"Murky."

"I can't make head or tails out of it."

"I kinda feel like I'm watching a chainsaw being taken to a soufflé."

Mercifully, the bell finally rang and Andy slunk out of the room. Professor Tute caught up with him midway down the hall. "Don't take it so hard, Archway. These first-quarter classes are just grunt work. Routine stuff. Wait until you hit your second-quarter classes. Now *there's* a place to put some of your creative thinking to work. I'll be in my office from 3:50 to 3:55 if you need someone to talk to."

"Thanks," said Andy, smiling glumly. This is hopeless, he thought as he walked across the campus through a steady drizzle. All that money Sunnyside's going to spend on me and now I'm going to fail. I'll have to go back home and learn how to milk the sheep. He kept walking, head down, as the rain fell harder. He cut through a line of pine trees and skidded down a muddy hill, then realized he had reached the far north end of the campus. He continued beyond the administration building into a swampy area of low industrial-looking classrooms. He had never been out here before. He headed slowly down the sidewalk outside the buildings, shrugging his shoulders as his soaked clothes clung to his skin.

As Andy passed by one of the classrooms, he heard a chipping noise, chisel on stone. He stopped in the open doorway. Inside, a black-haired, dark-skinned woman wearing a white smock and red beret was standing at a workshop table, carving an inscription on a headstone. Andy watched her, fascinated. After a few moments, she said, without taking her eye from the stone, "Aren't you getting wet out there?"

"You're working."

"So get wet, then."

Andy took one step forward, so that the rain spattered the pavement just behind his heels.

"What's your major?" she asked.

"I'm in the embalming-casketing sequence."

"Like it?"

"It's okay. Not exactly what I expected, but I hope things work out all right."

"I know what you mean," she said. She stepped back and surveyed her work, then began chiseling again. "When I was a kid growing up in Mexico I used to run around to the local cemeteries after school, writing down the inscriptions in a notebook, and making etchings of my favorites. 'María Sánchez, wife of Don Sánchez, 1849–1932: I don't know how to die.' 'Pablo Muñoz, M.D. 1866–1939: This is on me.' 'Linda López, 1812, age 4: She tasted Life's bitter cup/Refused to drink the portion up/But turned her little head aside/Disgusted with the taste and died.' Isn't that beautiful?"

"I like the first one best," said Andy.

"They don't write them like that nowadays, at least not in this country." She stopped again and read her work. " 'John T. Margin, February 9, 1939–December 15, 1993.' That's it! And they tell us this is a typical inscription. *Yecch!* It's like painting a canvas gray."

"But you're doing it."

"Both my parents and my brother work in a chicken processing plant in Guadomilia. I will carve stones, thank you." She set down her tools and climbed up onto a stool. She looked at Andy for the first time, her eyes dark, curious. "So where are you from?"

Tentatively moving closer, Andy looked at her, then looked away. "Golbyville. My folks have a farm there. I'm not much of a farmer, though, so I guess that's why I'm here."

"We had a farm, too," she said. "Then the rains stopped and the money ran out and we had to sell out and get jobs in the city. Have you ever been to Mexico?"

"No, I haven't. I'd like to, someday. I haven't been many places, I guess."

"When people find out I'm from Mexico, they always say how sorry they are for me, and that's silly, because the people in Mexico are so wonderful. We don't have everything that America does, and life is harder, but the people, the *people.*"

"Why did you come all the way up here? Just for school?"

"Yes, for the school. After the school, I don't know. Maybe I'll go back home. Maybe California. I don't know. What about you?"

"Uh, I'm under contract to, uh, Sunnyside," he said, his voice dwindling.

"Oh really," she said, smiling. "A real hotshot, eh?"

"Gosh, no. Sometimes it seems like a great big accident.

Sometimes I wonder what I'm doing here."

"You must have talent or they wouldn't have signed you."

He did not reply, embarrassed. Then, quietly, he said, "I should let you get back to work."

"So what's your name?"

"Andy Archway."

The woman hopped off the stool and picked up her tools, saying, "I'm Maria Eldorado. Stop in anytime you need to dry off. I'm usually here Tuesday and Thursday afternoons."

"Thanks . . . Maria," he said, and drifted out into the rain.

five

WHEN GRADES WERE sent out at the end of the fall quarter, Andy expected the worst and was not disappointed. Beginning Casketing: D. Introduction to Embalming: D. Elementary Cosmetics: D. A bright spot, Consolation Literature: B-. But Professor Tute had promised that his second-quarter classes would be more conducive to his creative powers, so, while feeling somewhat downbeat, Andy still held out hope that he could salvage his first year.

It was a pensive Christmas vacation down on the farm, long nights spent by the fire reading vintage holiday issues of *Undisturbed* and *Respectful Casket Tales*, which contained some of his favorite Yuletide stories such as "The Little Coffin Drummer Boy" and "The Wake Before Christmas." He told his folks not to worry about his grades, that it was only his first quarter and now that he had adjusted to living on his own things would go much smoother.

Andy ran into Maria outside the cafeteria on his first day back from break. "I . . . I missed visiting you," he said. "What's your schedule this quarter?"

"Mostly book work, I'm afraid," she replied. "No time

in the workshop. You may have to get the nerve up to come visit me in my room."

Andy stammered a reply, and she laughed and touched his forearm.

Later that afternoon, Andy spotted Maria in the library, running a finger along the spines on the shelf. She smiled when she saw him. Almost whispering, he said, "I was wondering, um, if I could, um, come over . . . tonight?"

"How about right now?"

"Sure, I guess."

They left the library and walked together to her dorm room. She shut the door behind them. "It's not much, but it's *not* home."

"No, it's nice," he said. "I like it. It's you."

Rough drawings of headstones with inscriptions covered the walls. A life-size plastic penguin wearing a blue baseball cap stood guard in one corner. Snapshots were tacked up on a bulletin board. "Your family?" he asked.

"Yes," she said, lightly brushing against him as she pointed at the photos. "Those are my brothers, Pedro and Fernando. That's my sister Linda and her daughter Nona. Those are my parents, my grandma Lupi. That's our next-door-neighbor Carlos."

"Do you all live together?"

"Yes, it's crowded, but there is no other way. Even if there was another way, I am not sure it would be possible. We depend too much on each other. It's strange to live in a place like this, by myself. I try not to spend too much time in here. It's no good for me."

"I don't like being alone, either."

She moved away and looked at him from the other side of the small room. "Now this isn't so bad, is it?" she said with a grin. She pulled down a thin book from the shelf. "I want to read an inscription for you." She flipped through the pages, then stopped. "There it is. 'Here lies the mortal wreck of Sally

Dugby AE 69 yrs. In the midst of society/she lived alone./ Beneath the mockery of cheerfulness, she hid deep woe. In the ruin of her intellect/the kindness of her heart survived. She perished in the snow on the night of Feb. 25, 1854.' "

She paused for a moment, and set down the book. "I like you, Andy," she said, not looking at him for the first time he could recall. "I like you," she said again, softly.

"I should go now, shouldn't I?"

"Yes. You will come again?"

He nodded.

"Yes, I know you will. There is no other way."

❖   ❖   ❖

The first class Andy had on his schedule for the beginning of winter quarter looked promising: Business and the Bereaved. He arrived at class early, said hello to a few familiar faces, remarked at the thoughtfulness of the floral tribute on the teacher's desk.

"This should be great," said Dirk Deane. "I hear Professor Drainage is a load of laughs."

Soon the professor entered the classroom, attired in a tuxedo with tails, a black satchel, and magician's wand in hand. "For my first trick I'd like to show you something I like to call the Old Shell Game." He opened the satchel and dumped out three small plastic objects that resembled caskets and a miniature green human figure. Placing the figure beneath one of the caskets, he said, "Keep your eye on the deceased," then proceeded to slide the caskets swiftly across the table, changing their positions, mixing them up so fast that Andy lost track of the body almost immediately.

Stopping suddenly, the professor looked at the class with a wry smile. "Any guesses?"

"It's in the middle!" someone called out.

"Are you sure?" the professor asked seriously. "All right, then." He dramatically lifted the casket. It was empty.

"It's on the left!" another student yelled.

Empty again!

Professor Drainage paused, grinned knowingly at the class, and raised the final casket.

Empty!

Voilà!

Wild applause!

"My name is Professor Bob Drainage," he said, removing more play caskets from his satchel, setting them in order on the table, "and I am here today to tell you that many young professionals in the funeral business make the mistake of leaving casket selection to chance. The ultimate outcome of that strategy is that you will wind up with a showroom full of extremely expensive caskets and have nothing to place inside them. The ultimate result of leaving casket selection to chance is that you will, at best, see your business suffer immeasurably, or at worst, go out of business entirely. I've seen it happen, gentlemen. How do we prevent this calamity from occurring? Gather around the desk and I will demonstrate."

Andy did as instructed. The caskets, he noticed, seemed to be arranged in some arcane pattern, but he was not able to decipher its code.

"It's a fact of nature," Professor Drainage said, "that human beings naturally trend right. It's also a fact of nature that human beings trend toward claustrophobia. We can accommodate these tendencies by our placement of caskets in the showroom. As you may have observed, there are two corridors displayed here. One, wide and on the right, where your higher quality caskets are located. This is called the Avenue of Approach. The other corridor, narrow and on the left, where the less expensive caskets are placed, is called Resistance Lane."

"What if someone goes down Resistance Lane?" one of the scholars asked. "How do you get them back into the Avenue of Approach?"

"All in good time," said the professor. "This design, of

course, is not the only design that will work. There are many variations on this theme. I instructed the student bookstore to order enough sets of practice caskets for the entire class, and I recommend you purchase a set and experiment with them at home."

So far so good, Andy thought, even though he was still wondering what happened to the body.

A week later Professor Drainage told the class they were going to conduct an exercise in showroom role-playing. Andy had been struggling—his mind glazing over—with the assigned textbook, *One to a Customer: How to Get the Most Out of the Casket Purchase*, by Robert P. Drainage, Egyptian Press ($37.95). The book was crammed with columns of figures, formulas, and graphs. Maybe role-playing will bring this casket business into focus, Andy hoped.

"A question was raised last time about what to do if a customer should, by some fluke, wander into Resistance Lane," Professor Drainage began. "The answer is simple yet elegant, bringing the customer back into the above-the-median fold while at the same time allowing them to feel as if they have done their best for the deceased. It is a matter of showing them a casket that is well below the median, a bottom-of-the-line, nearly offensive container. Something a little nicer, you ask? Guide them to a rebound unit, above median, of course, back in the Avenue of Approach. Naturally, real life is never so simple. Now, let's try a basic role-playing exercise, one person playing the funeral director, the other playing the customer. Everyone will get a chance to play both roles by the end of the quarter. You will notice that I have marked the floor with masking tape designating each corridor. Mr. Inx, take your place as customer. Mr. Archway, you will be our first director."

Andy got up and took his place at the front of the classroom. At least I'll get it over with, he thought.

"Begin," said the instructor.

Mr. Inx immediately took a step into the pretend Resistance Lane. "This flimsy redwood job looks pretty sharp," he said. "It's exactly the one I want."

"Uh, okay."

"From the top, Mr. Inx," the professor said patiently.

"Right. Say, I like the looks of this casket here. Yessiree, this is the one for me all right."

"We, er, have many different models to choose from. Nicer than that one."

"No, I really don't want to spend a lot of time looking for a casket. And I don't have much money to spend."

"Are you sure?"

"Yep."

"Uh, okay."

Professor Drainage sighed. "Overcome his objections, Mr. Archway. Say: 'Isn't it worth taking the time to make a decision that will last forever?' Say: 'I can get you into a much classier model for just a very small additional investment in the service.' Never use the word *money*. Now, once more."

"This one looks decent," said the customer in a bored monotone.

"Isn't it worth taking the time, uh, to make a choice that will last forever?"

"Yes. You know, you're exactly right."

"May I show you some other models?"

"You may! You may!"

Andy led him into the Avenue of Approach. "This one, for instance. A fine model. Anyone could be proud of owning it."

"Looks pretty expensive."

"Um, um, well, we have some other models over here," Andy said, and, panicking, led the customer back into Resistance Lane, a fatal faux pas.

Someone cackled.

"Mr. Archway, you are obviously not grasping the concept!" said the professor with a slight tinge of hysteria. "You cannot rebound the customer into Resistance Lane! Once you leave Resistance Lane, it is off-limits to you from thereafter. Entry forbidden, dead end, closed for construction work. Resistance Lane is the Lane of Last Resort. All the models there are at median or below. You rebounded him in reverse!"

Now the whole class was laughing, and Andy stood there, feeling his cheeks flush.

"Why don't you review your text, Mr. Archway," Professor Drainage said, calm once more, "and you may try again next week. Ms. Yopp, you are the customer. Mr. Hysong, take the director's role and please try to bear in mind what I have been saying."

* * *

At this point in his college career Andy landed in Despair Lane, where the doubts that arose in the first quarter about his place at Holmes U were magnified tenfold. He began skipping classes, spending time in the nooks and crannies of the library, lost in the golden age of undertaking. He roamed the campus at odd hours, steering clear of people, afraid to run into Maria. He even began avoiding his buddy, Dan Slade. Andy would leave his dorm room early in the morning and wander through the woods in the chill January air, not returning until late at night. He ate his meals out of vending machines or not at all.

One day when Andy was trying to slip out around 6:00 A.M., Slade was standing in the doorway, arms folded across his chest, his usual cocky smile replaced by a look of purpose.

"What's going on, buddy?"

"I'm late," Andy said, trying to squeeze by, but the bigger student blocked his way.

"You're going to be later," said Slade. He snatched hold of Andy's arm and forced him back into the room. "Sit down." Andy slipped off his backpack and wearily lowered himself onto the edge of the bed, burying his head in his hands. "Now spill. What's the problem?"

"It's not working out," said Andy. "My grades are terrible and I hate my classes. I thought things would get easier this quarter, but they haven't. I don't belong here."

"Look, the quarter just started, Andy. You can turn things around yet. I did terrible my first quarter, too. But then, you learn what they expect of you, and you get into the right frame of mind."

"I don't know how. I didn't think it would be like this. I don't want to be here anymore."

"You need some extracurricular activities, that's what you need. It will get your mind off your problems. Have you ever thought about trying out for the competitive embalming team?"

"No. I'm not going to do that."

There was silence for a few seconds, then Slade said, "Listen, you're going to be staying in your room tonight. All night. Got it?"

"Why?"

"Never mind. Just be here. If you're not, so help me I'll wallop you until you can't see straight. Is that clear?"

Andy raised his eyes and looked at Slade. He nodded.

Slade relaxed and smiled. "Come on, let's get some breakfast."

❋   ❋   ❋

That night Andy was pacing in his room—two steps forward and two steps back—wondering what his buddy had planned. Maybe it's a hazing, he thought fearfully.

The phone rang.

"Hello?"

"Is this the future of the funeral business I'm talking to?" growled a voice on the other end of the line.

"What . . . Wake, is that you?"

"Sorry it's been so long, kid. I've been in Louisiana all

fall, slurping down gumbo and watching some pretty god-awful embalming. Do you know they still practice voodoo in certain parts of the state? How the hell are you, kid?"

"Pretty good, I guess."

"That's not what I hear."

"Yes, well, actually I'm thinking of leaving school. I'll pay you back any money I owe you, I promise. I've hardly spent any. I bought some old issues of *Shroud*, but I probably can return those, I think I still have my receipt."

"Why the gloomy forecast?"

"Wake, the teachers here don't understand, or maybe I don't . . . I'm pretty mixed up. Last quarter I did one of my visitation scenes for a class project and they didn't get it. Now I'm in a class where they're teaching us how to sell caskets, and *I* don't get it. My grades started at D and they're going downhill. I'm very sorry to let you down, Wake, but I'm not enjoying this at all."

"Kid, are you telling me you're in a funk because of your classes and no other reason?"

"I guess so."

"No female trouble?"

"I talk to a girl once in a while. We haven't had any trouble, though."

"Your folks okay?"

"Last time I talked to them."

"No nightmares?"

"No, I just dream about dead people."

"Well then, don't worry! You've got it made! College is vastly overrated, kid. The teachers haven't touched a corpse in twenty years, so don't take them seriously. It's just a crummy game; learn the rules and play the game their way and you'll be fine. But chuck it once you graduate because you'll be part of a much brighter, more important game. College has about as much bearing on your life to come as my dear deceased auntie. You're going to be learning everything on the job, on the run. The only reason you go to school is to get that piece of paper that says you're certified to practice the dismal trade. Just have fun, for chrissakes and stop worrying!"

"Oh," Andy replied. He thought for a minute and said, "Okay."

"I'm glad we got that straightened out. Got something else to ask you, kid. How would you like to intern this summer at Sunnyside Central in beautiful Rancho Norman Rockwell, California?"

"Really? California? I've never been there before. They have the oranges there, right?"

"Not so much anymore, kid. Lots of parking lots. But Sunnyside is a piece of heaven, grass from sky to sky. Did you know we've got the world's biggest lawn mower?"

"Wow, I want to see that."

"You will, kid. Now, I can't promise what kind of work you'll be doing, could be drudge work, but it will give you a taste of the big time. I told P.T. all about you. He seemed pretty interested in meeting you. Whaddaya say?"

"Of course I'll go."

"Super duper. We'll get it all set up for you. Hey, kid, I gotta run, my gumbo's getting cold. See ya later."

I told P.T. all about you. He seemed pretty interested in meeting you.

Me?

Pleased to make your acquaintance, Mr. Sunnyside, sir.

Nice to meet you, Mr. Sunnyside.

Glad to know you, P.T.

Resistance Lane feeling very far away, Andy left his room. I have to find Dan, he thought. I need to thank him.

"You called Wake," Andy said, standing in the doorway to Slade's room.

"Oh yeah?" Slade answered from the bed, hands cupped behind his head. "What did he have to say?"

"School isn't life and death. Just get the certificate and stop worrying."

"Good advice, don't you think?"

"I feel better."

"You know, bud, I'm going to be out of here in a couple of months. You've got to be ready."

Andy looked at him, concerned. "But you talked about going to graduate school. I figured you'd be here all next year."

Grinning, Slade sat up. "I got the call, bud."

"What do you mean? What call?"

"Drabford Diversified. They offered me a two-year deal. It's sweet, bud."

"Gosh, that's wonderful." Andy self-consciously stuck out his hand. "Congratulations."

"Thanks, buddy."

Glancing away, Andy said quietly, "I sort of have some news, too."

"Oh? Tell me."

"Uh, Sunnyside wants me to intern out in California this summer."

"Terrific! Nice going, Andy. You'll do great."

"It's hard to believe, really." Andy, his face solemn, looked at his pal. "I wouldn't be here anymore if it wasn't for you." Then lowered his head. "You've been my loyal friend." And shut his eyes. "I owe you a lot."

six

IT WAS NIGHT when the plane passed over the mountains and descended into the Gothic sprawl of Southern California. Andy was puzzled by the brown mass that hung low over the valley. It looked like smoke from a smoldering fire, mountaintops poking through in the distance, hazy lights on the ground, glowing, ghostlike. He thought he saw the mass move, undulating like an ocean-floor creature spotting its next meal. The plane passed through this layer without incident and found the runway at Ontario International Airport.

Stepping carefully down the stairs to the tarmac, Andy crinkled his nose as the sour air filled his nostrils. But the warm night air felt nice. The pilot had said it was eighty-five degrees. It was barely sixty when he left Minnesota. He headed to the gate, trying to locate Wake.

"Over here, Andy!"

Andy waved, and hurried through the gate. "Boy, it's good to see you," he said as they shook hands.

"Welcome to never-never land," Wake said with a grin, taking one of Andy's bags. "It's good to see you, too."

"Why does it smell so bad?"

"Don't worry, kid, you'll get used to it." As they followed the handful of other passengers through the revolving door to the outdoor baggage claim, Wake said, "You know, this ex-stripper in L.A. had an idea for getting rid of the smog. She said they should install giant fans in the San Gabriel Mountains, and whenever the air got bad they would turn on the fans and blow the smog away. She may have been ahead of her time."

They picked up Andy's bag and headed to the parking lot. "We're going right to Sunnyside from here," Wake shouted as another plane came in for a landing. "We have our own rooms for visitors. They're small, but you'll be spending most of your time on the grounds, anyway."

After loading the suitcases in the trunk, they made it out onto the freeway, heading west. They had scarcely gone two miles before brake lights began appearing up ahead, and soon they were at a dead stop. "Damn traffic," Wake muttered.

"I wonder if there's been an accident."

"Naw, I've been in traffic jams out here at three in the morning. You lose track of time. People have to get things done today, tonight, as soon as possible, because tomorrow is a big question mark. I don't know, maybe people out here aren't as crazy as they seem. Maybe the roads should be jammed in the middle of the night everywhere. Maybe it's a healthy sign."

"How far do we have to go?"

"Oh, about thirty miles or so. May as well settle in, kid."

Andy leaned his head back and stared out the side window. Traffic abruptly began moving again. Shopping centers, ramshackle houses, graffiti-covered walls flashed by. He felt disoriented and a little frightened, unable to wake from this odd dream. He found himself thinking about Maria, about her eyes, the sound of her voice, the way her hands held the hammer and chisel. He wondered where she was now. Perhaps they had been in the air together, following the same curve of the earth at about the same time. He wondered if she was thinking of him, too . . .

❃ ❃ ❃

Flying Maria, near Mexico City, following the curve of the earth, feeling Andy. She pictured him the first day, raindrops on his face, felt his hands, his curiosity. Is he the good one for me? No, it was the rain, it was the day. I let my guard down. I looked into his eyes, let him look into mine, let him see my heart. He is not the same as me. We should not be. It is not too late. He is somewhere else now; he cannot find me now. I do not know where he is, but I know where he will be. I could go to him. She clenched her eyes tight and shook her head.

It was the rain, it was the rain . . .

❃ ❃ ❃

Soon the traffic eased. As they cruised down the freeway, the terrain became more hilly, dry slopes with elaborate houses perched on their sides. The fog swept over the car, obscuring everything. Wake turned off the freeway at the Rancho Norman Rockwell exit and drove up into the hills, taking the curves slowly. He signaled and braked to a stop outside a long wrought-iron gate topped with a series of angelic figures and a white archway that said in script, simply, SUNNYSIDE.

A guard from the blockhouse alongside the gate approached the car. "Evening, Wake," she said, tipping her hat.

"Hiya, Juanita. How's business?"

"Not bad at all. Had a brush fire down the road last week, but the Santa Anas weren't blowing so it was nothing serious. How long are you going to be around?"

"Just a couple weeks, unfortunately."

"Well, we'll see you later."

" 'Night, now."

The majestic gates swung open, and Wake waited, then swung the car inside. "This is it, kid," he said. "Sunnyside Central. Heaven Hill. You can't get any higher than this."

Andy tried peering through the fog at the grounds as

they drove along, but the shapes were too indistinct to decipher. He tiredly rubbed his eyes. They climbed a rise not far from the main gate, pulling up to a row of simple white cottages at the top of a grassy hill.

"You get a good view of the place from up here," Wake said, "although you can't tell it now. Let's get the stuff unloaded and grab some shut-eye, kid. You've got a big day ahead of you."

* * *

The sun woke Andy early, streaming through his window. He rolled onto his back, feeling groggy and thinking he was still in his dorm room. Then, remembering the nightmare landscape, sat up quickly. *Sunnyside,* he thought. Sunnyside. He padded to the window and moved the gingham curtain aside. The fog had burned away, revealing a wondrous vista. Below the cottage the ground dropped off sharply, deep into a gentle valley, the grass nearly luminescent. Statuary dotted the hillsides: winged figures, soldiers, horses.

After quickly dressing, Andy hurried outside. The air smelled clean-scrubbed on Heaven Hill, the blue sky extending forever. Birds chirped a greeting. He started down the hillside, zigzagging back and forth to keep under control, losing his footing and tumbling down, rolling to the base of the hill, the long tufted grass cushioning his fall. Reaching the bottom, he got to his grass-stained knees and grinned.

Sunnyside.

Then, in the distance, he heard a low rumbling noise. He cocked his head, listening intently, unable to tell if it was an airplane or a car or . . . something else. It seemed to be coming closer, coming from beyond the hill on his left. It was getting very loud, very near. He stood up, alarmed. He retreated a few paces. Suddenly, it appeared over the hill, swallowing the sky.

It was a gargantuan machine, as big as a two-story house, shaped like a lunch box on wheels. It rolled supernaturally fast over the hillside toward Andy, producing an ear-splitting roar. There wasn't even time to panic. He shut his eyes and waited for impact.

But all Andy felt was a tickling sensation on his face and arms as he heard the machine zip by him. Feeling reprieved, he opened his eyes again, and catching the scent of freshly mowed grass, brushed the newly trimmed blades from his arms. He gazed in amazement as the biggest lawn mower in the world zoomed through the little valley, outlining wedge-shaped quadrants, slicing them down and moving to the next section without missing a single blade, veering off whenever it approached one of the statues. Andy watched in fascination for a while before trudging back up the hill to the cottages, looking back one last time as the mower finished the final section and sped back across the valley and cut clean the small circle where he had been standing.

Wake was just coming out of his cottage when Andy puffed back onto the paved path at the top of the hill. "Nice morning for a walk, eh pal?"

Glancing back down the hill, Andy said, "Uh, that's some lawn mower."

"World's biggest," Wake said proudly. "Fully computerized. Turning radius as small as a baby's hand. Problem is, they let the goddamn thing loose at six in the morning. A person can't sleep in around here."

"What are we doing today?"

"They're sending breakfast up, then we'll go meet P.T. I don't know what they're bringing, some fruits and nuts, probably."

"I'm not that hungry. I'm too excited. This is all so beautiful."

"Hey, kid, this is just the back lot. Wait till you see the heart of Heaven Hill."

❖　❖　❖

Right after Andy and Wake gobbled up the last crumbs of their breakfast—fruit and pastry, no nuts—and had stepped outside, a futuristic bubble-top vehicle emitting a low hum scooted up to the cottage door, as if on cue.

"Hop in, fellas," said the driver, a gray-haired yet boyish-looking man with a mustache and whimsical smile. The vehicle's side panel slid smoothly upward, and Andy and Wake climbed into the back of the odd-looking car. A line of monitors lined the dashboard and the back side of the forward seats, showing scenes from various areas of the center.

"How's things, P.T.?" Wake asked as the car sealed itself again and moved off. "How's Time Hill progressing?"

"Terrific. We're a month ahead on the Western and Future sections. We're having a few problems keeping to schedule in the Egyptian section, but nothing serious. It's a pretty labor-intensive project."

"P.T., this is the kid I was telling you about, Andy Archway. He'll be here all summer."

"Welcome aboard, Andy," P.T. Sunnyside said, his grinning face bobbing in the rearview mirror. "Wallace has spoken well of you. He rarely speaks well of anyone, professionally, so my ears pricked up when he started waxing effusive about you."

"Thanks, Mr., uh, Sunnyside."

"I'm P.T. Say, where did Wake say you were going to school? Grail State?"

"Holmes U."

"Godalmighty, Wake, couldn't you do any better for the kid?"

"It's close to home," said Wake.

"I'm surprised they're still accredited," P.T. mumbled, then brightened again as they whizzed by a gathering of fountains, from hubcap- to telephone-pole-size, each bearing a memorial plaque. "Andy, this is called Fountain Village. We built it back in the fifties. Most of the fountains are replicas of the fountains built for the Louisiana Purchase Exposition, held in St. Louis in 1904. Most of the folks buried here did in fact have their roots in Missouri, and later retired throughout the Southland. You'll see these areas as we go along, plots organized around a particular theme, such as Rose Row, Train Town, Patriots' Path. Of course, they're pretty crude compared to Time Hill. But the roots of these things are always buried deep. Time Hill is no different. It's been years and years in the making."

They passed a packed tour bus with a streamlined *S* on its side. P.T. waved to the tourists, who pointed excitedly and flapped their hands back at him. "So what have we got lined up for you this summer, Andrew?"

"Uh, I don't know. No one said anything."

"What do you think, Wake?"

"Well, I warned him not to expect too much. But no disposal work, if you don't mind."

"You mentioned you're behind on the Egyptian section," Andy offered.

"Hey, perfect," said P.T. "Hard work up there, though."

"I don't mind."

"Egyptland it is, then," P.T. said. He gestured out the front window, at a white three-story blockhouse-shaped building. "Here's the administration building. Houses all the offices, technical areas, plus a coffee shop and a nifty little gift nook. Everybody loves a souvenir. Let's get out and I'll show you the brains of Sunnyside."

They began the tour in an air-cooled lobby; all its walls were covered by a colorful mural that appeared to depict, Andy thought, the progression of the funeral profession. Beginning on the far left with some Egyptians wrapping up a corpse in the shadow of the pyramids, the time line continued through the Middle Ages and Puritan America, to a section portraying an Amish-looking fellow tending to a body in a corpse cooler, tracking to the end of the mural showing a modern embalmer, sunlight radiating behind his noggin, surrounded by streamlined devices and intricate electronic gizmos.

"This is really something," Andy marveled.

"Biggest funerary mural in the world," said P.T. "A woman named Bellite Transon painted it. She couldn't afford the bill for her husband, Trent, so we traded our services for hers. She's brilliant, don't you think?"

"It's wonderful."

"Look closely at the Puritan section," Wake said. "See anyone familiar?"

Andy did not recognize any of them. But there, peeking out from behind one of the black-clad early Americans was the mug of P. T. Sunnyside.

"I asked her not to do that," P.T. said with a grin.

They walked down the hall to a set of automatic doors. "This is the embalming area," P.T. said as the doors zipped open and they started down a glass-lined corridor perched above the scene. Andy looked from side to side at the rows and rows of embalmers working on the assembly line in the warehouse-size room, the bodies moving methodically down conveyor belts.

"Each worker is assigned a particular task," explained P.T., stopping. "Draining the blood, sticking on the eyecaps, setting the positioning blocks in place. "It's unfortunate in many ways, but we've found it's the only way to keep up with the volume of deceased we receive. We tend to aim our resources toward the grounds and the surroundings, and I'm afraid the embalming isn't done with as much of a personal touch as we'd like."

"Will I be working here eventually?" Andy asked.

"Not necessarily," P.T. replied. "You may begin on the embalming line, like many of our top people, but once you get a little experience under your belt, the career possibilities at Sunnyside are limited only by your imagination. I didn't bring you here because of your embalming skills; I'm looking to your future—and ours."

After touring the cryogenics building and the crematorium, they returned to the bubble car. Whirring by the front gate, Wake said, "Picnic areas on your right. People should feel comfortable in cemeteries, don't you agree? There's our camping grounds. Hook-ups for seventy-five tents, campers, what-have-you. We do have plans to build a motel, up where your cottages are. It will make things easy on the folks who visit us. They won't have to drive halfway to Cucamonga just to find a place to plunk down for the night."

"How are your competitors taking all this?" Andy asked.

"Those goddamn midgets, the Drabfords, have some choice politicos in their pocket," said P.T., his voice choked with disgust. "They're filing all sorts of actions against us. We're violating zoning laws, ethical standards, the American Way of Life, according to them. We've beat them at every turn. So far."

"What do they have against you?"

"We have a difference in philosophy, you might say. The Drabfords believe in making money, then inventing ideas, scams really, to bring this about. I believe in my ideas, and the fact that they make money is a gift. They came up with the drive-by wake; stick the corpse in the picture window and let folks drive right up, take a peek, and drive off. Terrible idea. Plenty of people have ideas that don't amount to anything. I'm your average Joe American, born in the Midwest, came out here to find my dream. Folks have been following the same path since the 1700s, from Abbie Floreshaker, inventor of the potato gun to Karo Monsen, who thought up designer distilled water. People still follow the dream, even though every generation is trying to build their dreams on a bigger and bigger pile of rubble. They'll always come out here, I guess. Most of them will get beaten down, but enough will make it that people will still say, 'Why not me?' "

"Come on, P.T., there's more to this than philosophy," Wake gently chided him.

"Oh, that was all worked out years ago."

"You think the Drabfords are the types who forget a royal screwing like that? Not a chance." Wake turned to Andy. "Back in the early 1950s the Drabford brothers wanted this property we're on right now to build what would then have been the world's largest cemetery. They had the plans drawn up, and the surveyors had been on the site. Well, they weren't the only ones who realized what a glorious location this was. So old P.T. here chums up to highway czar and park commissioner Robert Ezekiel, and convinces him that Heaven Hill would make a perfect spot for a new park. Only problem, of course, is that the Drabfords have bought the land from the farmer who owned it. No problem, says P.T., announce that you're going to build a new freeway right through the center of Heaven Hill, and that you have declared eminent domain on the property. The midgets try to fight it, but then the bulldozers arrive and start tearing up the ground at the base of the hill. They settled fast, and Heaven Hill became property of the state. Naturally, funds for the highway dried up almost immediately; these things happen. In gratitude, Ezekiel splits the property in half and sells one portion to P.T. at a bargain price. There actually is a public park on the other side of the hill. It's nice, but it's no Sunnyside. Did I get that right, P.T.?"

"Oh, it wasn't as Machiavellian as you make it sound. Ezekiel couldn't stand those goddamn midgets any more than I could."

"Well, it was beautiful to watch," Wake told Andy. "I've been with P.T. since he was running a funeral home out of the back room of a bakery in Tarzana. When I'm out on the road I know exactly what he's looking for. There's a lot of adequate talent out there, but precious few Sunnysiders. You're a natural Sunnysider, kid. You were born for this."

"And I trust Wake more than anyone else on my staff," P.T. said. "He's the best scout in the business. I can keep an eye on most things around here, but I don't know the scoop in Clapboard, Maine, or Atlantis, South Dakota. He's my eyes across America. He keeps us supplied with unique talent, the engines that will drive us into the next century. We're always looking to the future. The business must outlast me."

They glided up a steep incline. At its summit, P.T. stopped the vehicle and announced, "Welcome to Time Hill."

Andy leaned forward, looking over the front seat. There were three widely spaced gates, each with a different motif. On the left, a gate constructed in log-fort-style, with a wood-burned sign that said "Frontiersville." In the center, amoeba shapes and flying saucers floated above an art deco sign proclaiming "Futureville." On the right was "Egyptville," its pyramid-shaped gate covered with hieroglyphics. Beyond the gates Andy could see clouds of dust, dump trucks, backhoes, men and women in white jumpsuits and hardhats—hammering, hauling, and studying blueprints. The sound of jackhammers and diesel engines filled his ears. A few vague shapes were beginning to take form: a log fort and Wild West main street; glistening spires and domes; a pyramid and sphinx.

"A theme park for the dead," P.T. said proudly. "Or more correctly, for the living survivors of the departed. I have been accused of possessing a flippant attitude toward the dead, and nothing could be farther from the truth. Time Hill will be respectful of the deceased. Would you rather be buried in a depressing, forgotten cemetery or on Boot Hill in a replica Wild West town? In Shady Gate cemetery or in the well-ordered wonder of the Town of Tomorrow? Lost among hundreds of thousands of other headstones or enshrined in a genuine replica of a pyramid from Ancient Egypt?"

"I see what you mean," Andy said. "I've done little scenes with my dead, but nothing like this. Do you bury the people normally?"

"Yes, all the burial procedures are conducted in a traditional fashion. There's a fine line between innovation and insanity, in terms of public perception. Whether there's any difference in reality I'm not so sure. But this will not be a static project. We always leave room for projects like this to evolve. In the future we may hire actors to play various roles in the parks. Give it more realism. We may also provide more services to the park's visitors: food, amusements, and so forth. But that's looking far into the future."

"What will the actors be doing?" asked Andy.

"We really haven't gotten that far into the creative process. I suppose they would be pretending to perform various tasks, like minding the stores, shopping, playing games, and so on."

"Couldn't the actors tell the visitors about the deceased, what a swell guy he was, what his hobbies were?"

"Interesting."

"Or maybe the deceased could do it themselves. They could make a videotape where they talk about who they were and what they want people to remember about them."

"And substitute a video screen for a headstone," P.T. finished. "Yes, normally the screen would contain all the information a traditional tombstone would, plus maybe an image of the deceased. Push a button on the side of the screen and you get the autobiography."

"You could even cut in scenes from the person's life," Andy went on, "using home movies, videos, and photographs. It would be like a documentary of that person."

"We should get this on tape," Wake interjected.

"Tape's always running," said P.T. "Voice activated. Prints out automatically. I just had it installed last week." He flipped open a compartment beneath one of the dashboard video screens and handed Wake a sheaf of papers.

How's things, P.T.? . . . Terrific . . . Uh, I don't know . . . No disposal work . . . A theme park for the dead . . . maybe the deceased could do it themselves . . . we should get this down . . .

"Video tombstones," P.T. said softly, shaking his head. "Beautiful." He looked back at Andy, his face surprisingly stern. "Get that goddamn certificate and get back here. You've got a job waiting for you."

SEVEN

ANDY HAD ANOTHER job waiting for him first. After lunch he returned to Time Hill and entered a mysterious land where a half-built pyramid and sphinx rose into the shimmering sky. Here, sand had replaced the grass and the air seemed hotter than it had moments earlier.

"I'm looking for Kant Demars," he asked one of the workers. The woman pointed to a nearby bedouin-style tent as she rushed by. He parted the flaps and stepped inside.

A balding, beet-faced man wearing what appeared to be a uniform from an old foreign legion movie was seated at a plain wood-frame desk, his fingers flashing across a keyboard, the speeding reds and blues from the screen reflecting off his round eyeglasses.

"Excuse me," Andy said, dumping the sand out of his shoe. "Are you Kant Demars?"

The man held up one finger, pounded the keys for a few more seconds, paused to study the screen, then exhaled and sat back. "Ah, yes, the reinforcements have arrived," Demars said in a clipped British accent. "You are Mr. Archway, then."

"Yes. I'm interning for the summer."

"Came to forget a girl, I take it."

"Huh?"

"Joking." He stood and smartly clasped Andy's hand. "You'd better know this from the get-go. I am an Egyptologist from Oxford University. While at the university I was embroiled in a controversy involving the alleged theft of artifacts from the tomb of Allaz-Ben-Rottotiller. Let me assure you, I was completely innocent of the charges. Others, unfortunately, did not see it that way. My services were terminated and I found myself without employment and without reputation. I read about this . . . *project* in *Egyptology Illustrated*. It was the object of much ridicule. However, I choked down my pride and contacted Mr. Sunnyside immediately. There you have it. Yes, the sand is from Huntington Beach. Yes, the pyramids are made out of plastic. But I am trying my best. Any questions?"

"What am I going to be doing?"

"Manual labor, I'm afraid. We're automated to a certain extent, but pyramid-building is slave work and that fact cannot be altered. The stones are made of a synthetic material — they used it on the moon shots, I believe — and fit together like children's blocks. But they are heavy and they do require hauling and lifting. Do you have any physical ailments? A bad back, perhaps?"

"No."

Surveying Andy from head to toe, Demars said, "We'll have to get you out of those clothes, though. The sun is a devil in the middle of the day. You'll get heat stroke within an hour." After fitting out Andy in a khaki uniform matching his own, Demars said, "Better. Keep that canteen on your belt filled. Drink from it every fifteen minutes, whether you're thirsty or not. The troops on the line will show you what needs to be done." He firmly kissed Andy on both cheeks and shook his hand again. "Good luck and Godspeed, my boy."

Andy introduced himself to the half-dozen sullen, sweaty faces at the base of the pyramid and was met with a less than chummy response. They gave him the job of loading the synthetic stones, stacked on a nearby pallet, into a wheelbarrow and dumping them at the pyramid's base. On his first load Andy stacked the wheelbarrow to the top, then discovered that the weight caused the cart to sink into the sand, making it unmovable. He tried a half load, and that seemed to work better, but it was still a chore having to almost drag the cart through the sand instead of letting it roll. After a few trips he was exhausted. Plopping down onto the edge of the pallet, he unscrewed his canteen cap and took a big swig of water. Fortunately, Demars appeared soon and yelled that it was break time.

"They've got you hauling, eh?" Demars said, looking down at Andy with a grin. "Don't worry, they make all the new arrivals haul. Soon you'll be up on the pyramid." He tossed Andy a small tube. "Sunscreen," he said. "You're already burning. You funeral fellows certainly are a pale lot."

"Thanks," Andy said, spreading the cream on his nose.

"By the way, I don't know if they told you, but we all sleep right here on the grounds in our tents. Really gets you in the spirit of the thing. We try not to be too heartless. We work in the night when the thermometer tops a hundred, but some locals have been complaining about the lights, so we're going day by day on this."

By quitting time early that evening Andy was so worn out that he skipped dinner and simply crawled into his tent and fell into an exhausted sleep. When he woke the next morning he felt as though every muscle in his body had been stretched like taffy, and his head ached terribly. On the second night he felt no better. On the third night he secretly plotted his escape. On the fourth night he secretly plotted the murder of Demars.

And so it went until the end of the second week when Andy began keeping his fellow legionnaires up well past curfew, telling them wild stories about life in Golbyville. His muscles had hardened. His stamina was excellent. His skin, where it was exposed to the sun, had turned from its usual pallor to desert-rat brown. His hauling had become so efficient that he had time in between trips to scale the ever-growing pyramid and help snap some bricks into place.

"We're right on schedule, men," Demars announced one afternoon. "Congratulations." Andy and the other legionnaires whooped and flung their hats into the air.

* * *

It was about this time that Andy began to dream about the pyramid.

His first vision was that the pyramid was being destroyed, the plastic stones crashing into a pile. He watched the disaster in awe from outside his tent, feeling the ground shaking beneath his boots. Then he felt his dream merge into a dim wakeful state, realizing he had been asleep, but the trembling sensation remained. It was daylight, barely. He sat bolt upright.

Voices outside the tent, shouting, "Earthquake! Earthquake!"

The support beams on his tent were bouncing, and the tent fabric shook as if in a stiff wind. Suddenly the tent collapsed, pinning Andy underneath. The vibrations abruptly faded. He lay dazed for a moment before kicking free from one of the stanchions and crawling out from under the heavy canvas.

Andy expected to see their work reduced to a pile of rubble, but it appeared to be undamaged. A pile of bricks by the pallets had fallen, and he could spot no other disturbances in the immediate vicinity. People were dashing about without much purpose. He walked over to the pyramid, where Demars was standing, hands raised victoriously in the air.

"You're lovely!" he shouted. "Lovely!"

Coming to his side, Andy said, "I dreamed that it collapsed."

Demars whirled and clenched Andy's arms. "It's too strong!" the man bellowed gleefully. "It's *not* a load of cheap crap! It's worth something! You fellows made it work! Five thousand years is nothing! The pyramid of Heaven Hill will endure forever!"

❀   ❀   ❀

The second dream occurred exactly a week later. In this dream Andy was standing outside his tent on a new moon night, gazing up at the incomplete pyramid. On top of the edifice stood a mysterious figure in silhouette, female in form. Although he could not see her eyes, he felt her beckoning to him. He heard her voice, faint in the wind, calling his name. Abruptly he woke, soaked in sweat. Still, he heard his name in the wind.

Andy went outside. He looked up at the pyramid, where a shadowed figure stood: a woman. Her voice quieted as he stepped away from the tent and approached the pyramid. Near the base he lost sight of her. He began to climb, quickly, deliberately, the handholds and footholds burned into his mind. At last feeling the flat surface of the top layer of bricks, he pulled himself onto the summit.

It was Maria, barefoot in a black dress. She stared at him, and for a moment there was no recognition in her dark eyes. He came closer, and then she smiled. He slowly reached out and touched her shoulder, running his hand down to her fingertips.

Unexpectedly, they separated and he looked to her for understanding, for some sign. He took both her hands, hold-

65

ing them palms up, running his fingers along their contours, examining every line, every crease.

Her hands had changed somehow, transformed into something both familiar and new. What was it? He looked at her again, uncomprehending.

"I've been dreaming about you," she said.

eight

THE EARTHQUAKE WAS an omen, Wake thought as he jetted back to the Midwest. Leave California, it told him. Fortunately, the temblor has caused only minor damage at Sunnyside. A thirty-foot-high reproduction of Michaelanski's "Paul Bunyan" had broken off at the ankles, falling face first into a goldfish pond. Seven rare Antarctic goldfish had perished. Up on Time Hill destruction was surprisingly light. Some scaffolding was knocked down. A few ersatz buildings that had not been reinforced collapsed. Nothing serious. Most of the damage on the hill was centered in the future area. They won't build them like they used to, Wake mused.

Arriving back home in Flankville, Iowa, Wake mowed the lawn, paid his bills, and visited his daughter and granddaughter in Newton. Within a week he had tuned up his station wagon and was back on the road, traversing farmland in northwestern Iowa and southwestern Minnesota. As he visited funeral homes in towns like Real Falls, Nodal, and Standard Springs, something odd began to work its way into his consciousness. Like a cat before a quake, Wake began to sense that something was amiss in the funerary gestalt. Something just beyond his vision. He felt it deep inside, insistent, dangerous.

As he went from town to town, he asked questions, vague, sideways questions. Anything new? Any changes? Anyone interesting stop by lately? Just for my log book, of course. Strictly off the record. The responses were usually noncommittal, as indefinite as the inquiry itself. I need more information, Wake thought. I'm groping in the dark. He thought about calling P.T., but what would he tell him? Be patient, he told himself. Keep listening to the ground. Whatever it is will come into sight before long, hopefully before it tramples me.

His first break came back in Houdin. He had not intended to stop there — he was just passing through on his way to Bald Lake. However, driving by Knock's Bakery without loading up seemed unconscionable, so he bought a bag of salami doughnuts and went next door to the newspaper office to pick up a copy of the *Houdin Herald*. As he dropped fifty cents into the container and plucked a paper from the pile, glancing at the headline, "Local Man Distraught Over Demise of Talking Horse Show, Three Held Hostage," he caught a conversation taking place on the far end of the counter.

". . . stressed out or something. He must have stamped their name thirty times on this notice. When he came in he slammed it down and said, 'Goddammit, what's wrong with you people?'"

"That's funny, he's always seemed like such an easygoing guy. All we did was leave Carrots's name off Moms Stulkutz's notice."

"Maybe business has fallen off."

"Yeah, right. It's such a seasonal line of work."

"Funny. Say, did someone drop off the city council agenda?"

Wake folded the paper in half and walked out. They

were right. Carrots was as happy-go-lucky as they came. He enjoyed chatting and interacting with people, no matter what their status, breathingwise. An outburst as described was quite out of character. Perhaps his dog got into the scrap bucket. Anyway, it was worth investigating.

Getting back in his car, Wake made a U-turn on First Avenue and cut down Third Street to the funeral home. As he neared the entrance he noticed a man in a dignified black suit sitting on the curb at the side of the building, frantically trying to light a cigarette. It was Fred Carrots.

Pulling up to him, Wake stuck his head out the window and said, "Afternoon, Carrots. Nice day for a funeral, eh?"

The man looked up, dark circles under his sunken eyes. "Oh, Wakefield, it's you. Yeah, nice day."

"You look like horseshit. Which means either you're neck deep in customers or nobody's being thoughtful enough to pass on within trocar reach of you lately. Or are Strum and Dang beating your brains out?"

Carrots laughed bitterly. "Strum and Dang? Strum and Dang? You haven't been around lately, pal."

This could be it, Wake thought. All his instincts were leaping toward this sorry figure, who had given up attempting to ignite his weed, letting it slip from his trembling fingers.

"Nice day for a drive," Wake said. "Care to join me?"

Anxiously glancing back at the funeral home, Carrots shook his head. "Can't. Some other time."

"I want to talk to you."

Carrots quickly stood up. "I gotta go," he said, striding swiftly back to the building. After the door closed behind him, Wake sat in the parking lot for a few minutes, engine idling, figuring his next move. Under the right circumstances he'll talk, Wake guessed. Something drastic has knocked him into this desperate state. But he owns the place. If there was an employee problem, he could fire the offender. If a procedure needed altering or a piece of equipment required repair, he could take care of it himself. The mention of Strum and Dang had provoked a strong response, so Wake headed over to the west end of town.

Wake drove past the location of Houdin's oldest funeral home twice before realizing he could not spot the building because it was no longer there. No, that was not exactly correct. The building was there, but it was no longer Strum and Dang Funeral Home.

The sign now said: OhBoy Family Restaurant.

He went in and ordered meat loaf, baked potato, and apple pie.

It wasn't bad.

❊   ❊   ❊

Wake checked into the Bostonian Hotel at the main intersection in Houdin, right across the street from Liberty and Truth Savings and Loan. As he was checking in, the postman tossed a sack of letters onto the counter and tugged Wake aside. "Let me give you a little friendly advice," he whispered. "This joint is full of Mexicans, mostly illegals. They work in the chicken processing plant. Most of them are in gangs. It's true; I read it in the newspaper. They're causing a lot of problems around here. There's a nice little motel on the north edge of town, the Spindletop Motor Lodge. They just renovated the . . ."

"Aw, go look for a federal holiday," Wake snapped at him, going back to the counter. He signed the registration card, grabbed his suitcase, and headed upstairs. After unpacking his clothes and showering, Wake proceeded to implement the first stage of his hastily conceived plan. First, he went to the hardware store and bought a pair of cheap binoculars, then drove back to the funeral home and parked alongside the armory, which was kitty-corner to Carrots's. From there he had a full view of whoever came and went through both the front and side doors.

Late that afternoon a pair of men in matching black three-piece suits exited from the side door. Peering through his binoculars, Wake got a good look at their faces, but did not recognize them. The men climbed into a white sedan and headed north. The remainder of the afternoon was slow, although Carrots did sneak out again and sulk at the curbside. Wake considered confronting him once more, but decided he would get better results if he first knew more about what exactly was taking place.

Early the following morning Wake returned to his post and was rewarded for his vigilance at just past 9:00 A.M. An unmarked red truck pulled into the side parking lot, backing up to the delivery door. A trio of burly men began unloading canvas-covered crates, perhaps a half dozen in all. They stood around and chatted for a minute before removing a refrigerator-size box from the truck and rolling it into the loading bay.

Just then, a long flatbed truck rolled up, conveying an object about the dimensions of a small car, draped in burlap. It took the three men from the first truck plus both men from the second to unload the mysterious object and place it on the asphalt. One of the men began rigging up some type of pulley system, and suddenly one of the other men whisked the tarpaulin from the cargo.

A satellite dish.

Wake watched them all morning, as they maneuvered the dish onto the roof and installed it. He didn't know what to make of it. Although he had never seen a funeral home utilize a dish, he could imagine a variety of uses for it. Perhaps a new information service for the funeral industry was starting up. It could provide live coverage of seminars, conventions, and conferences throughout the world. Or perhaps it was intended as a service for the bereaved, giving them a break from those long visitation days with a dose of *El Sábado Gigante.* That seemed unlikely, though. The real question was whether or not it was related to Carrots's mental state. It was dangerous to try to tie every activity at the home to him. This could be perfectly innocent. It seemed routine. The delivery men, once they had finished installing the dish, went inside the home for perhaps ten minutes, after which time they returned to their truck and drove away, heading south.

After a tedious afternoon Wake decided it was time to force the issue. He checked the obituary notices in the *Herald*, found one for the following morning, a Moms Stulkutz, eighty-six. How very sad for the family, he thought.

Wake showed up for the wake at 10:00 A.M., alibi in hand. I'm just a scout, he told himself, going into the home. Just doing my job. Very professional embalming work here. A bright future. We should talk contract some time.

As soon as he entered the visitation room, Wake pulled up short. There was Carrots, talking softly to family members at the side of the casket. Wake retreated into an adjacent waiting room. Seconds later a tall, youngish man in a black suit came into the room. Wake had seen him before. It's that Slade kid, Wake thought. The big stiff. Wake smiled dolefully and nodded.

Slade looked quizzically at him. "Don't I know you?"

"I don't believe we've met," Wake replied, trying to rub his face into unfamiliarity. "I'm Jolly Winston, a cousin of the departed."

"Oh. I'm sorry. You have my sympathy."

"Thank you."

Slade left the room, but not before he shot another glance at Wake.

Have to move fast, Wake thought. He ducked out of the room and crept down the corridor. He poked his head in the first door on his left, a broom closet, and the second door, the women's bathroom. Further down the hall was a set of double doors. Opening one a crack and peeking in, he saw the room was empty, so he slipped inside and quietly closed the door behind him.

This is it, he thought, heart racing. I found it.

It was a conference room with a polished dark wooden table at its center, and a giant video screen at the head of the table. An array of electronic equipment lined the walls behind the screen. On the table sat a thick, sealed manila folder. Wake picked it up. It was marked: CONFIDENTIAL—POST-NEED PROGRAM MATERIAL.

Post-need?

"That will do, Mr. Wakefield."

Wake whirled around. Slade and Carrots were standing in the doorway, Carrots slightly behind the younger man. Slade snatched the folder from Wake's hand. "Get out. If you ever set foot in this building again, I will personally see to it that you do some quality jail time."

Wake ignored Slade. He looked at Carrots, whose eyes were downcast. "What's going on, Fred?"

"You'd better leave, Wake," he said somberly.

Wake glanced down at the folder, then at Slade. "Post-need? What the hell does that mean?"

"Please leave. *Now.*"

Relenting, Wake let Slade escort him out onto the front steps. Turning back, Wake said, "Only the blackmailed or the dead can keep secrets, Slade, and sometimes I'm not so sure about the dead."

"Good-bye, Mr. Wakefield."

Going back to his car Wake thought: *Post-need. This smells like trouble.*

nine

ANDY NOTICED THE announcement on the dorm bulletin board his first day back from summer vacation. LOOKING FOR COMPETITIVE EMBALMERS, it said at the top. He read on: "The Holmes U Nightshades varsity embalming team will be holding tryouts this Wednesday and Thursday at Lunt Field beginning at 4:00 P.M. Registered students only are eligible. Must be available afternoons and weekends for practice. For more information contact Coach Marty Crok at x5551."

Last year, Andy thought, I wouldn't have even given a notice like this a second glance. I would have been too scared. But things looked different somehow after his summer as a slave. I can do this, he told himself.

So following his afternoon funeral etiquette class on Wednesday, he changed into a black T-shirt, shorts, and sneakers, and headed over to Lunt Field. By the time he got there the field was crammed with hopeful underclassmen standing about pensively. Separated from this group were perhaps six fellows attired in identical black jumpsuits and black high-top sneakers, chatting and laughing confidently.

He recognized some of them from the *Blade,* the student newspaper: Mattle, Redgate, Rhodes. The stars of the varsity squad. The team, Andy recalled, had fared poorly last season, finishing near the cellar in the conference.

A portly man in a baseball cap and black warm-up jacket, clipboard tucked under his arm, came jogging across the field. He tooted his whistle and the boys hushed.

"Okay, listen up, fellas," he said. "For those of you who don't know me, I'm Coach Crok. It looks like we've got a good turn out today, and I know there's a lot of you who will have a decent shot of making the varsity squad. We also field a junior varsity team for you freshmen out there. Now, I know there are those of you who probably think that competitive embalming is a walk in the graveyard. Let me assure you that nothing could be further from the truth. It's one thing to embalm in the privacy of your own office or home, but when you've got five thousand fans screaming at the top of their lungs and you see the clock ticking down, three, two, one, why by God then you find out if you've got guts in your belly or just sawdust. Okay, enough yakkin'. Two laps around the crematorium, let's go!"

Some of the hopefuls got pooped after just one lap and could not run any farther. "Move it! Move it!" Coach Crok bellowed. "I've seen stiffs with better wind than some of you!" Andy completed both laps without much difficulty, finishing third overall.

"Conditioning is one of the most vital aspects of our sport," said the coach. "Fatigue makes for sloppy workmanship. We may have had a lousy record last season, but nobody, I repeat *nobody* beat us because we were not in shape. We will be running every day, lifting weights, doing agility drills. Now line up here in groups of five and we'll give you a taste of the real thing."

A couple members of the varsity team hauled out an embalming dummy, positioning it in the center of the field, along with a practice casket with training wheels, a suit of clothes, and a tray of tubes and needles.

"Before I blow the whistle," the coach said, "you will have decided which of you will assume what position. When I do blow the whistle, you will simulate your assigned activity. First team, on your marks."

Andy found himself in the second group, taking the position of casketeer. He watched as the first team ran raggedly to the dummy, bumping into one another as they tried to take their positions. As they pretended to work on the dummy, three of the boys were standing back, apparently waiting for the others to finish. The four working on the dummy then stepped back, giving the others space to step forward. The second group made some uncertain motions above the dummy and when they finished the entire team stood there for a moment, looking at each other and the corpse, before trotting back into line.

"What did they do wrong?" the coach asked patiently. "Anybody?"

"They should have all been working on the deceased at the same time, shouldn't they?" someone said.

"You are correct. Their left and right needlemen were out of position, leaving the creamer and dresser no choice but to stand back and wait for them to finish. The casketeer, you may have observed, was also standing back. This is the correct position, but he is generally the captain of the team and so it is his responsibility to direct the team and keep his teammates coordinated and working as a single unit. Next group!"

Andy picked up on the suggestion and tried to keep his group from stepping on each other's toes as they worked on the dummy. Midway through the exercise he noticed that the left needleman had completed his task, while the dresser was having a problem with the pants.

"Dresser needs help!" he called out.

The needleman jumped over and gave the slacks the last little tug they needed. They casketed the dummy—Andy grabbing him under the arms and dragging him into position—and sprinted back to the sidelines.

"Better, better," said the coach. "Good direction, uh, what's your name, son?"

"Andy Archway."

"Nice job, Archway."

After every group had a chance to perform a mock embalming, the coach took a trocar and pointed it at them, saying, "F-U-N-D-A-mentals. You can't win in this game without your fundamentals. You can have all the talent in the world, but if you can't insert a trocar without spilling your fluids, then you will be in a sorry state. Let me tell you a story. I was on the sixty-three team here at Holmes U, yes, that championship season. In the title game we were up against Grail State. They were a real powerhouse back then. They were bigger than us, stronger than us, more talented than us, probably smarter than us, too."

Everyone laughed.

"Nobody gave us a chance to beat them, not even our own fans. We didn't care. Coach Blackstone told us not to worry about the other team or the fans, just keep our eye on the corpse. We practiced three hours a day, five days a week that season. Positioning, timing, technique. The fundamentals. Grail State knew the fundamentals, too, but maybe they were a little too cocky, or maybe they had been partying too much that week counting on a championship celebration. Whatever, they weren't prepared for the crematorium they ran into when they took the field at Memorial Stadium. We were up 20–0 before they knew what hit them. We beat them every way possible. When the final gun sounded Coach Blackstone had his heart attack and died, beginning that long-standing tradition. Legend has it that as he was being carted off the field a reporter asked him why his team won the title that day. The coach motioned for the reporter to come close, and when the reporter put his ear to the coach's mouth he heard him say in a hoarse, barely audible whisper, *'Funda-mentals.'* " Coach Crok dabbed away a tear. "That was the last word Coach Blackstone ever spoke."

After letting the story sink in for a few moments, the coach began passing out practice jerseys. As Andy took his, Coach Crok said, "I don't remember you from last year. Are you a freshman?"

"No, I didn't try out last year. I was having a problem with my studies."

"I should warn you that there will only be a couple of spots open on the varsity squad. Boys who were on last year's junior varsity will be fighting like funeral directors for those open spots. That first year is important, although heck, you sure looked like you caught on quick out there."

"I'm going to make the team, coach," Andy said flatly.

"You'll get your chance," the coach promised.

After everyone had gotten a jersey, Coach Crok waved the boys to his side and motioned for them to kneel down. "Tomorrow is the big day," he said. "Do or die. You'll get your choice of positions, working alone with the equipment we use in game situations. We'll run a stopwatch on you to check your speed and I will judge the quality of your work. You'll get one chance—no more, no second tries. The results from these trials will make up eighty percent of my decision on whether or not you make the team. The rest will be based on those qualities that are required for the position you try out for. Your character, temperament, personality, and so forth will come into play here. I will be fair. I wish I had positions for each and every one of you. Now take another lap and we'll see you back here the same time tomorrow."

❈ ❈ ❈

Left needleman, Andy thought to himself in his dorm room the night prior to his big chance. Definitely left needleman. Make the incision in the jugular vein. Let the blood drain out. Insert the tube in the carotid artery and pump the embalming fluid in. Simple. He knew he could do it fast and he figured it was the one area where he was least likely to get marked down based merely on a subjective aesthetic judgment. Yet it required enough technical skill that it should impress the coach if he didn't slip up.

He knew some of the fellows would take the easy way out and opt for dresser. It was Andy's opinion, and he knew it was controversial, that it didn't take much talent to put clothes on a dead body. Or rather, though it might take some talent, the result was singularly unimpressive. It was a childish task, like showing the world you could put your underwear on straight.

Rummaging through his closet, Andy found his homemade embalming tubes, and he spent the rest of the night practicing on his pillow, just going through the motions step-by-step. I'm only going to have one chance, he thought. His main worry was Art, the artificial corpse used in embalming classes and competitions. Andy had learned in lab class that Art was finicky; if the temperature or humidity got too low or too high, he would not cooperate at all. His synthetic skin would soften or harden, the veins and arteries would expand or contract. But then, everyone would be embalming under the same conditions.

Insert. Drain. Insert. Pump.

Andy fluffed up his pillow and kept practicing.

❊ ❊ ❊

The next afternoon, Andy nervously limbered up on the edge of Lunt Field, awaiting his turn. It was a blood-chilling day, the wind blowing hard from the north, more like late November than early September. He carefully studied the other hopefuls as they raced to midfield and worked on Art. The fellow ahead of Andy chose right needleman, and Andy could tell he was having a hard time drilling the trocar into the cold-hardened abdomen.

Andy blew on his hands as the fellow finished up. Coach Crok inspected the job while an assistant ran up and reset the scene, draining and refilling Art, and replacing the trocar and tube back on the cart, which also contained the portable pumps and bottles. The coach wrote something on his clipboard and raised his hand.

"Archway!" Andy cried out. "Left needleman!" He crouched low, knees bent, waiting for the signal.

The coach lowered his arm and gave a burst on his whistle.

Andy forgot about the cold, the other players, Coach Crok standing nearby with his stopwatch. His consciousness focused into a tunnel, onto his fingers, the pump, the needles, and the artificial thing on the slab before him.

Insert. Drain. Insert. Pump.

It was all over in an instant. Andy stepped back, in a slight daze.

"Outstanding time," said the coach. "Good job, Archway."

"Thanks," he replied, gaining his bearings again. He gazed at his work as if it was someone else's, and bounded off the field.

The next morning Andy headed straight to the locker room after breakfast. The list was posted on the wall outside Coach Crok's office.

Mattle
Redgate
Rhodes
Anson
Archway

Andy reached out and pressed his fingertips against his name on the sheet, as if he wanted to be certain it was real.

I'm on the team, he said to himself. I did it.

*　*　*

However, being on the team and actually getting a chance to play turned out to be two entirely different prospects. Andy fully expected to ride the bench his first few games, but when the fourth game, a squeaker at lowly Silas Tech, came and went without his name being called, Andy began to get worried.

The next day at lunch, Andy poked at his tuna-fish sandwich without enthusiasm.

"Look," Maria finally said, "if you feel strongly about it, why don't you have a talk with Coach Crok?"

"Maybe I will, tomorrow," Andy agreed.

"What's wrong with right now? You know his home is always open to his boys. You'll sleep better if you settle it tonight."

Smiling weakly, Andy said, "I suppose you're right. All right, I'll do it." He pushed his chair back from the table and stood up.

Andy walked to Osiris Street. Coach Crok lived in a small bungalow at the edge of the campus. Crok was a bachelor, but his home was always clean and neat. There was a big stone fireplace with an array of trophies on the mantel. Deep, comfortable leather chairs were scattered around the spacious living room. And the small study was lined with bookcases and photographs of the great embalmers of the past. The house always smelled of pipe tobacco and formaldehyde. Often, after a triumph on the playing field, the coach would hold an open house for his players.

Andy felt nostalgic as he walked down the short lane that led to the bungalow, remembering the good times he hoped to one day spend there. The coach was sitting on the front steps, smoking his pipe, when Andy walked up. October had come in clear and balmy, and it was pleasant to be outdoors in the late afternoon.

Coach Crok smiled. "Well, this is a surprise. Pull up a step and sit down."

"Yes, sir," Andy said self-consciously.

"Looks like we're going to have fine weather for the homecoming festivities this Friday," the coach said.

"And the game on Saturday," Andy added. "That's what I want to talk to you about. I want what's best for the team, Coach, but how long do you think it will be before I'll get in a game? I'm getting pretty frustrated sitting on the bench all the time."

"And you're probably getting a few splinters, too!" Coach Crok joked with a kind smile. "Andy, you've got to be patient. Remember, this is your first year on the team. There's a lot to learn. I will say that you've been doing a fine job in practice. One of the problems is that we haven't had any blowouts yet this season. The games have all been so tightly fought that we haven't had a chance to slip in our backups for a few minutes at the end of the game."

"I really feel like I could help the team, Coach."

"Tell you what. No promises, but if it's at all possible I'll try to run you in for at least one play Saturday. Then we'll take it game by game from there. Believe me, if you prove you belong in the starting lineup, I'll only be too glad to find a spot for you."

❉ ❉ ❉

As homecoming festivities got under way that week, Andy maintained a low profile, keeping his concentration on the upcoming game. The opponent was the Grail State Rattlers, a rematch from that championship season. Although Grail State had first place in the conference locked up and already had accepted an invitation to the Funeral Bowl, you could throw out the memorial book when these two bitter rivals clashed.

However, Andy did want to see Friday night's bonfire, so around dusk he picked up Maria, who brought a broken wooden folding chair, and they strolled hand in hand across campus to Lunt Field. A big crowd had already gathered there, milling around a pile of old furniture, boxes, and other combustible debris. A fire truck stood waiting nearby, just in case.

Maria handed the chair to a member of the Cremation Club, which had sponsored the event, and the fellow tossed the chair onto the stack.

Cremation Club president Red Binderstaff hopped up onto a flatbed trailer. He brandished a dummy wearing an orange-and-black Grail State jersey. "Okay! Okay! This is Ralph the Rattler. You know what's going to happen when we light the fire, don't you, don't you?"

"Yah!" the crowd cheered.

"That's right, the same thing that's going to happen tomorrow afternoon!"

The fire was lit. It rapidly grew into an inferno, aided by a brisk evening breeze. Sparks from the blaze shot in the air, scattering the crowd standing downwind. The firefighters started looking nervous, but the bonfire stayed contained.

Roger Redgate, team captain, was given the honor of heaving Ralph the Rattler into the flames. The crowd cheered wildly, the Crematorium Club members perhaps more loudly than the rest. The dummy ignited instantly, and the crowd let out another whoop. A man with a camera slung around his neck circled the fire, snapping pictures.

As the bonfire burned on, the crowd grew silent, staring into the flames. Someone began singing softly, and soon others began to join in.

"Sing in praise to thee our College, Low on swampy banks,

Emblem of our search for knowledge, Symbol of our pale ranks
Filled with fires of true cremation, Let us ever be,
Loyal to thy fine tradition, Hail, Holmes U, to thee."

t ε n

SATURDAY BROKE CRISP and sunny, a perfect fall day. Andy headed down to the locker room early, too nervous to do anything else. As he came into the room, Coach Crok, in his office, called out, "Archway, come in here."

"What is it, Coach?" Andy asked, poking his head in the door.

"You're going to get your chance sooner than you think. Mattle smashed his car into a telephone pole after the bonfire last night, that reckless numbskull. He wasn't hurt seriously, but he broke two fingers on his right hand. You're taking his place at left needleman."

"My gosh," Andy exclaimed.

"I know you're ready for this or else I would have chosen another replacement. Don't worry, Andy, you'll do great."

Andy slowly went to his locker and placed his uniform on the bench. He knew coach was right. He knew he was ready. He knew it was his time.

The team gathered around Coach Crok before running into the stadium. In the distance the pep band was charging through a revved-up version of the Funeral March. "Now I know we've been dealt a tough break here," he said, "but it's a sign of character to overcome adversity. I know all of you have full confidence that Archway can do the job out there today. I know I do. We need to help him any way we can. If we play as a team, we can beat those Rattlers. I don't care if they're in first place or not. They're not supermen. They put the pants on their corpses one leg at a time, just like we do. Right?"

"RIIIGHT!!!"

"Now hush up and bow your heads, fellas. Lord, allow us to perform to the best of our ability today, to respect our opponents and the lifelike simulated human being we will be working on. Allow us to be good sports in victory or, if for some reason it's your will, in defeat. We ask that you protect us and our opponents from injury, and help us remember that no matter what the outcome, there are bigger homecoming games in life, the homecoming when we join you in heaven. Amen."

"Amen," repeated the team.

"Now let's get out there and knock 'em dead!"

The team dashed through the tunnel onto the Memorial Stadium turf to the roar of the crowd while on the stadium's crest bright pennants fluttered in the breeze. They circled the field once and went to their bench area, each player kneeling for a moment at the row of tombstones for departed coaches located behind the bench. Also behind the bench were the cheerleaders, who were forming a human headstone. They waved their pom-poms, chanting, "Blood out, fluid in! Go team, win!"

Before the opening whistle sounded, Redgate, the captain, pulled Andy aside. "Just relax out there," he said. "Don't let the crowd throw you. Keep focused. Don't forget we're a team. We can whip these guys." He clapped Andy on the shoulder. "Now let's go get 'em."

The Rattlers won the toss and elected to go with a standard corpse. When the whistle trilled the teams raced to the center of the field in precision form and began to work. Andy discovered that his fingers were not cooperating with his brain. They felt wooden, clumsy. Gotta relax, he reminded himself. He made the incision in the jugular, and his hand jerked suddenly, opening a big gash in the neck. He quickly stuck the tube in, but the blood began streaming down the neck and onto the ground.

"Archway, you've got a problem!" Redgate yelled. "Tommy, help him out!"

Tommy Bones, the creamer, had just fitted the eyecaps into place. He jabbed his thumbs against the ragged wound exposed around the perimeter of the tube. The bleeding dwindled to a trickle.

"Before you pump the fluid," Redgate said, stepping in Bones's spot and beginning to cement the eyes shut, "let Tommy stitch up the wound. Then make your normal incision for the fluid. But be careful. Are you okay?"

"Yeah, I'm fine. It just slipped."

"Okay, we're doing good now, guys."

However, the lost seconds cost them. The Rattlers beat the Nightshades on time by more than a minute for a 10–0 lead. When the referee finished his grading and the marks were posted on the scoreboard, the crowd groaned in disappointment. Holmes U had been docked twenty penalty points, while the Rattlers were penalized only five, giving them a twenty-five-point lead after the first round.

During the timeout, Coach Crok told his troops, "Look, let's not hold our heads down. One corpse doesn't make a match. I've got an idea. Here's what we're gonna do."

At the start of the second round, the referee trotted to midfield and made a chopping motion, right hand striking left wrist. The crowd roared. This meant Holmes U had designated the teams to work this round on a corpse that was missing its left hand. That meant making a plaster cast for the hand, and Coach Crok knew that his plaster specialist, Ronny Diggs, was one of the best in the conference, and that this was a hole that Grail State had been unsuccessfully attempting to fill all season. Ronny did his usual lifelike job, while the Rattlers seemed to be having trouble. However, at the end of the round the referee signaled only a five-point penalty for Grail State.

Coach Crok threw his cap to the ground. "What the hell are you looking at?" he screamed at the official. "What's wrong with you? Get over here! Get over here!" Coach started out onto the field, but the referee jogged over, motioning him back. "Stay off the field, Coach. I don't want to give you a penalty."

"Where did you come up with this five points crap? Are you seeing something I'm not?"

"It's a judgment call, Coach."

"But look at it! That hand looks like a deformed foot! My blind aunt could do better than that! That's a ten-point penalty, minimum."

"Five points," he said and ran off.

"*Un*-believable," the coach said to anyone within earshot. "That's a ten-point penalty right there."

As the game wore on, Andy grew more comfortable and his tubing picked up considerably. By halftime, the Rattlers' lead had been cut to ten points.

"We're right in there," Coach Crok told his team at halftime. "We're making up ground on them. Tommy, terrific work on the cast. We got jobbed on that one, I'm afraid. We have to keep our poise in the second half. Let's not panic. We can't make up ten points the minute we run out there. We've got to stick to the fundamentals. The results will take care of themselves."

The teams returned to the field as the halftime show was concluding. It was a historical tribute to the coffin torpedo, a device containing an explosive charge and a mechanism set to go off when there was any tampering with the coffin. First manufactured by the Clove Coffin Torpedo Manufacturing Company of Columbus, Ohio, its purpose was to discourage the practice of grave robbing. In the halftime show's grand finale, a torpedo-shaped formation of coffins blew up simultaneously as mimes portraying grave robbers did a synchronized somersault and expired. The crowd applauded politely.

As the second half began, Andy went from being comfortable to actually enjoying the competition. He wanted to win. He worked faster, more efficiently—in fact, so quickly and efficiently that he had enough time to tie up a shoe or sew up a mouth. When he did this, the crowd went crazy. Even his teammates were looking oddly at him. But he was not even consciously trying to do well. He did not think. It seemed so easy. The veins and arteries looked as thick as garden hoses.

Holmes U closed the gap to five points. Then they tied the score. The crowd went bonkers. Grail State frantically tried to hold off the onslaught that was the Holmes U Nightshades, but it was too late. Holmes took the lead on a standard corpse and cruised to a 45–30 victory, scoring the biggest upset of the year in the conference.

In the triumphant locker room afterward, the *Blade*'s sports editor George Slocum cornered Andy, who was peeling off his sweat-soaked jersey. "Where's the coach been hiding you?" he asked. "You were a regular Mordecai out there."

"Gosh, I don't know about that."

"Watch out, Andy," Coach Crok said, coming over, wearing a wide grin. "You won't recognize yourself after Scoop Slocum gets through with you." He placed a firm hand on Andy's shoulder. "You really did the job out there today, son. I'll admit that I was a little concerned after the first round, but you displayed some real poise out there. In fact,

I'm not sure I've ever seen anything quite like it. I'm proud of you."

"Thanks, Coach. I didn't want to let you down."

"Let me at him now," said Slocum. "This is news."

❖ ❖ ❖

Andy picked up the *Blade* Monday morning from a bin outside the cafeteria and was stunned to see his own face staring out at him from the front page under the headline, "Newcomer Spurs Homecoming Win." He self-consciously folded the paper in half and walked off.

Andy soon got used to seeing his photo in the paper. After Mattle recovered from his date with the telephone pole, Andy stayed in the starting lineup. There was no other choice. Andy had already broken three school records for fast embalming. As the records fell, old-timers said they had never seen a speedier embalmer than Andy Archway, and that included one Janus P. Mordecai.

The sports pages in the *Blade* were packed with coverage about Andy's exploits and praise of the emerging legend himself. The Golbyville Ghost, they called him. Dandy Andy. The Next Mordecai. He clipped out every word and sent them to his folks.

People began recognizing him around campus. They slapped his back, shook his hand, remarked at what a marvelous season he was having.

It was a heady time, and he was happy to let the tide take him out. What other choice did he have? For the first time in his life, Andy believed, the world was making room for him.

❖ ❖ ❖

"I haven't seen you much lately," Maria said over the phone one evening. How have you been?"

"Fine. Things have been pretty hectic lately, you understand."

"Oh, I know. I understand that. I'm so happy for you,

90

Andy. I was always afraid for you, afraid you would be lost."

"That's nice of you. I do appreciate it."

"You sound different. Am I calling at a bad time?"

"No, it's not a bad time. I'm glad you called."

"I want to see you. Can I come over tonight? I can leave in twenty minutes or so."

"Tonight? No, not tonight. I have to go to an interview. A writer from *Western Undertaker* called. He wants to meet me at his hotel in an hour."

"I could come over until you go."

"No, I'm too busy getting ready. It's just not a good time for me, Maria."

"How about tomorrow, then?"

"I don't know. I think I have a meeting with someone."

"All day?"

"Well, I've got a term paper to finish up for a class, too."

"So what day would be good for you?"

"I don't know. I'd have to check my schedule. Why don't I call you back sometime?"

"Why don't you want to see me?"

"Look, I don't want to talk about it right now. I gotta go."

"Andy . . ."

He hung up the phone.

"Who was that?" asked the red-haired coed perched on the bed.

"Just a friend," Andy replied.

909

ELEUEN

*If the Mountain Won't Come to Mohammed, Then Build a Better
Mousetrap*
—*title of self-published book by Bob Drabford, 1965, 909 Ranch, Fla.*

IT WAS WITH an unexpected sense of apprehension that Dan
Slade first set foot in the primordial modernism of contempo-
rary Florida. The Sunshine State had always held a mythic
quality for him. It was part of the United States, yet it seemed
to belong to somewhere else as well, to some other time, to
some other land. Steamy winters, alligators, hurricanes,
Everglades, baseball-playing chickens. At one time the landscape must have inspired its people, provoked some outland-
ish dreams, but now, as he drove through Swamp City,
Palmetto, the West Dunes, he saw only fragments of the
strange past: Cypress Knees Museum, the Serpentarium, the
Citrus Tower.

Now, Slade wondered, where would the Drabford
Brothers fit into this realm? He had considered them to be
merely successful businessmen when he signed with them
after he graduated from Holmes U. He was flattered when

they offered him the lead position in a funeral home they had just acquired in Houdin. Who wouldn't be? The pay was above median and the possibilities for advancement were unlimited. Of course, he had never met the brothers face-to-face, but the representatives he had talked to seemed normal enough.

So it caught him off guard when the trucks showed up that day and the men unloaded the satellite equipment, and he was handed a packet containing something called "Post-Need Program Materials." He had been excited at first, seeing proof that the Drabfords were willing to make capital improvements in Houdin. It seemed like a good sign. Yet even while the equipment was being installed, a vague sense of puzzlement played in the back of his mind. He could think of fifteen other things the home needed more than a load of high-tech video paraphernalia. Their fluid pumps were twenty years old, minimum. The hearses had been overhauled twice in the past year, Carrots had told him. Slade stopped the practice of using the hearses for personal use, but that didn't alter the fact that they needed to be replaced.

His befuddlement changed to dismay when he began to read and digest the program materials. Slade had thought, reading the first few pages, that it was a joke, but he kept reading, faster and faster, skimming through the manual in disbelief. Whoever wrote this stuff is delusional, he had thought. It was grandiose, hallucinatory nonsense. Then, several days later, Drabford's regional office called and told him to pack his bags and catch the first flight available for Florida. Bring your cowboy boots, they said, if you want to get in good with the boys. They gave him an address in southern Florida, outside the town of Ringling. The 909 Ranch, it was called. Ask around. You can't miss it.

As it turned out, Slade did miss it, or at least he thought he had. He followed the instructions, which sent him from four lanes of blacktop to a rutted, muddy, gravel road winding through a grove of cypress trees. But he had been bouncing along these desolate roads for what seemed like hours without any indication that he was any nearer the 909 than when he had begun his trip. Finally, he decided he had taken a wrong turn somewhere, and pulled into a ramshackle gas station called Hap's. Slade peeled his shirt off from where it was sticking to his sweat-soaked back and went inside, the screen door banging behind him. Behind the counter stood a man with skin that looked as rough as an alligator's hide. A shock of black hair lay pasted to his sunburned forehead. A knife handle protruded from a sheath buckled around his waist. His meaty, scarred hands were clenching a beaten-up copy of a book bearing a title that began, *If the Mountain Won't Come*, etc. He looked at Slade as he came in and said, "Hi."

"Hello," Slade said, scanning the store for something to purchase, not wanting to admit that he was lost. I am thirsty, he decided, and plucked a bottle of grape soda from a cooler, setting it and a dollar bill on the counter.

The man stared at the items, a strange look on his gnarled cypress face. Then he looked at Slade and half-smiled. "What is this, some kind of joke?"

Slade dropped his eyes to the counter. What had he done? He stared at the bottle of soda, at the dollar bill, and saw nothing amiss. He looked at the counter man again. "I'm sorry?"

"Come on, pal, it's not *that* funny. Give me some *real* money."

Now Slade thought he understood. He picked up the bill and gazed at it carefully. Odd. Nothing phony about the bill, as least as far as he could tell. Maybe the man was an ex-con, used to run a counterfeiting ring, probably. He smiled hopefully. "Boy, you've got better eyes than I do. It looks like the genuine article to me."

"I'm beginning to lose my patience. Either buy the pop or get out."

Slade quickly retrieved the bill and slipped it back into his wallet. "Suits yourself. I didn't want it anyway. I just came in looking for directions—909 Ranch, have you heard of it?"

The man said nothing for a moment, then quietly asked, "Where you from?"

"Houdin, Minnesota, not that it's any of your business. Look, I have a meeting to get to this afternoon. Do you know where it is or not?"

"You're not lost," said the man. "You've found it."

"I did?"

"This is 909 Ranch property," he replied. "You musta come in on Tiki Road. Every other way in is marked. When it rains, the road washes out. Not many of us drive on it anymore. You're lucky we've been dry lately."

"I guess I am. How far is it to the Drabford house?"

"Not far. Twenty miles, maybe."

"*Twenty miles?* You've got to be kidding. How big is this place?"

"Oh, a hundred thousand acres, give or take a few hundred."

"*A hundred thousand?* Shit, why do they call it a ranch? I was expecting to see herds of cattle, horses racing down to the bunkhouse, cowboys trying to lasso cowgirls."

The counter man grinned. "You'll get a taste of that, up by the main compound. But that's mostly for show. Tourists like that sort of thing."

"How long have you lived here?"

"I was born on the 909. I've lived here all my life. Probably been a good eight years since I set foot outside the Ranch, and that was to see my daughter get married out in Missouri. I spared no time in getting back."

"I'm a little confused," Slade said. "Are you saying the Drabfords own all this?"

"Yes, and it's not just the land," said the man, his demeanor transforming into that of a gracious host and civic booster. "There's citrus groves, a mining operation, a wild animal park — I couldn't begin to list them all. We run our own hospital, publish our own newspaper, and print our own money. We're completely self-sufficient, you see."

"My dollar bill . . ."

"Yes, that kind of currency is no good here, I'm afraid. You need to exchange it for real money. I can do that for you here, if you'd like. Unfortunately, the exchange rate is not very favorable at the moment."

❖   ❖   ❖

Back on the road, Slade gulped down some grape soda and sneaked glances at the *909 Observer* on the seat beside him. "Biggest Dam in State Nears Completion," said one headline. "Citrus Group Posts Record High Profits." "Governor to Present Humanitarian Award to Drabford Brothers." A scattering of change also lay on the seat, visages of the brothers on each coin.

Slade quickly began to revise his opinion of the brothers. They weren't fools. It was clear they never did anything on a scale less than gargantuan. And if they were capable of building an empire like this, then perhaps the Post-Need Project wasn't so farfetched after all. Beyond the borders of the ranch, such a plan bordered on the lunatic. But here, within the boundaries of the 909, anything, it seemed, was possible.

❖   ❖   ❖

The ranch aspects of 909 became visible as the odometer on Slade's car hit eighteen miles. Fields of low, leafy plants, which Slade could not identify, were set in neat rows on both sides of the road. A half-dozen sheep grazed in a pasture, black faces nodding into the grasses. Suddenly, the road ended, blocked off by a gate with a sign warning NO MOTORIZED TRAFFIC BEYOND THIS POINT. There was a narrow dirt lot adjacent to the gate, occupied by a green, rust-eaten station wagon. Slade parked there, removed his suitcase from the trunk and started walking.

Sometime later, as he trekked to the top of a modest incline, he saw in the distance a complex of white modernistic buildings. Must be the place, he thought, and started down the hill. He walked a little farther before his ears caught a sound, indistinct at first, now growing louder. It was coming from behind him. He stopped and turned back. Over the hill came a trio of horses, hooves pounding on the dirt, kicking up clouds of dust in their wake. Riding the steeds were some children, and Slade felt an instant of fear for them, fear that they were not strong enough to keep the horses under rein, that they would get thrown.

But as they approached, Slade realized they were not children at all, but the Drabford Brothers, each attired in appropriate Western gear, riding low, urging more speed from their mounts. They raced by Slade, who turned with them as they flashed by, feeling a rush of wind on his face. Slade watched them as they headed toward the white buildings, then he sat down right there and opened his suitcase. He kicked off his loafers, tugged on his genuine Trail Boss cowboy boots, and moseyed on after them. By the time he caught up with them, they were watering their horses near a rustic-looking ranch house.

"Howdy," he said. "Name's Dan Slade. I'm the director out in Houdin, Minnesota. I'm here for the meeting."

"Good to make your acquaintance," said the older-looking of the three in a high-pitched voice, stroking his horse's side as it drank from the trough. Slade recognized him as the eldest brother, Bob. He looked younger than his picture. Although he was diminutive, Slade saw nothing cute or child-like about him. His eyes were bright but hard. His face and hands were pale, smooth, not the hands of cowpoke but of a businessman who spent long hours indoors, behind a computer and in meetings. They shook hands, the small hand disappearing into Slade's palm.

"These are my brothers," Bob said, "Preston and Everett." The duo tipped their hats and offered their hands. Preston and Everett were difficult to distinguish, keeping the same placid expressions, the same deep-set eyes. Slade guessed they were twins, although that may just have been their cowboy outfits. All three looked extremely fit and utterly sane.

"How'd you end up on the East Fork?" asked Bob. "Most folks come in through the main gate."

"I wanted to get a lay of the land first," Slade said. "It's quite a spread you've got here. Very impressive. I've never been to Florida before."

"Yes, Florida is pleasant, too," Bob said.

"I like your boots," said Everett.

Pulling his pant leg up, Slade said, "Yeah, I wear them a lot when I'm out traipsing around. Wouldn't go anywhere without them."

"From the looks of them," said Bob with a bemused smile, "you get out traipsing about as often as we get out riding."

"It's a go-go business, that's for sure," Slade agreed. When he let his pant leg back down, he reflexively scuffed his boot in the dirt.

"Shouldn't we be getting in?" Preston asked his brothers. "The program is scheduled to begin at one." He checked his watch. "It's almost 12:47."

"I suppose so," Bob said with a sigh. "But we do need to have Cookie rustle us up some grub first. Mr. Slade, you may join us or you may wish to freshen up at the bunkhouse. It's up to you."

"Some grub sounds mighty good," Slade said. "Lead the way."

After the group sat down at the rough-hewn benches inside the ranch house, a heavy-jowled man in a crisp white apron came to the table and said, "What'll it be, boys?"

"Four bowls, Cookie. And plenty of water."

"Gotcha."

"Forgive me for ordering for you," Bob told Slade, "but you must try the chili. We have it flown in direct from Texas every morning. You can't get authentic chili in Florida, I'm afraid."

"Thank you," Slade said. "Chili is my favorite food."

In less than a minute the cook returned, setting a steaming bowl of imported chili and a frosted glass of ice water in front of each of them. As they began eating, the elder Drabford said matter-of-factly, "So, Mr. Slade, you've had an opportunity to mull things over. What are your views on our Project Post-Need?"

Downing a spoonful of chili, Slade coughed, then guzzled some water and said, "It's a bold plan. Daring. Innovative. If anybody can pull it off, it is you fellows. Have you had a chance to run a pilot program yet?"

"There will be no trial runs," Bob said. "You see, for the project to be successful, all facets must be integrated. The scope of the project is so large that if we were to experiment with a small pilot project, the results would not be of much use to us. We have run, and will continue to run, computer simulations. The simulations have been quite successful. Of course, in the real world, unseen factors will crop up unexpectedly."

"Such as?"

"The human factor, for instance. The psychology of the masses is an indefinite science, unfortunately. In recent years, significant strides have been made in the fields of advertising and public relations; I'm thinking of the Spunky Cola episode in particular. Yet these abilities to shape the mass consciousness have been successful only in a peripheral sense. Once you enter the area of social mores and long-held beliefs, then the picture changes."

"Funeral professionals have always been in the advance guard of civilization," added Preston. "The public expects us to lead. They have no stomach for this. They will see us two or three times in the course of their lives, and in-between those times they will not reflect on us at all."

"Of course," said Everett, "we'll be mitforded from time to time. We have to expect that and be prepared to respond immediately. Right, brother Bob?"

Bob smiled. "My brother and I have a disagreement on this point. My view is that by the time the information works its way from the mitfords to the elite press to the popular press and into the homes of America, it will be too late. Even in this age, the channels of information must work on their own time. Any response from us rouses the attention of more and more media. They're a sleepy lot; they need to be shaken awake in order to notice an issue. If we remain still and walk through the room on tiptoe, they will dream on."

"It's 12:59," said Everett. "We should be going."

"Yes," Preston said, getting up, "we don't want to be late for the program."

"You can leave your suitcase here," Bob told Slade. "I'll have someone bring it over to the bunkhouse. You really don't want to miss the program."

As they walked across the compound, Slade expected them to head toward the white buildings beyond the ranch house, which appeared as if they might house meeting rooms and auditoriums. He was steeling himself for a long, dull afternoon of lectures and overhead slides. Instead, they swung around the horse barns to a grandstand area, half-filled with somber men in dark suits. When the Drabford Brothers entered and took their places in a roped-off box ten rows up in the center of the grandstand, ushering Slade in ahead of them, the crowd rose as one and applauded. The Brothers carefully removed their hats, and suddenly began waving them wildly above their heads. The crowd paused self-consciously for a moment, then began making hooting and whooping noises. The Drabfords abruptly sat down, and the crowd instantaneously went silent.

Happy fiddle music began playing over the loudspeaker, and Slade could see the Drabford Brothers were tapping their toes in unison, so he did the same. An old man in a cowboy outfit twirling a rope over his head came out into the center of the dirt track. "Howdy, folks," he said into a cordless mike attached to his head, "my name is Pawnee Bill, Jr. My pappy was Pawnee Bill, befriender of the Indian and companion to Buffalo Bill Cody himself. Pawnee Bill and Buffalo Bill traveled throughout the world, delighting millions with their Wild West show. Sadly, the Wild West show died in the 1930s, killed by the moving picture show." He held his hat over his heart and bowed his head. Then he replaced his hat and held his head proudly. "This ain't no moving picture show. I ain't on no TV screen. I ain't no little gremlin you shoot down on your videos. And I ain't no dead guy, either! I am Pawnee Bill, Jr., son of Pawnee Bill, benefactor of the Indian and best friend of Buffalo Bill! Get ready partners, this is Pawnee Bill's New Wild West Show!"

The "program" began with a display of the finer techniques of the buffalo hunt, proceeded to present a genuine demonstration of the Indian way of life (starring the descendants and a few neighbors of a tribe of real-life Seminoles), followed by examples of calf roping, sharp shooting, and yodeling, and concluded with a re-creation of Little Big Horn. Amid the carnage in the finale, Pawnee Bill, Jr., came riding slowly onto the scene, gazing sadly at the fallen soldiers, as if to say that if he had only been there, he might have been able to prevent this tragedy. A poignant, if historically inaccurate moment.

The assembled funeral professionals gave Pawnee Bill, Jr., and his troop a spirited ovation. No one, though, was cheering louder than the Drabford Brothers. They brought him back for three encores, and had him blast to bits another set of clay pigeons on horseback before allowing him to depart.

"Wow, that sure was something," Slade said as they left the grandstand, not sure if etiquette required him to break off and go his own way or hang at their heels.

"He's not really Pawnee Bill, Jr.," said Bob. "He used to be a ranch hand here before he retired. But the details of the show are authentic. We hired a history professor at Oklahoma State University as a consultant. It's just a way to break the ice, share our interests with our people."

"Where now?" Slade asked.

"I'm afraid this is where we must part company. The seminar starts in fifteen minutes at the main auditorium, and we need to change into more modest clothing. Please look for us this evening at the barbecue. Enjoy your stay."

"Thanks, I will. See you later." Slade headed off, whistling "Happy Trails." This is good, he thought. The Brothers noticed me, and they seemed to like me. This could get me out of Houdin in a big hurry. Would I be risking everything by asking if they could use me somewhere else in the organization? Depends, depends. Got to get the conversation going in that direction. Career goals, the future of the company. They'll like someone with ambition, who takes the long view on things. This is a rare opportunity. I can't blow it.

Back at the bunkhouse, Slade found his suitcase on a narrow cot at the rear of the long room. He changed clothes, traded boots for loafers, and splashed some water on his face from a basin. Heading outside, he followed the crowd to a spherical white building nestled into the side of a hill.

The interior of the building was glass and steel. The cool air smelled of synthetics rather than manure. In the lobby area streamlined mobiles dangled from the pitched ceiling. Tubular metal chairs were placed here and there, apparently more for effect than function. A dispassionate female voice intoned from above: "Please enter on your right. Extinguish all smoking materials. Leave all recording equipment with an attendant. Please remember that all information must be kept confidential."

Slade moved slowly down the sloping aisle with the others, and found a seat toward the front of the auditorium. He nodded to the fellow sitting beside him, a husky youngish man with a crew cut. "Boy, I'm sure looking forward to this," said the fellow, who was holding a copy of the same book Hap, the money-changer, had been reading.

"Say, what's the deal with that book?" Slade asked. "I'm seeing it everywhere."

"I picked it up at the gift shop when I came in," he replied, holding it up. For the first time Slade saw the full title and the author. "It's terrific stuff." He grinned. "Don't ask me to lend it to you. I'm going to try to get Drabford to autograph it."

"What's it about?"

"Well, that's sort of hard to explain. It's a self-help book for practical visionaries, I guess. I've only read the first couple chapters. He's talking about how he dreamed up the 909 Ranch. He says he saw the practical beginning, the actual ranch that 909 began as, and he saw the end point, which even goes beyond this incredible empire we see today. He says that's all you need, the rest will take care of itself if you keep both aspects in mind. And the wild thing is, he wrote the book in 1965! He knew all this would come to pass! He lived it himself!"

"That's something," Slade agreed. "I'll have to pick up a copy." Extending his hand, he said, "By the way, I'm Dan Slade, Houdin, Minnesota."

"Bart Brittleman, Neckstra, Montana."

"How's business in your parts?"

"Not bad. Most of the older folks in town worked in smelting and mining for the Conadora Copper Company. Lots of lung problems, kidney problems. Keeps you hopping. But now that the mine closed down, things don't look quite so rosy. When the Drabfords came in, they promised some big changes were coming, and it looks like they're going to live up to their promise. How are things in Minnesota?"

"Pretty steady. Houdin is an aging farming community, people pass on pretty much when they're supposed to. I guess I'm looking for something with a little more adventure to it. I'm not ready to settle down yet."

"You're in the right place, then. I . . ."

At that moment, the Drabford Brothers, now dressed in suits and ties, walked out onto the stage. The audience cheered enthusiastically. Bob the elder, flanked by his brothers, smiled merrily and after a brief interval held up his hands for quiet. "Thank you for that warm greeting," he began, "and thank you for accepting our invitation to visit us at our little home here, the 909 Ranch. I hope your stay will be memorable. Now, some of you are probably wondering why, in this age of whisker-quick communications, did we bring you all down here this weekend. Well, while we use the most up-to-date equipment here at the 909 and in our businesses throughout the country, we are in fact pretty old-fashioned at heart. If we are going to be embarking on a great adventure with you, we at least want the opportunity to shake your hand and look you in the eye and get to know you a little. So enjoy your stay here and make yourselves right at home. Now here's my brother Everett."

The crowd clapped, and then Everett Drabford stepped out front and said, "All of you have studied the Post-Need Program Materials that were sent to your various locations nine days ago. These materials explained what the Post-Need Project is, and what your role, as community funeral professionals, will be in the project. We deliberately kept the scope of the materials narrow, referring to the overall strategy of the project only in the most general terms. That situation will be remedied now. Lights, please."

The lights in the room dimmed, then faded to black. Seconds later a screen that had been lowered at the front of the stage was illuminated with the image of a funeral home set near a cornfield. "You are the front line of Project Post-Need," Everett Drabford said, his piping voice echoing through the room. "This is Phase One, securing a base across America. To that end the Resting Place Funeral Consortium, a group consisting of five companies wholly owned by Drabford Diversified, has been acquiring funeral homes from Maine to California over the past five years. The number now stands at 1,003. We make the purchase, install our own people, and drive out the competition. In most cases we have absorbed the competition, although some holdouts have refused to sell and are now out of business. We are now fairly comfortable that this base has been firmly established. You, the branches, will be primarily communicating with us via satellite, providing the command and control center with up-to-the-minute updates, holding teleconferences with command and control and other branches, and receiving strategy instructions in return."

The image on the screen changed to a single phrase in large block letters:

ESTABLISH THE NEED

"Read those words carefully," said Everett. "Recite them in your sleep if necessary. This is the second phase of the project. Establish the Need. Or should I say, establish the *Post*-Need." Laughter rippled through the hall. "The manuals on this phase of the project, if stacked together, would be as high as myself or my brothers . . ."—silence, then some nervous chuckles—". . . standing on each other's shoulders!" Peals of laughter filled the auditorium. "But to give you a brief overview, let me first say that we sincerely believe this is a need we're addressing, and we realize it may create some controversy, so these tactics are designed to smooth things out a bit on the road to the inevitable, ultimate destination of the funeral business."

A montage of newspapers, magazines, and television sets flashed onto the screen.

"The first step is pro-active. We will place articles in weekly newspapers and small, family-oriented magazines across the country compassionately outlining the reasons why Post-Need is necessary. The newspaper articles will bear the letterhead of our local home and bear the byline of the local director. We will establish an entity called the Post-Need Institute, which will canvass the country with favorable information about Post-Need. This group will include scientists as well as media professionals."

A field of speaking mouths.

"Voices, voices. Everywhere we can be heard. With the heart of America listening and through repetition now mildly sympathetic if not yet converted, the need will be established in more sophisticated media circles. It will begin in California . . ."

The Hollywood sign.

". . . presented as the latest, most fashionable trend. A high-profile, celebrity-packed Post-Need event will staged. We hope, and fully expect, that this event will be treated as simply another example of California flakiness. We expect the event to get its biggest play in the tabloid newspapers and television programs. In fact, we expect them to leap on the story, which will to some extent scare off the more respected journalistic outlets. A second event will be held, again encouraged if not staged by us. At some point, this new 'fad' will cross the border of California and enter America."

Again, the words:

ESTABLISH THE NEED

"Phase Three. At a crucial point, we will respond professionally. We will begin to offer full Post-Need services. We are simply responding, we will say, to the wishes of the public. Who are we to decide what is proper for the families of America?"

A question mark.

"It will be then, when we offer the service to the public and wait for the public to respond, that we will know if we have done our jobs well. If the response, the *need,* is not there it will be too late to reclaim it. But we're optimists. We think this will work. We're betting our reputations on it."

The lights came up and Bob Drabford once again took centerstage. "No guarantees in the business world, folks. We're going to work our tails off and probably get frustrated once in a while. But if we keep the faith and don't let ourselves get discouraged, then anything will be possible. The 909 is living proof of that. It's like I say . . ."—and here a sizable portion of the crowd joined in, chanting sing-song— ". . . IF THE MOUNTAIN WON'T COME TO MOHAMMED, THEN BUILD A BETTER MOUSETRAP!"

❀   ❀   ❀

Given the remainder of the afternoon off, Slade headed down to the gift shop. There he found a full array of souvenirs, the words "909 Ranch" emblazoned on everything from bucking-bronco snow globes to a set of rubber stamps showing the smiling visages of Bob, Preston, and Everett. He also found stacks of the 909 best-seller, *If the Mountain Won't Come to Mohammed, Then Build a Better Mousetrap.* He bought a copy and started out the door, when a stocky man with a bushy beard and horn-rimmed glasses, wearing a bright blue tie and red polyester slacks stepped in front of him. He was carrying an open notebook, pen poised, camera hooked around his neck.

"Excuse me," the man said, "I'm Slack Dougherty, from the *909 Observer*. I was wondering if you'd like to answer this week's People Poll? It's just an informal survey we take every week for the paper, kind of a man-on-the-street type deal where we ask average, everyday citizens what their opinion is on an issue of the day. It'll only take a second."

Slade was not in the mood for this. He felt tired from the trip, and wanted to go to the bunkhouse and rest for a while. "Well, I'm really just visiting. I'm from out of town."

"That's no problem. Would you do it? Please?"

"Oh, all right. Fire away."

He gazed down at his note pad, tapping the words with his pen as he spoke. "This week's People Poll question is: What is your favorite dairy product?"

"Uh, ice cream, I suppose."

"Why?"

"I like the way it tastes."

"Do you like it better in a dish or a cone?"

"Dish."

"Any particular reason?"

"No, it's just one of those things."

The reporter carefully copied down Slade's responses, then held up his camera. "Smile, okay? Pretend you're eating a dish of ice cream!" He took two pictures, and asked, "Could I have your name?"

"Dan Slade."

"And where are you from?"

"Houdin, Minnesota."

"Who did?"

"Houdin. H-o-u-d-i-n."

"What was that last part again?"

"D-i-n."

"Got it." He tucked his note pad into his shirt pocket. "Thanks for taking part in the People's Poll!" he said, and skittered off.

Slade went over to the bunkhouse and laid on his cot, reading from the 909 bible. As bibles went it was okay, although a little short on details. One thing that impressed Slade was that the elder brother had an unshakable, almost maniacal faith in his own destiny. A few of the specifics were inaccurate. There was no mile-high 909 skyscraper. There was no rocket launching pad on the 909 Ranch with flights hopping back and forth to the 909 Moon Base. But the idea of empire, the idea of establishing a friendly kingdom in the swamps of southern Florida rang clear through his prose.

Slade began thinking about his own life, his dreams, and a sense of sadness filled him. In comparison to a visionary like Drabford, his own dreams seemed small and inconsequential. Why am I settling for this life? he wondered. Why did I choose it? I'm a big man in Houdin, maybe bigger than I imagined I would be, but it's nothing compared to all this. Absolutely nothing. Do I lack courage? Brains? Connections? But I'm still young, he thought. I just need that one big break. I can be like Drabford someday. There's no reason why I can't.

No reason . . . no reason at all . . .

* * *

When Slade awoke, the wagon wheel light hanging from the ceiling was shining, a moth fluttering crazily around it. He sat up suddenly. He looked at the window, and it was all darkness. I'm late, he thought. Must be at least eight o'clock. Panicking, he yanked on his cowboy boots and headed to the door. My one big chance, he thought, and I screwed it up. I could have sat beside the Drabfords at the barbecue, made sure they noticed me, told them about my ambitions, the future. Now I'm late and I'll be stuck in Houdin or some other dead-end town for good.

Stumbling to the dark field where the barbecue had been held, all that was left, Slade saw, were some smoldering coals in the barbecue pit. There was no one around. What was next on the schedule? Campfire. But where? Wait a minute. Slade cocked his ear to the wind. He heard music, people singing. He headed toward the sounds, past the corral, past the grandstand, to the hill where he had first come across the tiny cowboys, the music getting louder, and finally, beyond the crest of the rise he found them, circled around a dozen campfires spread out across the hillside.

Slade tried to act nonchalant as he wandered slowly among the knots of his fellow funeral cowpokes, pale faces bathed in yellow and orange, all the while trying to spot his bantam hosts.

"Howdy, Slade."

Slade turned, an instant of hope that it was a Drabford evaporating when he realized that the voice was too deep. Who was it?

"Didn't see you at the barbecue. You missed a nice spread."

It was that fellow he met in the auditorium. Bart. Crew cut. Brittle hair. Brittleman. "Oh hi, Brittleman. Good to see you again." I don't have time for this, Slade thought. Have to get rid of him. "I hate to be rude, but I'm . . ."

"Look what I got," Brittleman said. He proudly held up his book, open to the title page. "Signed by Bob Drabford himself. I won't let it out of my sight, you can bet on that."

"You've seen Drabford? Where is he?"

"Over there," Brittleman said, pointing off to his right. "Two fires over. Next to the guy with the guitar. See him?"

"Yes, I do. Thanks, Brittleman. I'll catch you later." Slade found a spot at Drabford's fire, sitting down Indian-style. Drabford was seated beside Pawnee Bill, Jr. There was a conversation in progress.

". . . was no Rogers," Drabford was saying. "Autry

didn't even look like a cowboy. He was too chunky, you could never picture him being out on the trail. Too much Hollywood in him."

"But his voice!" argued Pawnee Bill. "In *The Big Show*, he sang a love song to his dying horse before he shot the poor thing. 'Old Faithful.' It was a part of a show at the Dallas Centennial. It went something like, 'When your round-up days are over/there'll be fields as white as clover/Old Faithful/Pal o' mine.' Man, there were some tears in your eyes after that one."

"Rogers was no slouch, either. Remember, he started his career as a singer with the Sons of the Pioneers . . ."

Great, Slade thought. How am I going to turn the conversation from singing cowboys to the dismal trade? He half-listened as the men volleyed their arguments back and forth, when it came to him. Perfect. He waited for a pause in the conversation, then said, "Say, didn't I read something once that Roy Rogers had his horse pickled or something?"

"Ah, Mr. Slade," Drabford said with a gentle smile. "I didn't see you sit down. Actually, Trigger is stuffed and standing on his hind legs outside the Roy Rogers Museum in Victorville, California. It's quite a museum, built to resemble an old fort. There's a translucent bowling ball with Trigger's photograph in the center on display. Remarkable place."

"Has there ever been a case of anyone embalming a horse or a dog or something?"

"Not that I'm aware of. Fur is the main drawback, I suppose. No complexion to improve. And pets generally have a limited social circle, which would make a wake somewhat pointless. However, the owners do care and the few pet cemeteries around try to help them through this difficult time."

"Sounds like a pretty untapped market, though," Slade said, seeing the opening. "The fur could be cleaned up, brushed. A new collar. An argument could be made for embalming fluid, in terms of disease reduction. Hell, a lot of pets get treated better in life than a lot of humans. So why should they get short shrift at the time of death?"

"Interesting," Drabford said, poking meditatively at the fire with a branding iron.

"I'd be willing to develop the idea for you," Slade said, trying to keep his voice under control. This was not exactly where he expected the conversation to wind up, but it was better than nothing.

"We need to keep focused on Project Post-Need," Drabford said without hesitation. "It's a fine idea, something to mull over certainly, but this isn't the time. Somewhere down the road, perhaps."

"Speaking of untapped markets," said Slade, winging it, "I was curious as to why the project is confined to the United States. Why not go worldwide with it? If you don't mind my asking, that is."

"It's no secret. We have no foothold outside this country, no reputation as a foundation to build from. The same goes for the customs, the history. We see the project as the evolution of some very definite traditions. Other cultures will take a different evolutionary path. Did you know that the concept of Pre-Need is almost unheard of in England? If they have no familiarity with Pre-Need, how will we indoctrinate them to the concept of Post-Need?"

"You answered it yourself this afternoon," Slade said, rising. "Make it the trendy thing to do, you said. Well, what kind of jeans does the world wear? What kind of soft drinks do they drink? What kind of music do they listen to? American. You know what's going to happen? You're going to get ripped off. Some sharpie in Spain or Australia or Japan will see what's going on here and take the idea for his own. It's happened a million times before. Only he won't do it with quite the care that you take, and there will be scandals and investigations and the waves of protest and anger won't stop when they reach our shores, you can bet on that." Slade stood there, looking at Drabford, who was still gazing into the fire.

After a long time, Drabford also stood up, coming even to the hat of Pawnee Bill. He's going to kick my ass out of here, Slade thought, his heart thumping against his chest. Punched out by a midget. Fine with me. I'll learn how to sell tires or something.

Eyes inscrutable, Drabford said evenly, "Mr. Slade, would you mind coming with me, please?"

Slade nodded and followed him into the darkness, where the fires' light barely penetrated. The small man stopped. "I need to talk with my brothers about this. But I think they'll agree that your arguments are sound. How would you like to get out of Houdin?"

"I'll go wherever you think I can help the organization."

"Fine. Since you seem to have some pretty strong thoughts in this area, why don't you develop it? You'll need a partner, someone you can trust. Who are you working with now?"

"No good. The former owner. He's weak." Then the face flashed into his mind. "I know the perfect man for the job. Andy Archway."

The elder Drabford said nothing.

"We went to school together," Slade continued. "He's made quite a name for himself, you know. The next Mordecai, they're calling him, of course those are just press clippings. He's signed with Sunnyside, but it wouldn't hurt to . . ." Slade's sentence trailed off when he saw the expression of pure white-hot hate in Drabford's eyes, campfires reflecting in his pupils, at the mention of the name Sunnyside.

"I'm sorry," Slade said under his breath. "I'll come up with someone else. I promise."

The venomous look still pouring from his eyes, Drabford said, his reedlike voice coming in heaves. "You will . . . get Archway for me. Use whatever means . . . necessary."

Slade felt himself shrinking under the midget's glare.

"*I want . . . Archway.*"

twelve

"How do I say good-bye to what we had? . . ."

The Archways put on their Sunday clothes, got a neighbor to do the chores, and drove up from Golbyville for the 77th Commencement Exercises at the Thomas Holmes University of Embalming and Funerary Practices. It was a beautiful, sun-soaked June morning. Proud parents strolled across the campus flanking their equally proud offspring, serenaded by a flock of scavenging crows. The Archways met their famous son at the cafeteria for breakfast. They exchanged hugs and handshakes, and Mrs. Archway said, "We're so proud of you, Andy. So proud."

"You're the first one in our family ever to graduate from college," added Mr. Archway. "I respect you more than you could know, son."

"Thanks a lot. I'm glad you could come up. Who's looking after the farm?"

"Herman Kopishkee. He said to say congratulations."

"Tell him I said hi."

Mrs. Archway snapped a picture, the flash momentarily

blinding Andy. "Mom, let's do this outside later on. We should get our food and sit down."

Over lukewarm scrambled eggs and soggy toast, Mrs. Archway said, "Dear, I hope you're doing the right thing. Jobs are so hard to come by these days. Maybe you should have gone into computers."

"Mom, haven't you been getting the clippings I've been sending you?" Andy asked, sipping his orange juice. "I broke most of the embalming records at Holmes. People think I'm going to be the next Mordecai. Besides, I have a signed contract with Sunnyside." Andy spotted Coach Crok sitting several tables over, called his name to get his attention, and waved him over.

"Coach, these are my parents. This is Coach Crok, Mom and Dad. I wouldn't be where I am if Coach here hadn't gambled and given me a chance to prove myself. Actually, I should thank Mattle, too, eh Coach?"

"Your boy is too modest, Mr. and Mrs. Archway," said the coach, wearing a black T-shirt that read COMPETITIVE EMBALMERS ARE SLAB HAPPY. "He would have fought his way into the lineup somehow. He's got too much talent. You should be proud of him."

"We're very proud of him," said Mrs. Archway. She patted Andy on the forearm. "Go stand by the coach. I want to take your picture."

"Oh, Mom."

"Let's go, Archway," the coach said playfully. "Mind your mother or I'll make you do laps in your graduation gown."

Andy relented, his pained expression dissolving into a grin, and they posed together, Coach Crok placing a fatherly hand on his shoulder. Then, the coach took Andy aside and said, his eyes glistening, "You're going to do great things in this world, Archway. You've got a very special gift, and a long life ahead to use it in. But you have to promise to keep in touch with your old coach once in a while, okay?"

Andy nodded, blinking away tears. "Thanks, Coach. Thanks for everything. I promise I won't forget you."

They embraced, and the coach wandered sadly out of the cafeteria, leaving his corn flakes to grow soggy in their bittersweet bowl.

Glancing at his watch, Andy said, "I have to get back to my room and change. We're supposed to be down at the stadium by eleven."

"I should help you with your tie," his mother offered.

"For gosh sakes, he's a grown man," said his dad.

"I can handle it, Mom. You guys should head down to the stadium and make sure you get a decent seat. P. T. Sunnyside is going to be giving the commencement address. Maybe I can introduce him to you afterward."

"Don't go to any trouble for us," his mom requested.

"Why would it be any trouble for him?" said his dad.

"It's no trouble, Mom. He knows who I am."

So Andy started back to his dorm room while his parents took the long walk down to the stadium. He was glad his parents had come, even though they did get on his nerves occasionally. Although he too believed there were much greater things in store for him, Andy reveled in this day. It had been just two short years ago when he had arrived on campus, feeling lost: a naive, insecure kid from a little town. The experience, he speculated, had been a matter of facing down his fears. He had never ventured beyond the borders of Minnesota before he came to Holmes. He had never been comfortable talking to people. He had never touched a girl. Andy felt sort of a perverse affection for this person he used to be, but was grateful that his old self had now receded permanently into the memory books.

As Andy ambled down the shady sidewalk in front of

his dorm, he heard a short hissing sound. He walked on, then stopped when he heard it again.

"Archway, over here."

Andy turned and a familiar but unexpected figure appeared from behind a tree trunk, frantically gesturing at him.

"Slade, is that you? What are you doing here? Why are you hiding behind that tree?"

"Come over here," he repeated in a low voice. "I have to talk to you."

Andy did, and Slade pulled him behind the tree, out of view from the sidewalk. "Have you seen Wakefield today? Have you talked to him?"

"No, I haven't. Have you seen him? I'm supposed to be flying out to California with him tonight. Say, what's going on here anyway? You look like you haven't slept for a month."

"If you don't hear me out, I may as well be put to sleep permanently."

"What the problem?"

Slade peeked around the tree and said, "Shit, here he comes again. Look, Archway, don't go anywhere tonight until we get a chance to talk." He stole another look. "I gotta go. Don't tell him I talked to you. I'll try to find you later." With that, Slade slipped away, duck-walking along a line of lilac bushes and disappearing around the corner of the dorm. Andy stepped out from behind the tree.

"There you are," Wake said, coming down the sidewalk, compromising his fashion sense by adding a wide green tie to his usual rumpled shirt and corduroys. "I've been looking for you all morning. I ran into your parents and they said you came back here."

"I've got a gown and funny hat waiting for me upstairs. Why don't you come on up?"

As they went to his room, Wake said, "You've certainly made a name for yourself here, Andrew. It's a good sign. It shows you can adapt to a situation and do your best. Of course, the situation out at Sunnyside will be a little more favorable in terms of your true talent. You'll be able to let your creative skills breathe again."

"I'm looking forward to it. Is Mr. Sunnyside here yet?"

"No, he's flying his private plane out this morning. If I know him, he'll show up at the exact moment they're introducing him. What have you got planned after the ceremony?"

"I have an aunt who lives in town, and my folks and I are going over there for a little party. You're welcome to come."

"Sounds fine. Our flight leaves at seven, so we'll have to keep an eye on the clock."

As Andy got into his cap and gown and chatted with Wake, he wondered if he should betray Slade's confidence. Although Andy no longer admired Slade as much as he once did, realizing that much of his appeal was a self-confident facade, he still felt a certain affection for the fellow, and still owed him a certain debt. What could he want? Why was he so worked up? Why was he afraid that Wake would see him? Would it hurt anything to wait and see what he had to say? Probably not. I have to take care of things myself now, Andy thought. Slade is my responsibility.

✿   ✿   ✿

Andy parted company with Wake at the stadium. His fellow graduates were milling about just outside the stadium at an opened maintenance gate, while beyond them he could look out at a sea of empty folding chairs on the grass itself, a stage now occupied only by a man dragging a tangle of electrical cords to the podium, and the stands filled with the graduates' parents, relatives and friends. A reggae version of the Funeral March played over the loudspeakers.

Nearby, a woman carrying a megaphone said, "Okay, graduates, we're going to be marching into the stadium in a few minutes. We will be marching two-by-two, in alphabetical order. So I want the *A*s up in the front followed by the *B*s and *C*s and so forth until we reach the *Z*s. I don't know if there are any *Z*s or not here today, but if there are they should go way to the back."

"Zorkman here!" someone yelled.

"Then you belong toward the back with the other *Z*s, if there are any. Now, once we get all lined up, watch me for the signal to start filing inside. I'll give a signal, waving my hand like this, which will mean begin walking. If for some reason we need to stop, I will hold my hand up like this. If we need to slow down, I will wave my hand very *slowly*. I'll do them together. This is walk normally. And this is walk *slowly*. I don't anticipate us having to walk *quickly*."

Andy moved forward, as everyone found their places. "*A* here," he said, weaving his way through the crowd. "*A* coming through." Finally, the lines formed, and Andy found himself one row back from the first couple, matched up with a dark-haired woman. Their eyes met.

"Hey, you're not an *A*," Andy told Maria.

"I am today, asshole," she replied.

Now the signal came, the band broke into a traditional rendition of the Funeral March and the assembled graduates began marching at a normal cadence, for the moment, into Memorial Stadium. After the graduates settled into their seats, the Dean of Students began with some brief introductory remarks. "There is a time to study, a time to play, a time to embalm, and now, a time to say good-bye."

Andy felt a tapping on his shoulder. "Archway," a voice whispered. "We need to talk." Andy craned his neck around and saw that Slade had somehow gotten his hands on a cap and gown, both ludicrously small, and was seated directly behind him.

"What are you doing here? What do you want?"

". . . moving on into the real world . . ."

Crouching forward, so that he was inches from Andy's

right ear, Slade said, "I don't have much time. I ran into Wakefield on the way in and he said he's going to get someone to kick me out of here. Listen, I came here to offer you a job. The Drabfords want you really bad."

"I've already got a job all lined up, thank you."

"With Sunnyside."

"Yes, with Sunnyside."

"I suppose you're going to deny that there was ever anything between us," Maria said into his left ear.

"Huh?"

". . . down the road of life . . ."

"Have you really stopped and thought about what it would be like to work for Sunnyside? From what I hear, there's only one person that matters to him and that's P. T. Sunnyside. He builds monuments to his own ego. Everyone else works in his shadow."

"I waited for you to call, even when I saw you walking with other girls."

". . . take with you these very, very important lessons. Thank you."

A round of applause drowned out the voices for a moment. When the valedictorian began, Andy bent over and unlaced his shoes and tied them, then retied them. When she finished and the clapping began again, he sat up.

"How much freedom do you think you're going to have with Sunnyside? Don't count on having any, from what people have told me. He's an egocentric supreme."

"This is all just a big ego trip for you, isn't it?" Maria hissed.

". . . to introduce a true funereal legend, the one and only P. T. Sunnyside!"

A long ovation ensued as Sunnyside strode briskly onto the stage. He grasped the podium with both hands and said, "The folks who invited me here today told me they wanted me to speak to you because I know something about the future, the future where they believe most of you will be spending the rest of your lives. Well, I'm here to tell you to forget about the future. The past is where the fun is."

"The Drabfords want us to start up a branch of their operation in Europe. They'll leave us alone. We'll be able to do things our way."

"You should at least have had the backbone to tell me to my face that you weren't interested in me anymore. Don't you think I deserved that much?"

". . . project called Time Hill . . ."

"I'm not interested."

"Fine. That's just fine."

"I didn't mean you. I don't know, maybe I do. But I wasn't talking to you."

"It'll be like old times, buddy."

On the stage, Andy saw, Wake had suddenly appeared and was whispering into Sunnyside's ear. P.T. nodded, then said into the microphone, "And in conclusion, let me say, er, have a nice day everyone!" He quickly exited.

The dean returned to the podium and announced that it was time to distribute the diplomas. The band struck up again, and Andy finally was able to break away from Slade and followed Maria up the stairs onto the stage. He was presented with an envelope, shook the hand of the university president, and went back down the stairs on the other side, where Wake was waiting for him. He hooked Andy's arm as Maria looked back at them, and when he ushered Andy toward a side exit, she turned and walked on, head bowed. "What was Slade talking to you about?" Wake asked, biting off the words. "What did that sonofabitch want?"

"He offered me a job," Andy said matter-of-factly.

"You didn't . . ."

"Of course not."

"I don't know what's going on," Wake said, "but I'm not letting you out of my sight until we're on that plane tonight."

Aunt Agnatia and Uncle Rex were waiting on the porch, beaming, when the Archway's car pulled up to the curb, the Wakefield vehicle following right on their bumper. As the group tumbled out of their cars, the relatives offered salutations and congratulations and ushered them inside.

"We made up a special cake just for the occasion," Auntie said, going into the kitchen and bringing back a sheet cake. She set it on the dining-room table for everyone to admire.

"My, it's lovely," said Mrs. Archway. "You always have such clever ideas, sis."

The cake was done in black frosting with a white-frosting inscription that said, CONGRATULATIONS, ANDREW — THE ESSENCE OF EMBALMING IS EFFERVESCENCE. Frosting art covered the rest of the cake: a graduation cap, diploma, and tombstone.

"The saying was my idea," said Uncle Rex.

"Why don't we open gifts first and then I'll cut the cake," Agnatia suggested.

So they sat down, Andy and his parents taking the couch by the window, Wake claiming a card-table chair directly in line with Andy, the relatives hovering. Andy began opening his gifts and made the appropriate responses. Nothing too surprising: a briefcase, a tie, a monogrammed trocar. Then he tore the paper from a flat package, and saw, as he feared, that it was one of Uncle Rex's homemade books. Rex had retired five years early from the insurance company to become a writer. He was writing, certainly. The book was bound with shoestring and paste. The cover read: *Effervescence — A Book of Verse* by Rex T. Rodan.

"Thank you," Andy said quickly and tried to grab the next gift.

"I'd like to read a poem, if you don't mind," Uncle Rex said, lifting the book from Andy's hand. "It's a special tribute, just for you. It's the title piece, in fact. I call it "Effervescence." He cleared his throat and began:

" 'Effervescence,' by Rex T. Rodan.

What will we remember most this day, this day
Some would say the weather
but I would say it's you, An-day, An-day.
You and your effervescence
like champagne bubbles bubbling effervescently,
Your effervescent personality
bubbling effervescently.
Like the effervescence of champagne bubbles
bubbling like you
so effervescently."

Rex closed the book with a pleased grin and bowed. The gathering clapped lightly.

"Time for sweets!" Auntie announced. After pouring punch, she began to slice into the cake. Suddenly, windows began shattering all along the far side of the house. Everyone leaped from their seats. "My goodness, what's happening?" Aunt Agnatia exclaimed. "Careful, mother," said Rex, and, followed by Mr. Archway and Wake, charged through the kitchen and out the back door.

"I'll help you clean up, sis," said Mrs. Archway, moving toward Agnatia, who was heading outside with a dust pan. "It's probably just a college prank or something."

"Archway," a familiar voice whispered.

Andy turned and saw that Slade was at the window behind the couch. He knelt on the couch and peered out. "Did you break all those windows, Slade? Are you crazy?"

"Name your price. What will you be getting from Sunnyside? $30,000? $40,000? We'll make it $60,000."

"I thought we had straightened this out."

"Seventy thousand."

"You'd better get out of here before they come around to this side of the house."

Slade's nose made the screen bulge. "Okay, $100,000. You can't turn me down for $100,000."

"In the first place it's not a question of money, and in the second place I think you're pulling these numbers out of the air."

"There he is!" a voice shouted.

"I'll find you later," Slade said and dashed off.

After a few minutes the men came back in. "We just missed him," Rex said. "He hopped a fence down by the lumberyard. We're getting a little too old for that kind of shenanigans."

"What a terrible thing to do," Auntie said, holding a dust pan of glass fragments.

Coming over to Andy, Wake said, "It was that Slade character. Doesn't he know when he's licked? What did he say to you?"

"He offered me $100,000 to take the job."

"You didn't . . ."

"Of course not."

＊　＊　＊

Andy felt relieved when the final good-byes were said, and he and Wake loaded up the car and headed to the airport. For several weeks after his trip out west last summer, the California he remembered, the California that lay beyond the gates of Heaven Hill, was a sordid, dank land. He recalled palm trees choking under the perpetually hazy, vile skies; the helicopters that buzzed the bungalows with high beams sweeping over the rooftops and across backyards. Gravel pits, concrete, despair. Even though he had rarely ventured beyond the confines of Heaven Hill, these were the recollections he brought back with him.

But time passed, and while the memories—the images—remained unchanged, his perception of them did not. It was a different country, perhaps a worse land than the one he was coming from, but it was exotic, stimulating. He could think freely there. He could create. The air stinging his nostrils as he got off the plane would be a signal that he was in the right place.

They parked and walked to the airport escalators. "We've made some temporary housing arrangements for you," Wake said. "A new crop of interns is coming in next week, so you can stay on the grounds until then. Maybe next weekend we can go looking at condos for you in the area. I think there's a list of Sunnyside people who want roommates, if you prefer not to live alone."

"I lived alone in the dorm this past year," said Andy. "It wasn't so bad. I just don't want to drive a long way to work every day."

"Shouldn't be a problem."

After they checked in, Andy and Wake headed down to the blue concourse where their gate was located. Wake had allowed them plenty of extra time, so it would probably be a good half hour before their plane would begin boarding.

"Watch my stuff," Wake said, setting his satchel down on a chair in the waiting area by the gate. He pressed a hand against his stomach and grinned. "Overloaded on the punch, I guess."

"I'll be right here," Andy said, sitting down. He slid his carry-on bag under the chair and tried to make himself comfortable. He shut his eyes.

Moments later, someone sat down beside Andy.

"I'm sorry about your aunt's windows."

Andy jerked up in surprise. He gazed incredulously at Slade. "I can't believe you. For chrissakes, why don't you leave me alone? Can't you take no for an answer?"

"I have a proposition," Slade replied with a desperate smile.

"I don't care what you have."

"It involves . . . Mordecai."

Glaring at him, Andy said, "Leave Mordecai out of this."

Slade slowly slid back in his seat, looking out at the planes. Finally, he quietly said, "How would you like to break the record?"

Andy said nothing.

"One-seven-six-nine. Isn't now the time to break it? Aren't you the person to do it? You're the next Mordecai, they say. Why not strive for a Mordecai-like goal instead of settling for working as an errand boy for a washed-up legend?"

Andy shook his head. "This is stooping pretty low, Slade. Even for you."

"I've talked to the Drabfords about it. They'll set you up with everything you need. Equipment, personnel, transportation. They even have a place in mind. The number-crunchers say there would be a seventy-five percent chance of someone breaking the record there, and they didn't even factor in an individual with your level of talent. A hack like me would even have a shot at it. For you, it should be easy."

"Why do the Drabfords want me? Why should they care if I break the record?"

"It doesn't involve us. They've been feuding with Sunnyside for years. They'd jump at any opportunity to deny him something he wants. But it's not our fight, buddy. So why not take advantage of the situation? You don't ask questions when someone hands you a solid-gold dream, do you?" Slade abruptly rose. "Wakefield will be back any second. I think I'm starting to develop a sixth sense about him."

Andy did not look at his buddy.

"I'll be waiting for you down by the ticket counter. We can fly out to Florida tonight."

Andy shut his eyes.

A short time later, Wake returned, newspaper tucked under his arm. "Have they announced boarding?" he asked.

"No, not yet."

Wake sat down, unfolded the paper, and began to read. Andy stared out the window at the blunt-nosed planes rolling across the tarmac.

Before long a voice came over the loudspeaker. "Good evening and welcome to Oswald Airlines flight 909 non-stop service to Ontario. We will be boarding in a few minutes, starting with those of you who are Nobility Club members, those of you traveling with unruly teenagers, and those of you who are so damn old that you need a little extra time to board. Again, boarding will begin in just a few minutes. Thank you."

"It's about time," Wake said.

Andy abruptly stood up. "I should use the bathroom before we get on."

"Well, hurry up, then. They won't hold the plane for us."

Hesitating, he looked at Wake, who was reading the paper, glasses perched on his sunburned nose.

"I'll be right back."

thirteen

WAKE MADE NO attempt to disguise his foray into enemy territory. He figured they were probably expecting him, and no doubt had plotted a suitable surprise. Besides, he was too steamed to care. Nobody walks off with one of my prospects, Wake thought as he flew down the cypress-lined road. Especially a punk like Slade. Whatever bait he used, Andy sure swallowed it big time. But Wake knew that whatever promise they made Andy, it would be as empty as a funeral home on the fourth of July. That was just the way the Drabfords operated, those goddamn midgets.

The farther Wake drove, and the closer he came to the 909 Ranch, the madder he became. To beat out a bird dog for a prospect fair and square is one thing; Wake had been on both ends of the game many times in the past. But to do it when the contract has already been signed, to do it when the bird dog is in the biffy minutes before their plane takes off, well, it broke every unwritten rule of scouting imaginable. Even a weasel like Bing Daniels wouldn't dirty his ugly nose in such a scheme. It was completely unethical and gave a black heart to the dismal profession.

So Wake felt not only justified but obligated to go after Andy. He hoped he could pull out the kid and hop back to California without P.T. knowing about it, and he fretted what he would tell P.T. if he failed. *I really like that kid*, P.T. had told him so often that Wake suggested he use it in an advertisement hailing the arrival of the Golbyville Ghost.

But what had gotten into Andy? He had seemed a much more confident person since the last time Wake had spoken to him, no longer that shy kid he had stumbled across in the Archway grove. Nothing wrong with that. His extraordinary success as a competitive embalmer was fine, but it had few applications in the real world, especially at Sunnyside where the emphasis was on imagination rather than speed. The only time these skills would have any use would be in a time of emergency, when large numbers of deceased needed to be embalmed quickly, such as following a natural disaster or during a war.

The image of Andy's shrine shed back in Golbyville, the walls plastered with the visage of Mordecai, flashed into Wake's head. Shit, that's it, he thought. The record. They promised him the goddamn record. What else could get him to defect? Hell, Wake thought, I'd probably jump caskets too if someone came along and offered me my lifelong dream.

Those goddamn midgets.

Suddenly Wake stomped on his brakes. In the road up ahead an alligator sat sunning itself, sweeping its long gray tail along the gravel. Wake laid on the horn, and the animal just blinked at him. The gator sized up the car for a moment, as if pondering a dessert tray, then thought better of it and shambled into the weeds.

Wake had of course followed the development of the 909 Ranch in *Shroud* and other magazines, but nothing prepared him for the immensity of what he saw. He had spotted the 909 water tower, the informal entrance marker to the Drabford holdings, a good hour ago, and there was still no sign of the ranch proper. A vague sense of unease drifted through his heart, knowing he was deep in the badlands. Even if he did manage to nab Andy, it would be a scramble to reach safe haven again. The midgets had a lot of resources at their disposal and knew the terrain like they had designed it themselves, which in fact they had.

Wake flipped on the radio, all static until he reached 909 on the dial. ". . . today, with a high tomorrow expected to reach eighty-eight again with a chance of thunderstorms in the afternoon. And boy, when it gets hot I like to mosey on over to Hap's Service Stop and get me some of that dee-licious Hap's ice cream, twelve flavors, many different. While you're at Hap's why don't you fill up your tank and let Hap treat you to some of that down-home service you've come to expect over these many years. That's Hap's Service Stop, located on Gunta Porda Road five miles east of Snakeland in the Northeast Quadrant. Again, today's top story, another record profit for the tourist division of Drabford Diversified. Couldn't happen to sweller set of brothers. Nice goin', fellas. Now, keep listening to 909 KBOB for the finest programs this side of the Rio Grande. Coming up at three P.M. is an hour-long tribute in song and verse to Tex Ritter. Then tune in at four for 'Chuck Wagon Theater,' which will present for your enjoyment another thrilling tale of the Old West, 'Ambush at Shifty Creek.' Hang onto your hats for that one, pardners."

Ambush is right, Wake thought, snapping off the radio.

Before long Wake swung into the central grounds at 909, pulling up outside a rustic building with a sign that said GENERAL STORE. He tramped up to the building, the floorboards creaking as he stepped inside. It certainly was an accurate replica of a general store. Shelves were stocked with everything from bridles to flyswatters to wooden pull toys. A pickle barrel stood by the counter, which was lined with a bright assortment of candy-filled jars. A white-haired man in a vest and visor was wiping the counter with a towel.

"Good afternoon," said Wake, going up to the counter, "I was wondering if you could help me."

"How would you like a good old-fashioned licorice stick?" asked the storekeeper with a condescending grin.

"No thanks. I'm here on business. I'm looking for someone."

"Well, stranger, I can't make no promises, but I reckon I'll help you out if I can. Now who might you be looking for?"

"Two young guys, college age. Both dark haired, one well built, the other lean. They probably came in late last night."

"Last night, you say," replied the man, stroking his chin. "Can't say as I recall. I see a lot of folks come through here every day, though." He chuckled, and tapped a finger to his head. "And this ol' memory ain't what it used to be."

"Who's in charge here?"

"I am the proprietor here, sir. Name's Conway Cody. Just because I run the general store don't mean I didn't have a wild streak in me. Why, when I was a young 'un I once shot a man just for . . ."

"Look, pal, save this cowpoke shit for the tourists. This is business. I'm a scout. Your boss stole one of my kids when he was under contract to us. This country has laws against that sort of practice, you know.

"Rustling, eh? That's not good." Cody leaned across the counter and whispered, "Listen, mister, this is a lawless town, been that way as long as I can recollect. The Drabford gang runs things as they see fit, don't take folks' rights into account. What we need here is a lawman, someone who will stand up to the midgets and make them act like decent citizens. Don't suppose you'd be interested in the job."

"You'd need a pretty big posse to fight the Drabfords."

"Naw, naw, I ain't talking 'bout six-shooters, I'm talking 'bout rev . . ." Cody abruptly broke off and looked over

Wake's shoulder to the door, then he dropped his gaze and resumed polishing the counter.

Wake turned. One of the midgets, outfitted in full Western regalia, had entered the store. It looked like Preston but Wake always had trouble telling the younger Drabford brothers apart.

"Afternoon, Cody," the small one squeaked.

Cody looked up and smiled with forced surprise. "Why, Ev Drabford, it's been a spell since you been 'round these parts. How are Bob and Preston faring these days?"

"Fine, thanks," the midget said, approaching. He glanced at Wake, then reached way up and slapped an odd-looking coin on the counter. "Beef jerky, if you don't mind."

"Why sure, Mr. Drabford," Cody said with relief, and grabbed a fistful of jerky from a nearby canister and tentatively handed it to Preston, who took it and thrust it into his belt. The midget turned and quickly left, his cowboy boots making a short tapping rhythm on the floorboards.

Cody sagged slightly as the door banged shut. "You'd better skeedaddle out of here, mister."

"Why do you say that?"

"Didn't you see the way he looked at you? You don't sleep around here at night when you get that look. Were they expectin' you, mister? Are you gonna have a shoot-out with them, is that why you came to town?"

"They may have been expecting me," Wake said, "but I didn't come here looking for trouble. I came to claim what's rightfully mine."

"That sounds like trouble to me. The Brothers don't back down or give anything away." His voice dropped low. "Look, I'll help you make your getaway. I'll take your car and send them on a wild-goose chase. Don't worry about me, I'll act drunk if they catch me. The Big Eyes will think it's you, and then you can hop on one of them tourist buses and make it to freedom."

"The Big Eyes?"

"It's a saying we have around here. 'The Little Men Have Big Eyes.' " He gestured at the ceiling. "Brother, they got cameras in the trees and satellites in the sky! It's no wonder he came in right after you. They probably saw you comin' the minute you crossed over into their territory."

"I appreciate your offer," said Wake, "but I prefer the direct approach. No sense running from them. I'll have to face them sooner or later to get what I want."

Cody came half-running around the counter, charging out the door, shouting hoarsely, "We's gonna have us a shoot-out! We's gonna have us a shoot-out!"

Wake followed him out the door to the dusty street. Tourists, thinking it was a show, scattered to the safety of buildings, laughing and playfully screaming. It was hot, hushed.

Not far down the street stood the Drabford Brothers, all in a row, Bob in the middle with Preston on his left and Everett on his right. They had their thumbs tucked into their gun belts, hats tugged low over their eyes.

Wake did not hesitate. He made the first move, coming out from the shadow of the store and walking purposefully toward the brothers. They responded in kind. When they were within twenty feet of one another both sides stopped.

"Get 'em, Drabfords!" someone from the crowd yelled.

"I want Andy Archway," Wake called out.

"Can't have him," Bob Drabford replied.

"We have a legally binding contract for his services. Make it easy on yourselves and turn him over to me now."

"Watch 'em, he looks like a slippery side-winding back-stabber!" another voice warned, then hooted with laughter.

"Contract's broken, Mr. Wakefield," said the elder Brother. "You forced him to sign it under duress. He's part of our family now, and he's perfectly happy about it."

"Let me talk to him."

"He doesn't want to talk to you or anyone associated with *Shady*side. I can't blame him. A terrible organization run by a despicable man. You can quote me on that to your boss if you'd like."

"We'll take you to court to get him back."

"Of course you will, dear."

"We'll take him back the same way you took him from us."

"Oh, I don't think so."

"Did you tell Andy you're just using him to get back at Sunnyside for taking Heaven Hill? Did you tell him that, Drabford? Was he perfectly happy about it?"

"Mr. Archway has a goal in mind, and we simply want to assist him in reaching that goal. The rest is irrelevant."

"What's the goal, Drabford? You tell him he's going to be the next Mordecai? Did you whisper in his ear and tell him he's going to break the record? It's not going to happen. That's not the Andy I found. He can't deny who he is. He wasn't put on this Earth to break records, he was put here to kick our profession into the next century."

Drabford feigned a yawn.

"It's not going to end here," Wake warned. "We won't give Andy up without a fight."

"Of that I have no doubt," the ultimate Drabford replied with a smile.

Wake backed off, going over to his car, accompanied by boos and cries of "yellow belly" from the assembled sightseers. Spinning his tires as he sped away, Wake glanced at his rearview mirror and watched as the tourists emerged from their hiding places and swarmed the Drabfords, flapping papers and pens in their wee mugs.

After driving several miles, passing from grazing land to dank tropics, Wake saw a roadblock up ahead. The sign pointed left. Wake made the turn, swinging onto a narrow gravel path. He eased down the rutted trail carefully for a short distance, the car rocking as it hit the crevices, then braked to halt. That sign must have pointed right, not left, Wake thought, shifting into reverse. He placed his arm across the seat, craned his neck, and proceeded to edge his way out to the main road.

Just then a pickup truck turned onto the detour and pulled right up against Wake's car, blocking his path. Two men exited the truck, one thin, the other rotund. Wake slipped the car into neutral and waited for them to come up to the car, one on each side. The skinny man came to the passenger side and tapped on the window, gesturing at Wake to open it. When Wake turned his attention toward the man, he suddenly felt himself being yanked out the driver's window by the second man.

"Leggo, you sonofabitch!" Wake yelled as his head banged against the top of the window frame. Another mighty heave and Wake's left knee thudded onto the steering wheel. One more tug and his right heel smacked down on the bottom of the window frame. Finally, the men roughly deposited their cargo onto the muddy road.

Wake lay twisted on the ground, holding his knee, which felt like it had been hit with a baseball bat. "Come on, old-timer, we're goin' for a ride," said one of the men and they hauled Wake to their truck, where they lashed his hands behind his back with a cord and tossed him into the pickup bed.

The ride was a short one, ending on another side road. The men dragged Wake out of the truck by his feet and freed his hands, then hustled him to the rear of a moss-choked shed. There was a curious bit of landscaping at the back of that shed. Instead of a gazebo or fountain there was a ten-foot deep pit with a pool of water at the bottom. Inside the pit was a regulation-size alligator.

Grasping Wake by his shoulders, the men forced him toward the precipice of the pit.

"Hold on!" Wake shouted, digging his heels into the

soft earth. "Are you guys nuts or something?"

"Betsy hasn't had a bite all day," one of his captors said cheerily.

Wake could see the alligator's maw and nothing else. They pushed him closer. One foot slid over the edge.

"No!" screamed Wake.

"Yes," the men replied, and kicked his other foot away. Wake clawed at the weeds, the dirt, the air, and shortly found himself sliding down into the pit, and landing in a shallow pool of muddy water. It was dark, clammy. He could see the creature breathing; even this seemed to be a killing motion. The gator made a quick lunge toward him, and Wake stood up, his lower lip shaking.

I'm a goner, he thought.

The creature stared at him, but moved no closer.

Gazing into its cold killer's eyes, Wake realized that this creature, or the ancestors of this creature, had experienced this confrontation many times before. Despite his churning gut, Wake felt a strange, primeval sense of familiarity. They both knew what would happen next: The gator would clamp down onto his arm, drag him into the dank pool, and, hopefully, death would take over quickly.

Suddenly, the alligator retreated to the far end of the pit. It settled down into the mud with an odd finality.

"I'll be damned," came a voice from above.

I am death, Wake thought, but not the kind of death it wanted. Not fresh, tender dead. I am formaldehyde-soaked, trocar-drained dead. I smell of it. It's in my eyes, the way I breathe.

Grabbing hold of a protruding tangle of roots, Wake pulled himself back onto terra firma. Drabford's thugs looked uncertainly at him. He glared back and walked between them, heading to the main road.

❊　❊　❊

So Wake returned to Southern California unscarred but empty-handed. As he drove his rented car along the Barnum Arroyo Expressway to Heaven Hill, Wake thought he had learned every lesson a scout could have drummed into him after all these years, and realized he was wrong. Forget handshakes, forget contracts; the prospect must be in your camp, under the friendly influence of possessive overseers before a deal could be considered safe.

It wasn't like this in the old days, Wake mused. Back twenty years ago or so there was an unwritten code among bird dogs and throughout the funeral trade as a whole. This code applied both to the arcane, intramural affairs of the funeral professional and the treatment of customers. Respect for a scout's territory. No swearing in front of a corpse. No pushing the bereaved into a metal vault when a simple redwood box would serve just as well. No pre-need, the selling of caskets and burial plots to individuals while they still walked among the living.

Things had definitely grown meaner in the death field over the past few years, Wake thought as he took the Rancho Norman Rockwell exit. Once, many years ago, he had personally witnessed a shoving match between the two funeral homes in Rolling Rail over the disposition of an elderly woman who had reportedly promised that each home could take her body when she died. One home's hearse pulled up to her apartment as the other was leaving with her body, prompting a hair-raising chase over the back roads of Fetch County, which ended with both hearses in the ditch and Mrs. Forgetful getting a good dousing in six inches of dirty water. A cute story—Wake had told it many times to friends and neighbors and civic groups—but it took place fifteen years ago. He could not fathom the type of hijinks that must be transpiring nowadays.

The simple fact was that people didn't die the way they

used to. The advances in medicine and improvements in diet, which had extended the average life span, spelled big problems for the funeral business. It cut off the vital flow of deceased, the lifeblood of the trade. It was, for example, as if fish were to evolve and become more intelligent, smart enough not to chomp down on that hook. Fishermen could use the fanciest rigs invented but it wouldn't fill their stringers. Their only options would be to settle for less, find another hobby, or buy a package of frozen fish sticks at the supermarket.

Same with funeral professionals. They could cast for the dead all they wished, but if a fundamental change in the lot of the living had taken place, they wouldn't fill their caskets. So they would have to settle for less, unlikely; find another profession, uncertain; or get their dead someplace else, unbelievable.

As Wake pulled into Heaven Hill's entrance, his thoughts snapped back to what he was going to tell P.T. about Andy. The shaded truth would probably be the best bet. Confess that Andy defected while at the same time playing up the ruthlessness of the midgets and leaving a ray of hope that he could still be reclaimed. No matter how much fancy talking I do this will still be a humiliating experience, Wake thought glumly. He hoped there weren't any reporters nosing around.

To his surprise and eternal gratitude the anticipated humiliation did not occur. Wake entered P.T.'s office, walls covered with plans and blueprints for various ongoing projects, saying, "Look, chief, I've got some bad news. Andy Archway left us for Drabford."

"No time for that now," P. T. Sunnyside said from behind his desk. He waved a magazine, folded back onto itself, at Wake. "We've got big problems. Look at this."

Taking the magazine, Wake read, "Why Post-Need is

Necessary for Your Family," by Dr. Halo Shoots, Ph.D. Wake flipped to the cover.

"Goddamn."

It was *Family Fanfare*, the most widely read Sunday supplement in the nation, reaching an estimated one hundred million homes, the cover boasted. The cover also boasted a color photo of Gen. Raymond Bellwether, star of last year's three-week war against the guerrillas in famine-struck Soma, hugging a fuzzy white kitty.

"Read the article," P.T. suggested.

Wake did, rapidly, with increasing disbelief. He numbly set the magazine on the desk and gazed at P.T. "They can't be serious."

"We hired a clipping service last week to send us any references to post-need and this is what arrived this morning." P.T. shoved a thick file folder across the desk. "One week! Imagine the engine driving this campaign, it must be colossal! Imagine the effect it's having on Mr. and Mrs. America! This is real trouble, Wake."

Flipping through the folder, Wake said, "This is insane. It can't work. The public won't go for it."

"I'm not so sure. Those goddamn midgets are hitting all the right buttons: family, morality, guilt, public health, keeping up with the Joneses. This is a first-class job, all right."

"But providing funeral services to people who are already *buried*," said Wake, wincing.

"It's perfectly logical, in a twisted sort of way," P.T. said. "When you put grandma in the ground twenty years ago, you just forgot about her, didn't you? She would have never forgotten about you no matter what your state, would she? What has been happening to her over the course of these years? Casket's rotting, and so is she. They didn't have the technological know-how back then that we do now. Doesn't she deserve all the care in death that she gave to you in life?

So we will rescue her from her plight, fix her up good as new, give her a brand-new casket made from the same stuff that went to the moon, then return her to her eternal resting place safe and sound."

"Wild," Wake said with a whistle.

"And they didn't miss the environmental angle, either."

"How so?"

"Think of all the contaminants to be found in a rotting human body. Think what it's doing to the ground water. Help your loved one and your planet at the same time."

"Post-need," said Wake softly.

"Post-need," echoed P.T.

"How do we respond?"

"There must be a maximum response. We can't sit on the fence on this one. Ours is a company that has to keep out front. We can't follow, and we can't look like we're slow. The midgets are so diversified now that they could still survive if this scheme fails. I never believed in diversification, and it may be my undoing. If we make the wrong move here we could be out of business for good. Maybe that's behind it, maybe they're trying to drive us out of business with this." P.T. leaned back in his chair, rocking slightly, and Wake could see the tension in his face. "I don't know," he said quietly, "maybe we should just sit tight. It's not my nature, though."

"Can I ask you something, P.T.?"

"Shoot."

"How do you feel personally about post-need?"

P.T. pondered this for a minute, thumping his thumb on the desk, and replied, "I'm not sure that's the right question. I think we need to ask how the goddamn midgets feel about post-need. If they truly believe in the concept, which I don't think is even remotely possible, then I would tend to cut them a little slack. God knows I've had some bad ideas in my time. Remember the drive-in funeral home?" P.T. shuddered.

"How did the motto go again, I forget."

"'In by 12, under by 5.' And that was the best of the bunch."

"Maybe it's time for another bad idea."

"No more drive-ins, please."

"We need to find the post-need alternative," Wake suggested. "Give people a clear choice. Even if they feel the *need* to do something for their buried relatives, that doesn't mean that exhuming rotting corpses is the only solution."

"Do you have something in mind?"

"Not really. Not yet."

P.T. stared pensively at the copy of *Family Fanfare,* then swept it across the desk. He looked at Wake. "You mentioned something about Andy Archway when you came in."

"We lost him."

"Damn, I really liked that kid. Who got him?"

"Drabford."

"Shit. How did it happen?"

"They are apparently going to help him break Mordecai's record. Mordecai's been an obsession of Archway's since he was a kid."

"Can we get him back? He did sign a contract, didn't he?"

"They're claiming duress."

"I see." P.T. sat up suddenly, swiveling his chair to the computer on the edge of his desk. After punching in a series of numbers, he sat back and waited.

"What's wrong?" asked Wake.

"Hang on," said P.T., jabbing another button, then grabbed several sheets of paper that the printer spit out. He leafed through the pages, and a grin broke over his face. He passed the sheets to Wake.

"Video tombstones, remember?" P.T. said. "Now that's what I call a post-need alternative. Why go to the expense of digging up your loved one when you and the world will remember them always with living memory pictures? A documentary for the deceased. Splice together photos from family albums, interviews with friends and family, footage of the town she grew up in, whatever we can dig up. Just press a button on the tombscreen and watch her come to life. The family will feel like they're doing something for her, as well as preserving a bit of family and community history, and they won't have to turn over a single spade of earth."

"This could work," Wake said, looking up from the transcript of their conversation from last summer.

"It's the best idea we've got."

"There's just one problem, P.T."

"Just one?"

"One big one. Archway is on their side now. He may have already told the Drabfords all about the best idea we've got."

THE RECORD

fourteen

I SEE THINGS clearly now, Andy thought to himself as the plane flew on to its destination. Everything in my life has been preparation for this. I have no choice. I've tried to break free from this path many times, aligning myself with those who would lead me astray but who unwittingly steered me to the bright pure path. If Wake had not been lost, if Mattle had not lost control of his car, if Slade had not lied. There is a guiding force inside, of which coincidence and luck are just manifestations. And now the purpose of my life can no longer be denied.

There is no choice.

The record will be mine.

I met Mordecai once, Andy recalled, a long time ago. The memory lay in his mind, sharp yet unreal. It was summer, hot. He was in decline, yet the greatness still fell from his shoulders like snow shaken off an overcoat. Something passed between us, Andy remembered, almost like a blessing. I told him I would break his record. An insane thing for a kid to say. I wasn't an arrogant child, I didn't like to boast or exaggerate, and I felt very uncomfortable immediately after uttering the words. Where did they come from? It was almost like I was repeating something I had been told.

Andy had no illusions about breaking the record. He figured his fame would be momentary and his future uncertain. I will be despised when I break the record, he thought, just like Mordecai. The pressure will take its toll. One day I may find myself drunk and derelict, haunting the midways of America. Perhaps a young boy will come to see me, kneeling in my shadow, begging for a look, a word, a blessing. Maybe he will be the one, and the cycle will begin again.

The plane rocked slightly, nudging Andy from his reverie. He looked out the window to the nighttime landscape below. There were no lights, no signs of life. Was this Soma? The Drabfords had made good on Slade's deception, and had hired a researcher from Florida University to locate the most probable spot on Earth for the record to be broken this year. The answer came back: Soma. Andy had never heard of the place before. Was it a country? A province? An island? His new bosses said not to worry. They would get him in, get him the record, and pull him out. Easy.

Soon, the nearly empty plane landed. Andy waited for an announcement from the pilot, but nothing was said and so, following the lead of the other passengers he unbuckled his seat belt and pulled his bag from the overhead carrier. Going down the ramp into the terminal, a young olive-skinned woman wearing a black scarf on her head rushed up to him at the gate and latched onto his arm. "Doctor? You are doctor?"

He shook his head, trying to break her grip.

"You are doctor," she insisted, and began attempting to tow him through the airport.

"I am not a doctor," he said, roughly prying her fingers from his forearm. Red tracks remained.

Now she took his other arm, dark eyes imploring. *"Please."*

Suddenly, another woman approached and spoke in

short, rapid-fire, unintelligible syllables. The other woman responded with equal insistence, pointing to Andy. The interloper, white-skinned, perhaps in her early forties, was wearing a solid black business suit, wrinkled and a bit worn, her short blonde hair cut choppily. She had a scattering of welts on her face and neck. She spoke again, making a waving motion for the other to go away. The first woman glanced at Andy again, then finally retreated.

"I apologize," the woman said smoothly. "You are Mr. Archway?"

"Yes, I am," Andy replied. "But what was that all about?"

"She said there is a medical conference in the city. She was told to pick up a Dr. Flushing. Perhaps she met the wrong plane."

"You know who I am. You must be Ms. Roon. Mr. Drabford said I would be meeting you."

"Just *Roon,* if you please."

"Very well, Roon." Andy looked around at the deserted airport. "Say, I'm a little confused, it was a long flight. Are we in Soma?"

"No, Soma is some distance yet, beyond the mountains. We will fly in by helicopter. It's waiting for us now."

"This was all done in such a hurry. I didn't know what to bring. They didn't tell me anything about where I'll be working, where I'll be living . . ."

Roon smiled, revealing a gap where her right bicuspid should have been. "It's all taken care of. We are being compensated very well by the Drabfords. You will have no worries. Now we must be going. We've a long trip to come."

After retrieving his suitcases, they passed through customs and went to a secluded tarmac where the helicopter sat, rotors whirring. The air was chokingly humid. Andy could see little beyond the airport in the darkness, but smelled stagnant water. Large gnats swarmed his face. He waved them away, then felt a sharp stinging sensation on his ear. He slapped at it. "Jesus, those things are nasty."

"Those are harmless," his host said as they reached the helicopter. She nodded to the pilot, a stocky woman with a long ponytail, and placed his bags behind the seats. "The ones you don't feel are the ones to fear. But they haven't been seen in this area lately." Roon removed a white tube from her coat pocket. She unscrewed the cap, squeezed the lotion onto her palm and applied it to his ear with her index finger. "This will help the swelling. When we get to Soma I will give you a spray for the other bugs, should you decide to go outside."

The pain in Andy's ear eased quickly, and they climbed inside the helicopter. It rose immediately, and Andy felt his stomach roll.

"Tell me about the people I'll be working on," Andy said to Roon, fighting to be heard above the roar of the copter. "How will they be passing on?"

"It's routine," she replied. "Not to worry. We'll take care of you."

"Look, any detail about the deceased person I can discover is a great help in my work. I need to know this."

She did not respond.

"Is there a civil war going on? An epidemic? What?"

"One-seven-seven-zero," she said. "Not to worry."

＊　＊　＊

Andy expected to see city lights or at least a sign heralding their arrival into Soma, but there were no lights or signs, only dimly seen ramshackle buildings and piles of rubble when Roon announced, "We've just crossed over. We are in Soma."

"What is this place?" Andy asked. "It looks like a bomb hit it."

"It's a place to make your future," she said, and her laughter was short and brittle.

They flew high over the muddy streets, not seeing any

signs of life. Soon they approached the only modern-looking building Andy had spotted since crossing the border. It was a white, cube-shaped building, verging on skyscraper in dimensions, set amid the decay.

The pilot circled the tower once before landing on a yellow circle in the center of the roof. "Thanks, Wilhelmina," Roon said, and they gathered together Andy's luggage and a pair of small boxes. "See you next week." They hurried away from the copter, which zoomed off as they went to an elevator, where Roon used a key to gain access. They stepped inside and she pressed the number seven on the glowing display. The car descended speedily and in a short time the doors opened and Andy found himself standing in the lobby of what could have been any modern office building in the United States. They walked down the vacant corridors, the air conditioner humming steadily.

"You will be spending all of your time in this building," Roon said, "and most of it on this floor. You will work here, live here, be entertained here. Everything will be fully provided for you."

"You talk as if I have no choice."

She stopped and looked at him evenly. "Theoretically, you do. But really, there is no reason to go beyond these walls. There is nothing to do out there. There are no activities, the climate is insufferable, and you do not understand the language. It's a completely different culture. Certainly, we will not *prevent* you from venturing outside this building, but we will strongly discourage it. It's for the best, Mr. Archway."

"I'll keep that in mind."

When they reached an interior hallway, the lighting became diffuse, the walls a warm forest green. Roon swung open a door in the middle of the hall. "These are your living quarters," she said. The quarters consisted of a bedroom, living area, and kitchenette. An exterior photograph of the building hung over the couch. Opposite the couch was a television screen recessed into the wall.

"I'm afraid the television is out of commission," Roon said. "Someone should be coming to fix it by the end of the week."

"This will do," Andy said, setting his bags on the floor. "I'm not looking for luxury. I intend to work days, nights, whatever it takes."

"Then I should show you where you will be working," she said. "Unless you'd like to eat dinner and relax first."

"Show me."

The preparation room was just around the corner. It was a standard setup. The pumps, trocar, and other equipment looked brand-new. Andy imagined himself pumping clean the last two individuals. One-seven-seven-zero was important, but one-seven-six-nine, to tie the record, would be sweet, too. He reminded himself to get film for his camera.

Andy nodded, smiling. "This is all very nice," he said. "I have to tell you I was a bit nervous about coming over here. I've never really been out of the country before, and I didn't quite know what to expect. The Drabfords have a reputation for being eccentric, but they really came through here."

Roon appeared to be greatly appreciative. "Oh, *thank you,*" she said, touching his arm. "It's wonderful of you to say that."

"I'd like to get started first thing in the morning, if that's possible."

"We're ready anytime you are. We have a reliable supply of subjects and a cooler. My assistant Esto will be providing you with your . . . material. He speaks adequate English and can be completely trusted. Of course, if you need me for anything, please feel free to page me. All you do is press the intercom button."

They walked back into the corridor. "Any other questions?" Roon asked him.

"What about meals?"

"You can order room service, the menus are on your dresser. Not much of a selection lately, due to some airport problems, but you should be able to find something you like."

"No restaurants?"

"Well, yes, there is one downstairs. I wouldn't recommend it, though. The service is very slow."

"I guess that's it, then. I'm going to eat dinner and turn in, if you don't mind."

"Not at all. Enjoy your stay, Mr. Archway."

"Thank you." Andy went back to his room, found the menu, and called the number listed alongside it.

"Yes?" A thickly accented male voice answered. He sounded Indian.

"Yes, this is Andy Archway up in room seven-twenty-two. I'd like to order a cheese omelet, toast and orange juice, please."

"Ome-let, toast, orange juice. Yes?"

"Cheese omelet."

"Cheese ome-let. Yes?"

"That's right. Room seven-twenty-two."

"It will be coming. Good-bye now."

After taking a shower and changing clothes, Andy looked for a phone book but was unable to find one. Someone knocked at the door, and he went to answer it.

A slight, dark-skinned man in casual black attire stood outside, carrying a tray. "Dinner. Yes?"

"Yes. You can set it on the desk, please." Andy tipped the man and closed the door behind him.

In the morning, Andy felt nervous ripples in his stomach. Eager to get underway, he skipped breakfast and headed directly over to the preparation area. The room-service man was seated near an interior door, patiently reading a yellowed, disintegrating newspaper.

"Esto?" Andy ventured.

The man rose, came over, and offered his hand. "Yes, I am Esto. I am here for you."

"I'm Andy Archway," Andy said, clasping his hand. "You have many responsibilities here, Esto."

"Yes, and I cook good, too, and Roon will not let me cook."

"Maybe you can cook something for us sometime. I have a small kitchen in my room."

Esto smiled in surprise. "I would like that."

Andy clapped his hands. "Well, let's get started, shall we?"

Esto tugged on a pair of rubber gloves and left the room while Andy prepared his equipment. He slipped his own gloves on, filled the vessel with embalming fluid, did a test on the pumps, lined up his instruments. Everything looked to be in order. A short time later Esto returned, wheeling in the first deceased individual on a gurney.

Andy stared at the man on the cart.

"Something wrong, Mr. Archway?" Esto inquired.

"Get Roon for me, will you?" Andy asked calmly. "Tell her I need to talk to her right away."

Esto disappeared as the image of the body burned into Andy's mind. It was a male, olive-skinned, emaciated. The ribs, hipbones, and shoulder blades were all clearly defined. He was Andy's height, but weighed no more than seventy-five pounds, max.

Andy turned away.

When Roon came into the room, he looked angrily at her and said, "What the hell is this about?"

She seemed puzzled. "Is there a problem?"

He gestured at the hollow figure on the gurney. "That man starved to death."

Roon looked at the man, then at Andy. "No, he didn't. Some people have a naturally light build. It's perfectly normal."

"Bullshit."

"Don't people lose their muscle tone when they die? It's just the way he's laying down; he's not that much slimmer than you, really."

"I didn't expect this. No one told me anything. I can't do this."

Roon's lips tightened, and her hands clenched. Then, she appeared to relax and said, "Listen, Mr. Archway. I'm going to level with you. Yes, many people are starving to death here. Disease is rampant as well. It's a tragedy, we all agree on that. However, you have a job to do. This is a government contract. The Soma government hired the Drabford organization to employ modern Western embalming practices in the treatment of the dead here. They're hoping to reduce the spread of disease by disposing of the dead in a sanitary way. I'm no expert, in fact I knew virtually nothing about your profession until two weeks ago, but I don't see anything wrong with that. Surely you've handled worse cases than this. Car accidents, shooting and stabbing victims, death the modern way. Is this really any worse?"

"Are they all going to be like this?"

"I'm afraid so."

Andy gazed at the shrunken body again. "It's going to be difficult."

"You'll get used to it. You're doing fine already. I threw up the first time I saw one."

Andy decided then to give it his best shot. She was right. This was no different than a car accident or stabbing victim. Of course, he did not tell her that he had never worked on a car accident or stabbing victim. The worst case he had ever taken was Jumbo Dellhammer, who bled to death after his right arm was pulled into a grain auger on his farm. But he was just missing a limb, a shortcoming easily remedied by mixing up a batch of plaster of Paris. The rest of him still looked like the same old Jumbo. It would be hard to ignore the state of this ghost of a man.

So number one was tough, a real challenge. The man's skin had lost much of its flexibility, making clean incisions a tricky procedure. On the other hand, pumping out the entrails and refilling the cavity was a snap because his insides had contracted quite remarkably.

Like everyone, after Andy had worked on his first few starvation victims it became old hat. The figures on the slab became abstract, part of the routine—really no different than Art the Embalming Dummy at school. There were definite advantages to the situation. The deceased were lightweight, easy to move about. A full-size individual could sometimes pose problems simply because of the dead weight, but this was like moving a child. Also, the government wanted the basic embalming procedure without embellishments. This meant no cosmetics, no eyecaps, no shaving, no shirt, no shoes, no service. Just a simple sanitary medical procedure. It speeded up things immensely.

Andy worked long hours the first few weeks, often not retiring until two or three in the morning, running on a burst of energy fueled by the realization that the record would be his if he kept his head and didn't let his emotions run the show. He had Esto keep a running count of his embalming total, posted on a bulletin board in the preparation room. He also sent weekly updates on his progress to the Society of American Embalmers, the official sanctioning and record-keeping body of licensed embalmers in the United States.

After about a month at a drop-dead pace, Andy hit the three hundred mark, and to celebrate he decided to quit early on Friday and take the night off. Television was out, since the repair people had not yet showed up to fix it. Maybe dinner at a fine restaurant would be fun. He remembered Roon telling him service was slow, but he was in no hurry tonight. Andy went down the hall to the elevators, and saw that a handwritten "Out of Order" sign had been taped to the doors. He took the stairs instead, descending one floor. This level appeared much the same as his own floor, with offices and conference rooms, but there, at the end of the corridor, was the restaurant. There was no one at the entrance to seat him, so he took a table in the center of the dimly lit vacant room, overcome with ferns and idyllic paintings of sunset oceans.

After waiting a few minutes, Andy called out, somewhat self-consciously, "Is there anybody here?" Hearing no response, he got up and took a peek in the kitchen. Empty. The ovens were clean, the coffee pots mute. Not a morsel of food to be seen, and no cooks to prepare it.

He called Roon.

"Roon, this is Andy."

"Good evening, Mr. Archway. What can I do for you?"

"Well, I came across something pretty odd. I'm at the restaurant and there's nobody here. I mean, literally nobody. No customers, no waiters, no cooks. Do you know anything about it?"

"You're at the restaurant now?"

"Yes, is there a problem?"

"I think they close early Fridays."

"But it's only six P.M. This is when people go out to eat, for God's sake. How can they be closed?"

"It's a local custom. Some religious thing, I think."

"Do you know when they'll be open again?"

"I'd have to check on that for you."

"That doesn't do me any good tonight."

"I'll have room service bring something up to you, Mr. Archway. What would you like?"

"Oh, I suppose steak, potato, green vegetable, you know. I'm sort of celebrating. I hit three hundred today."

"Well, that's fantastic. Congratulations."

"Thanks. Say, is there any entertainment in building? A

movie, music, I'd even settle for a video game arcade."

"I'm afraid you picked the wrong night to celebrate, Mr. Archway. Everything's pretty much closed down for the evening. It's sort of a sacred holiday, from what I understand."

"I see. . . . Well, I'll just go back to my room and do some paperwork, then. Maybe some other night would be better to celebrate."

"I think that's a very good idea, Mr. Archway."

After leaving the abandoned restaurant, Andy found himself feeling uneasy. Why do I get the sense that Roon is making up stories? he thought. This isn't good. If there is any possibility that this woman might endanger my opportunity to break Mordecai's record, then I must know. But if there are any answers, they won't be found down these antiseptic corridors.

Andy kneeled and tied his shoes tight, loosened a button on his shirt, and started down the stairs, step by careful step at first, then bounding down two at a time, his steps echoing in the shaft as he descended into the heart of the tower.

fifteen

"I'M SORRY, MS. Eldorado, we are simply not hiring new college grads at the moment," said Tito "Red" Ostrich, Director of Markers and Memorials. "The people we hire often have five or six years experience at a major headstone company. Feel welcome to check back with us when you've had more seasoning."

Maria sank into her chair. She knew it was a long shot applying for a job at Sunnyside, but she did not expect such a quick brush-off. "I'd be willing to do anything to get my foot in the door," she said. "Run errands, sweep up, whatever. All I'm asking for is a chance."

"I'd like to give you that chance," Tito said with a sympathetic smile. "However, as I explained earlier, we do operate under pretty tight budgetary constraints here at Sunnyside. It often ends up that what I would *like* to do falls a good distance short of what I *can* do."

Riffling through a card file, he added, "Tell you what I *will* do, though. I can give a call to a couple of my colleagues, see if they're looking for anyone with your skills. You may have to work in a little town for a while, but at least you will be picking up some good experience."

"But you're the only ones who are doing anything innovative with headstones these days," Maria argued. "You encourage the customers to leave a creative remembrance. I've walked the grounds, Mr. O'stretch. I've seen the poetry in the words and in the stone. I would fit in here so well. I'd just be wasting my time in a small town."

"That may be so, but it remains my best advice for you at this point. Would you still like me to call someone for you?"

"Yes, thanks, that would be fine," Maria said with modest enthusiasm. She took her portfolio as he handed it back to her, and rose. "Thank you for your time, Mr. O'stretch."

"Please keep in touch with us, Ms. Eldorado," he said, firmly shaking her hand. "We're always on the lookout for new talent."

Maria quickly left the office, feeling downcast. The big brush-off, she thought. I know I'm good enough to work here, I know I'm right for Sunnyside. Why can't he see that? Maria left the building and walked out onto the grounds. She almost hoped she would see Andy; she had some unfinished business with him. The sun was high and bright and a soft warm wind rippled the palm trees lining the paths. Kneeling beside a tombstone shaped like a shoe, Maria read the words aloud, sensitive fingers tracing the outline of the letters.

> **"Beneath here lies a mender of the Sole**
> **whose like you will not find from pole to pole.**
> **By every honest means he got his Awl**
> **and happy could he live tho' in a Stall;**
> **His ends he answer'd in this life that's past**
> **and now let's hope he's happy at the Last."**

Maria snuffled a bit and moved on, wandering among the many zones at Sunnyside, passing from Memory Bridge to Fountain Valley to Radio Ridge. There appeared to be some kind of disturbance taking place on the hill where many of the legends of radio were interned. A crowd of angry voices, photographers, cameramen, security guards—what was going on? Maria moved close enough to hear, but stayed well on the sidelines of the melee.

"I do so have a right!" an elderly red-haired woman in a clinging tiger-skin jumpsuit was shouting. "He's my husband! Just who do you think you are?"

"Trust me, Mrs. Rider," a gray-haired man facing her said. "We would like nothing better than to serve you and your late husband in the best manner we know how. And part of that service is advising you on matters related to the disposition of the departed. We've been in this business for many years." Maria immediately recognized the man who was trying to soothe the woman. It was P. T. Sunnyside.

"I don't care how long you've been anywhere!" the woman screamed. "What is this country coming to if the family of a deceased relative doesn't have a say over his body?"

"I would rather we discuss this privately, Mrs. Rider."

"I'm sure you would!"

"You've trusted us over the years to take care of Jinx, why not now?"

"Because I want the best after-death care available for my dear late husband! I'm not going to forget him! I want him dug up, cleaned up, and put into one of those nice new caskets made of the stuff they took to the moon! I want him to be safe and secure and preserved down there, and I want to save the environment!" She crinkled her nose. "I don't want anything to get at him. There's bugs down there, you know."

"As I told you before, madam, we do not perform those

type of post-need services here at Sunnyside and we never will."

"You dig up my husband right now, you hear me!"

"As long as I am owner of Sunnyside, I will not turn one spade of dirt on this spot."

"Then maybe I should take my business elsewhere!"

As Maria circled the crowd to gain a better vantage point, she noticed the fellow who had shadowed Andy on graduation day. She went over to him. "What's going on here?" she asked.

"The biggest farce since no-cal pizza," the man replied with a disgusted smirk.

"Who are they fighting over?"

"Jinx Rider. Ever hear of him?"

"I don't think so. No, wait, yes I have. He's on those TV commercials in the middle of the night. He yodels cowboy songs, doesn't he?"

"Yeah, well, he was actually a big radio star in the 1940s. Nowadays the college kids think it's camp; they buy his records and play them at parties for a laugh. Truth is, he was a damn fine yodeler."

"I know you," Maria told him. "I saw you with Andy Archway on graduation day at Holmes U."

"Thanks for reminding me." He looked apologetically at her. "Name's Wake Wakefield. I'm a scout. I guess you could say I discovered Andy, not that I'm bursting with pride about it anymore."

"Is he here? Have you seen him?"

"Archway? Naw, he's long gone. Jumped over to Drabford, the stupid kid. Did you know him?"

Looking away, she said, "I thought I did." She turned back to him. "My name's Maria Eldorado. I met Andy in school, he came to me in the rain. He was so sweet, so different. I even snuck in here last summer to see him when he worked on the pyramid. Please tell me, what happened to him?"

"That's what we'd all like to know," said Wake.

The dispute broke off, and reporters crowded around Mrs. Rider and a tall man in a bowler hat who identified himself as her lawyer, a Mr. Blankit. "If Mr. Sunnyside does not acquiesce to Mrs. Rider's wishes, then we will have no choice but to file a lawsuit in district court. It's a clear violation of her rights as the closest living survivor of the deceased. Not to mention the rights of the dead. They're people too, you know."

"This is pretty controversial stuff, though, wouldn't you agree?" countered a reporter. "Do you think this post-need business will stand up in court?"

"I have no doubt that it will. Controversial or not, this is a decision that should be left up to the individual family. No government, no judges, no politicians, and especially no egomaniacal grounds keeper should be allowed to interfere with this fundamental right."

"What about that old saying, 'Rest in Peace,' Mrs. Rider?" asked a television journalist.

"What sort of peace do you think my Jinx has now?" she replied beseechingly. "He's resting in a rotting box with bugs in it. What could be less peaceful than that?" She dabbed her eyes with a frilly handkerchief. "I can barely sleep myself thinking about it."

Over on the other side, P. T. Sunnyside was holding court with another gaggle of press people.

"We've made our reputation on innovation," P.T. was saying, "but these so-called post-need services are not an innovation, they're an abomination. Since this is a relatively new phenomenon, we still have a program in the works to respond to the needs that our customers may have about their dear departed. But I assure you it will be nothing like the gruesome spectacle you almost witnessed here today."

"What is this new program you're talking about? How will you respond?"

"We'll be making an announcement in the near future. Other than that, I have nothing to add, folks."

"Just a few more questions, Mr. Sunnyside."

Wake turned to Maria. "These reporters are going to be asking the same question fifty different ways for the next hour. So what's your line of expertise, Ms. Eldorado?"

"Headstones, markers, and epitaphs," she said. "At least that's what I studied in school."

"Oh really," Wake said with interest. "Don't quote me, but this may be a growing area at Sunnyside in the future. Have you signed with anyone?"

"No, that's why I'm here. I had an interview."

"How did it go?"

Shrugging, Maria said, "Not so hot. He said I needed more experience."

"Who did you talk to?"

"O'stretch. An Irish fellow, I think."

"Red Ostrich, you mean."

"Yes, that was it."

"He has a title but no clout around here. I'll talk to P.T. about it. Are you willing to do drudge work for not much dough for a while?"

Maria looked at him squarely. "Mr. Wakefield, if you're teasing me, understand I'm not in the mood."

"Well, I'm not promising you anything. I'm not the guy who actually does the hiring around here." He grinned. "But I do have P.T.'s ear, if you know what I mean." Looking over at his boss, he said, "Things appear to be wrapping up."

". . . last question and then I must be going."

"What are you going to do with Mrs. Rider?"

"I love the dear, but you should ask her why she didn't conduct this conversation with me in my office, in private."

"Are you saying this was a publicity stunt, Mr. Sunnyside?"

"That's your call. Afraid I have to get back to work now—enjoy your stay at Sunnyside." P.T. parted the circle of reporters and headed over to Wake. Grabbing him by the elbow, P.T. said out of the corner of his mouth, "Let's get out of here and have a lemonade, pal."

"Come on along, Maria," said Wake as the pair started back to the administration building.

When she caught up to them, Wake told P.T., "This is Maria Eldorado. She was close to Archway, back in his saner days."

"Glad to know you, Maria," said P.T. "We were very disappointed to lose him. I really liked that kid."

"I know how you feel."

"We might be able to use her," Wake said. "She's a topnotch marker maker. You know, in case we ever decide to make some changes in that area and need to staff up quickly."

"I brought my portfolio," Maria offered.

"Will you work for room and board for a month while we see if you're fit for the fire?" P.T. asked.

"You know I will."

He stopped as they reached the administration building and shook her hand. "Welcome to Sunnyside, Maria."

They went inside P.T.'s office and had made good progress on their lemonade and sugar cookies when the phone rang.

"Goosehaus from Legal? Put him on, Elsie." P.T. took a sip of lemonade. "Goosey, what's up?"

Maria watched P.T. as he listened, nodding, his expression growing grim. She could almost hear the other end of the conversation; the man was talking loudly, almost hysterically. She wasn't certain, but thought she caught the word "overturned."

sixteen

DESCENDING INTO THE Soma tower, Andy soon discovered that most of the doors leading to the other floors were locked. The ones that were open led into complete darkness, and Andy was reluctant to explore any further without a flashlight. He finally reached the bottom of the stairway, the door marked "To Atrium." He took the knob and twisted it. The door opened.

The light was improved here, supplied by a full moon streaming through the long vertical atrium window. Andy removed a shoe and stuck it in the doorway in case it would lock, and ventured out. It did not look promising. Lounge areas, check-in desk, a drained fountain, and no people. The front doors had been boarded shut. He moved to the windows and gazed out at Soma. Nothing moved in the pale streets, or among the derelict sheds which somehow still stood. Soma was a dead town.

Andy was ready to head back upstairs when he saw a photo on the wall behind the fountain. It showed a groundbreaking ceremony. A trio of men and a woman dressed in suits and hardhats were posing for the camera with joyous smiles, and holding shiny spades thrust into the earth. A border across the top bore the phrase, "Make Your Future in Soma." The woman, Andy suddenly realized, was Roon, but with an unblemished face, stylishly cut hair, and a full set of teeth.

This is not good, he thought. The record. By God I cannot allow this woman to cost me the record.

Andy was winded by the time he reached his own floor. As he left the stairwell, a pungent burning smell caught his attention. Following it through the hallways he ended up outside a set of swinging metal doors. He poked his head inside.

The cook was attired untraditionally, in a yellow bathrobe and slippers. She was crying. Smoke poured from a frying pan on the stove. A lumpy, coallike mass undulated in the bottom of the pan.

"Roon . . ."

She turned, and a panicked look crossed her face. Quickly, she attempted to recover her composure, wiping away the tears and smoothing back her ragged hair. "I apologize for ruining your dinner," she said formally. "You see, the cook had to go home tonight, his mother was sick." She began frantically throwing open cupboard doors. "I'll fix you something else. Would you like a cheese omelet, perhaps?"

"I was downstairs," Andy said, moving toward her. "I saw your picture on the wall."

"You really shouldn't go downstairs," she said. "Everything will be fully provided for you here."

"You're the last one left, aren't you? Why did you stay? What hope could you have here?"

She sank to the floor, leaning up against the cupboards, hugging her knees. She looked plaintively at Andy. "Please don't leave. You can stay as our guest. Complimentary continental breakfast. Free cable TV. Service is our middle name."

"I'm not going anywhere," he said. "We have a business arrangement. I will stay here until my task is finished. You will be paid every fee that's coming to you. But you must live up to your end of the agreement."

"I love this tower," she said. "I built it myself, did you know that?" She kneaded her palms with her thumbs. "With these very hands I built it, out of the mud. I'm sorry, the television repair man should be coming this week. It's a religious holiday, so it may take some time. I can try to fix it for you, if you'd like. I've never actually done such a thing, but I think I saw someone do it once, a long time ago." Her head drooped and she slid prone to the floor.

Andy left her and found a phone. "Esto, listen to me carefully. Roon is sick. We need to move her to her bed."

"Roon sick?"

"Yes, we're in the kitchen. Could you come right away?"

"Yes."

A short time later Esto arrived, a concerned expression on his face, and together they helped Roon down the hall to her room. "She needs to rest," Andy said. "We can't disturb her. She's very sick."

"Do not disturb," Roon mumbled.

After they got her into bed, Andy led Esto out to the hallway. "How long have you been with Roon?"

"Year, maybe more."

"Has she ever been like this before?"

"Maybe once, not so bad. Things don't work. She and tower are *oaope*."

"What does that mean?"

"Two as one."

"Are there doctors in Soma?"

"Not many. They seeing the people I bring to you. They will not be helping her."

"Now Esto, this is very important. Can you keep me supplied with people until she gets better?"

He nodded solemnly. "Yes, I get people for you."

"Wonderful," Andy replied, putting a hand on Esto's shoulder. "And we will need your cooking skills, too."

"Yes," said Esto. "I will cook."

"Then we're all set. We'll continue work in the morning. I want to get finished with this project and return home as soon as possible."

The new regime performed exceptionally well its first two weeks. Andy picked up the pace, regaining the form that brought him all the accolades in college. The bodies became a blur, and Esto had to hustle to keep up with him. On the bulletin board the tally reached the coveted five hundred mark. Andy did not pause to celebrate; seeing the number drove him even harder.

During his mealtimes, Andy visited Roon, talked to her even though she did not appear to be listening. He knew that she held information that he might need to reach the record, from the logistics of delivering the deceased to keeping the kitchen stocked with food. She was apparently organized enough that the tower could run on automatic pilot for a while, but Andy figured that soon they would need her guidance again.

As the days passed her condition seemed to worsen. "She and tower are *oaope*," Esto told Andy. "It die, she die. Nothing no work, circle get smaller. You help people when is too late. You need her, you cannot help her. You need tower, you cannot help it. What is it you help, Mr. Archway?"

"I'm helping the government. It's a sanitation project. If bodies aren't sanitized at death, disease could get into the water and many people would get sick. I'm saving lives, Esto. It may not seem so now, but it's true."

"You take Roon if she dies?"

"It depends on the wishes of the family. I assume she will be flown back to her home for disposition of the body. But she's not going to die, Esto."

"No family. They die here."

"I didn't know. How did it happen?"

"Disease come. Husband, daughter, son, get sick, die. You think dead people killed them?"

"Did *oaope* begin then? Is that what happened to her, Esto?"

"Yes."

It die, she die, Andy thought. So it logically followed that if the tower made a recovery, then Roon would improve in kind. But Esto was right. *What is it you help, Mr. Archway?* How could he be expected to repair an elevator or television set or to fill the tower with guests? And even if Roon's condition did not depend on the state of the tower, even if she had a broken leg or tonsillitis, he was helpless. He knew nothing about medicine where the living were concerned. All he could do was what he knew best. She would need to die in order for him to help her. The only answer, Andy decided, was to keep working as long and as quickly as he could and hope that Esto was wrong and that she would recover on her own.

In the days that followed, Andy noticed a marked change in Esto. He seemed edgy, expectant. Often he found him in Roon's room, hovering over her as if he was waiting for a sign.

Andy wrapped up number 594 around lunchtime one day, and waited for Esto to haul in number 595. He did not hear the familiar sound of the gurney rolling down the hallway. "Esto!" he called out. "I'm ready for the next one! Esto, are you there?" Have to do everything myself, he thought angrily and went over to the cooler, which was adjacent to the preparation room. He pulled open the heavy door, felt the rush of cold air. It was empty. Where could he be?

After grabbing a cold sandwich in the kitchen, Andy dropped in on Roon. Hesitating at the threshold, he saw Esto kneeling at her bedside, ear close to her mouth. He nodded and spoke softly to her, then listened close again. The only problem was that from where Andy was standing it did not look like Roon's lips were moving when she spoke to Esto.

"Esto, what are you doing? I've been waiting for you. The cooler is empty."

He froze, not turning back to look at Andy. "She is waking," he said quietly.

Andy went over and examined Roon. She appeared comatose, eyes closed, unresponsive. Gently shaking her, Andy said, "Roon . . . Roon . . . can you hear me? . . . Roon . . ." He turned to Esto. "You were talking to her. What did she tell you?"

"You must leave here."

"Don't be stupid, man. We've got a lot of work ahead of us."

"She like you. Want nothing bad to happen. So time to go."

"Nonsense. I want you to leave her alone, Esto. You can give her meals, but otherwise stay out of this room. Roon told me you could be completely trusted. You need to help me now. You need to bring me bodies. It's your responsibility. Understand?"

Head bowed, Esto said, "Perhaps I hear things, Mr. Archway."

"Perhaps you do. Now let's get back to work."

A sense of normalcy returned to the tower. Esto was more efficient than ever, anticipating Andy's needs at every turn. At the end of the week they got together in Andy's room for dinner, Esto cooking up a beans-and-rice dish on the little stove.

"This is excellent," Andy remarked, scooping up a forkful. "What do you call it?"

"Pelladi," Esto said. "Used to be very common meal in Soma."

"It will be again someday, Esto."

"Not so sure. Things bad so long. No dreams left, I think. People dream tower here, don't dream no more. I talk

173

to people, who come here finally. They dream of food, bellies are full in dreams. Easier to live in dream than in Soma. Stay inside and sleep and dream, chew teesin plant to help them. It best way in Soma now. Only way."

"Can't the government do something to help?"

Esto laughed softly. "Government helps itself. Dreams not like people. No common meals."

"I'd like to go out with you on your next run," Andy said. "I haven't been outside the tower since the day I arrived. I want to see what's going on. I want to understand." He left it unsaid, but in truth he needed to know where to get bodies in case something happened to Esto.

Shaking his head, Esto said, "No, you stay here. Esto will take care of you. No place for you out there."

"Take me with you, Esto. Please."

"Will not be same after. You see."

"I want to go."

Esto paused, then said, "We will go tomorrow morning."

* * *

They left early for the land beyond the tower. Before they departed, Esto stopped in at the kitchen and filled a knapsack with bread and vegetables. "You do not mind?" he asked Andy. "Not my food, but Roon say okay."

"It's fine," Andy replied.

After taking a stack of sheets from a closet, the pair headed down the stairs to the parking garage. Going over to a rust-eaten blue pickup, Esto tossed the sheets into the back, tucked the knapsack behind the seats and got in. Andy climbed in on the passenger side. The truck started after two tries and revved up noisily, the muffler rattling.

Esto put the truck into gear and they rolled across the underground lot to the exit, the door opening automatically, and suddenly they ascended into the daylight. It was a bright morning, windy and hot. As they drove along, going slow to weave around rocks and potholes in the muddy road, Andy wished it was night, when the darkness could obscure the countenance of Soma. Every tragic flaw was revealed in the daylight. The wrecks of dilapidated buildings loomed over the narrow streets, threatening to topple. Vacant zones appeared every few blocks—vast areas of broken concrete and dirt. Flies buzzed the windshield. They were the only sign of life Andy had seen so far.

"We go to the hospital," Esto said. "Sisters there very nice. Help me. I help them, too. Should be able to fill the truck, no problem."

After driving for several more blocks, Esto pulled to a stop outside a house-size tent standing amid the rubble. He got out, slinging the knapsack over his shoulder. "You stay if you like," he said to Andy.

"I'm going with you." Andy climbed out and followed Esto inside the tent.

The tent was crammed with cots and blankets, wall to wall. On each lay an individual in the process, or so it appeared, of dying. Sisters tended to some of the victims, giving them water or mopping their foreheads. Sunlight filtering through the tent gave the room an odd yellow glow. A sour stench filled the air. An ancient fan chattered on a nearby desk, where a nun was writing on a pad.

"Sister Mally there," Esto told Andy. "Come."

They approached the sister, who looked up and smiled tiredly at Esto. "My friend Esto is back," she said. "How good to see you again. You brought something for me?"

"Yes," he said proudly, and opened the flap on his knapsack, setting it on the desk.

"Wonderful," said Sister Mally. "You help us so much, Esto. You are a blessing to us."

Taking Andy's elbow, Esto said, "This my friend, Mr. Archway. Works with Roon at Tower. I help him. We eat pelladi together last night."

"You're an undertaker," she said plainly.

"Yes, sister."

"It's rare to see a new face in Soma. Will you be staying long?"

"For a while. But things are a little uncertain right now."

"Roon is sick, Sister Mally," Esto said. "You help?"

"Roon is sick? What's wrong?"

"Is Tower. She and tower . . ."

"We're not really sure," Andy broke in. "She had some kind of nervous breakdown. I understand her husband and children died here. I'm sure it's related to that."

"I don't know what I can do for her then," said the sister. "You're welcome to bring her down. The doctor will be here in two days. Perhaps he can do something for her." She looked at Esto. "I need your help, my friend. Our bus wouldn't start this morning, I'm not sure what's wrong with it. Could you look at it?"

"I will help."

"Come, I'll show you," said the sister and the two disappeared through a flap in the back of the tent.

Andy waited, trying to breathe in with his mouth, watching the fan, the desk, the shadows.

Someone began moaning loudly in a nearby cot. Andy stood still, listening, but not looking over. The sisters will take care of him, he thought. The cries persisted, and Andy glanced quickly around the room. The sisters were occupied at other bedsides. "There's a man in pain here," he said in a strained voice that didn't seem to carry far. Finally, Andy looked at the person uttering the sounds. A man not unlike one of the six hundred. His meager naked body was trembling, sweat beading on his dark face. Andy stared at him, then looked away.

The moans grew deeper, softer. Andy forced his eyes to

look. The man's face was clenched in pain. His body was rocking slightly.

Andy took a step toward him.

A line of bile trickled down the man's chin.

Andy moved unthinking to him. Kneeling down, he tore off a piece of his shirt, dipping it into the pan of water below the cot, and gently mopped the man's forehead and face. A skeletal hand took hold of Andy's wrist. The man began breathing in deep heaves. Andy held him in an awkward embrace, feeling the heartbeat, the warmth. The man gasped and went limp in Andy's arms.

"You're gonna be okay," Andy said, holding the man tight. "You're gonna be okay."

Gentle hands pulled Andy away. "You did as much for him as any of us could," said the sister, leading him back to the desk. "He would have died alone without you. I don't recognize you. You're not a doctor, are you?"

"I—I came with Esto," Andy said numbly.

"I think he went out back with Sister Mally. Come, I'll take you." She walked with him outside to where Esto was leaning over the bus's engine with a wrench. "Now try," he told Sister Mally, who was at the wheel. The engine sparked to life. She smiled and gave him a thumbs-up sign. Esto lowered the hood.

"You have a good friend, Esto," said the sister with Andy.

Esto turned and grinned. "Yes. We are friends."

"Thank you so much, Esto," said Sister Mally as she climbed out of the bus. "You're a talented fellow."

"We load up now, yes?"

"Yes."

Esto went to the truck and backed it up to a smaller gray tent behind the hospital. The bodies, perhaps twenty in all, were wrapped in sheets. When they had finished loading them Esto left the pile of clean sheets in the tent and said his good-byes to the sisters.

"Thank you again," said Sister Mally. "We will see you soon. You too, Mr. Archway."

Esto stopped along the way to pick up bodies at a mass burial site, filling the bed to the top. "I will get more tomorrow," he said. "You work now."

As they drove down the narrow street back to the tower, Esto gestured out the window. "Look," he said. "Smoke."

Andy saw it, too. Black smoke was billowing above the tenements. When they reached an open zone they could see that the tower was on fire.

"Roon!" Esto exclaimed and sped through the streets, the truck banging down the rutted road, bodies toppling out the back. As they reached the approach to the tower, Andy could see that the fire was concentrated on the upper floors of the building, the strong wind whipping it into a conflagration. Esto was about to swing around back to the underground lot when Andy pointed, shouting, "Wait, Esto. Look!"

Tires screeching, the truck bounced to a halt. They leapt out of the truck and gazed at the tower's roof. Someone was up there, dressed in blue, standing stock still on the edge.

"Get out, Roon! Get out!" they screamed.

She didn't move.

They hopped back in the truck and pulled around to the back of the building, but as soon as the garage door rose, smoke poured out into the street. Esto backed up hurriedly, frantically saying, "What we do? What we do?"

Andy had no answer for him.

There was little they could do but watch helplessly, and this they did while the blaze engulfed the building, and when they could not watch anymore they left to find Sister Mally, and when night fell the burning tower was the only light to be seen in Soma.

$\iota \varepsilon \upsilon \varepsilon n t \varepsilon \varepsilon n$

THE DREAM WAS gone, but the dreamer remained. Andy haunted the site where he had caught a glimpse of the dream, as if by force of will he could resurrect what had been lost. At first he had to keep his distance, waiting until the tower's shell cooled. Only then did he venture inside to paw through the charred, twisted metal, hoping to find a familiar fragment, something to tell him that he had not imagined the whole nightmarish episode.

"Sister Mally say to come," Esto told Andy one day while he was stubbornly trying to remove the back lid of a blackened embalming fluid pump with a butter knife. "Building not safe. She take care of you."

"I'll be there in a minute," Andy said. "I just need to fix this pump."

"Mr. Archway, you here for a week. Nothing left. Too late. You come with me."

Andy stopped working on the pump. "No, this was meant to be, don't you know that? I'm supposed to be here now." He looked hopefully at Esto. "Can you still get me bodies? I'll rig up something temporary until I can replace my equipment. We can get started in the morning. I'll do the cooking and I'll pay you whatever wage you ask. What do you say?"

Shaking his head, Esto said, "Please, Mr. Archway, you come with me."

Andy turned away, resuming his work on the pump. "I can't, Esto," he said in a subdued tone. "Not right now. Thank Sister Mally for me, will you?"

As the days wore on in the abandoned tower, and the scavenged food and fresh water dwindled away, Andy began feeling very close to Roon. Perhaps it was simply the fact that he had remained in her tower after she had perished in the fire, like a loyal dog resolutely keeping watch over his dead master. Or was it the understanding that two dreams died in the tower that night? Was it a kinship of the damned? But the price Roon had paid for losing her dream was much steeper than Andy had paid, so far, and he feared that at the end of the cycle of his broken dream he, too, would feel the flames.

Strangely, when they had discovered Roon's body two floors beneath the collapsed roof, Andy had not felt even the remotest desire to embalm her. Of course, her flesh had been badly seared, but it was more than just the fact that the task may have been unpleasant. The desire, that innate instinct to create something beautiful out of a cold, cold form, was gone. It was the oddest feeling. Although he knew he could still perform the task physically—his knowledge and skill were certainly still intact—the *need* had faded. So he and Esto had dug the corpse out of the rubble, wrapped it in a sheet, and brought it to Sister Mally.

Andy had been operating on remote control since then, his thoughts and actions an echo of a self that had disappeared. Gradually, the realization seeped into his core that his desire had evaporated.

Andy knew he had to leave the tower. Where will I go? he thought. Every step has not been a step toward my dream, it's been a step of betrayal. Wake, P. T., Maria, my folks. They all believed in me and I betrayed their faith and their trust. Where will I go? I can't stay here, Andy thought. That night, having not eaten for two days, Andy left the tower for good.

He headed to the hospital, a long walk through the silent starving streets. When he reached the tent and went inside, he saw a nun on duty at the desk, head in the crook of her elbow, asleep. All the cots were full. It was quiet. The tent, dimly lit by a string of bare light bulbs, swayed slightly as the wind buffeted it.

Andy felt very dizzy. He sat down on the floor planks and put his head in his hands.

Finally, the barker appeared on the small stage.

"Ladies and gentlemen," the barker began. Andy uncovered his face, slowly. The barker smiled at him. "Or should I say, sir. You are about to witness three of the most amazing and educational exhibits ever presented at any exposition in this country. The unusual, the beautiful, the mysterious. Something for every taste. Now, I present to you . . . the Amazing Wakefield, the Man Who Lives on Air Alone!"

From behind the curtains came an emaciated version of the old scout. His bones poking out of his skin like sticks into a deflated balloon, he stepped gingerly to the front of the stage and turned a complete circle.

"What perverse desire caused this man to attempt to subsist exclusively on the air we breathe? But no, perhaps this is not perversity but necessity!"

The old man clutched his heart and reached out to the dreamer.

The barker swept back the curtain with his cane and the scout shambled offstage. "Thank you, Amazing Wakefield." Leaning against his cane, the barker continued, "We gave you the unusual, now we present the beautiful. Feast your eyes on Maria, the Aztec Goddess!"

Drifting out from behind the dark space as the curtains opened, the Goddess appeared, adorned in a gold-feathered headdress and a shimmering bodice. A falcon was perched on her shoulder—its predatory eyes scanned the room.

"I am today, asshole," the Goddess intoned and released the bird. The spectator screamed, throwing his hands up to cover his face as the talons found his neck.

The spectator found himself in a dark place. He could hear a rustling noise, fabric being shaken gently. A voice penetrated the blackness.

"Our final attraction this evening is a puzzle wrapped up inside a quandary. Tell you the truth, I don't even understand him myself. See what you make of him. He is called . . . The Mysterious One."

Intense light blinded the spectator. He stepped forward, shielding his eyes with his hands. He stood there unseeing, unmoving, silent.

"Don't just stand there, kid," the barker whispered sharply. "*Do* something."

That voice, the spectator thought. It sounds so familiar. He circled to the front of the stage so that his back blocked the spotlight and a shadow fell over the form of the barker.

"Pop . . ."

     ❋   ❋   ❋

In the days that followed, Andy spent most of his time at the hospital, emptying bedpans, mopping the floor, helping distribute what little food came in. He also tried to do the extra things that Esto had always done, such as mending window screens and keeping the bus running; a week earlier, Esto had taken the money he had earned at the tower and moved his family out of Soma. After his long days and nights Andy went to the mission, where he slept on the floor using a ratty blanket for a bed, draping himself with a piece of mosquito netting to keep the insects at bay. He beat back his doubts and fears about his life and lost himself in simple tasks. In all the misery that surrounded him, Andy somehow managed to find a sense of stability, no matter how fragile.

"You are so good with the patients," Sister Mally told him one morning while he was changing the sheets on the bed of a woman who had died the previous night. "I never thought someone like you would be interested in this type of work."

"I enjoy it," said Andy, tucking a corner in. "Makes me feel useful."

"I don't know if you've heard the news, but Sister Effy is going to be leaving us next week. She's going to be working in our mission in New Guinea."

"That's too bad," Andy said. "I like her."

"Me too. But what it means, Andy, is that we will have a spare room at the mission." She laughed. "It's funny, I've been putting off all week telling you that you were going to have to leave us because we can't afford to feed any extra mouths. Now, I want to ask you if you'd be interested in staying on with us."

Looking at her in disbelief, Andy said, "Stay here? You mean like as a job?"

"Yes. You would be paid an extremely small stipend, plus room and board. You probably have plans, but I thought I would at least see what you thought."

Turning back to the sheets, Andy said, "Yes, you're right. I do have a lot of plans. Big, important plans. I'm very flattered by the offer, Sister, but I work for somebody else. I have to check in with them and see where my next project is going to take me."

"I thought that might be the case," Sister Mally told him. "I'm glad I asked, anyway." She hesitated, then said, "Andy, I realize you went through quite a trauma over at the tower. I think I've been very understanding of your situation, but I was serious about us not being able to feed any extra mouths. There's really no room for you here if you're not going to work for us. You're going to have to leave, and I'd appreciate it if it would be as soon as possible. Every day, every meal makes a difference here."

Andy froze for a moment, then nodded, and continued changing the bed. "Could I stay until tomorrow? I need to make travel arrangements."

"A supply truck will be coming in the afternoon. I'll let them know that you'll be riding out with them."

"Thank you."

"I'm very sorry, Andy, I wish it were some other way," the sister said sadly. "It's just that everyone in Soma is so . . ."

❊ ❊ ❊

"Hungry?

"Then make tracks to the OhBoy Family Restaurant, located a frog's hop from the lakeshore in beautiful West Houdin. Presidential dining at soup-line prices. Kids under one eat free. That's . . ."

Andy switched off the radio and cranked down the window. It was a Saturday afternoon, a bright Indian summer day. He drove his rental car with abandon, impatiently watching the odometer click away the miles. He was intact, and he was home, and nothing else mattered.

Soon he slowed, taking the familiar turn off into Golbyville, where Mrs. Zeeny's canning jar sculpture still stood guard over the passage into town. Pumpkins rested on front steps along the main drag in downtown Golbyville, piles of rust and golden leaves were heaped in yards. A football game drifted out of a radio at a house where a man in a flannel shirt smoking a pipe clung to a ladder, clearing clumps of leaves and twigs from his rain gutter.

An old-timer in overalls crossing the street waved at Andy. Andy did not recognize him, but still he raised a finger and smiled. Coming to the feed store, Andy turned left and started down the final stretch to the farm. He sped up as he left town, a cloud of dust trailing behind him.

"My goodness!" Ma Archway said as Andy pulled up. She came down the steps in a hurry, saying, "Andrew, what are you doing here?" They embraced. "I thought you were in Baghdad."

"Soma, Mom. Gosh, it's good to see you. Where's Pop?"

"He went into town to play pinochle. But what are you doing here? Did you break the record?"

"They told you what happened, that I defected and signed with Drabford?"

"Yes, that nice Mr. Wakefield called us, very upset. I told him we trusted you to do what was best, so he should just never mind."

"You're not mad at me?"

"Why should we be mad at you? You're in the adult world now. Things aren't always as nice and neat as when you're growing up. The decisions you make are so much harder, can hurt so many other people. It can't be helped. That's just the way life is. Would you like a cookie?"

"Sure, mom."

"Oh!" she said suddenly. "A telegram came for you last week. I put it in the pocket of the calendar. It sounded important." They went inside, and she handed him the message.

From: Dr. Kent Demars, Time Hill, Sunnyside, 1254 Rancho Norman Rockwell Drive, Rancho Norman Rockwell, CA 91767

To: Andy Archway, R.R. 3, Golbyville, MN 56081

Urgent. *Stop.* Need your aid immediately! *Stop.* Pyramid in danger! *Stop.* Come at once! *Stop.* Desperately yours, K. Demars

Andy folded the telegram sharply and stuck it in his pocket. "I've got to go, Mom," he said. "I can't just stand here anymore. I've got to do something. Tell Pop I said thanks." He started for the door.

"But Andrew, you're cookie . . ."

"If you need to reach me," he said, looking over his shoulder, a sense of purpose in his eyes, "I'll be on Time Hill."

eighteen

SOMETHING WAS UP at Sunnyside, Andy realized the moment he passed beneath the angel gates to Heaven Hill. Something big and dead. As he slowly wound along the paths to Time Hill, Andy saw excavations on both sides of the road, in the zones, up the hills. Exhumations. His first thought was that these had become low-status districts, survivors moving their dear departed for the exclusivity of Time Hill. But Demars's message had said that the pyramid was in danger. Danger from what? Maybe P.T. had changed his plans for Time Hill; his whims were legendary, and it was not out of the question that he had cooked up another scheme for the site.

When Andy reached the summit of Time Hill, he was stunned to discover a row of bulldozers, engines idling, poised at the gates to Futureville and Egyptville. Strangely, only Frontiersville seemed not to be threatened. Andy parked and rushed into the grounds, noticing that a portion of the stone barrier surrounding Egyptville had been demolished. He found Demars at the base of the pyramid, walkie-talkie in hand. The pyramid had taken on a brownish, aged appearance, perhaps due to the smog. Underlings dashed back and forth between the tents and the pyramid. Everyone had traded in their desert headgear for a hard hat, and everyone was hefting a shovel, pick, or some other potential weapon. Someone hurried by with a tray of coffee. "No thanks," Andy said.

". . . just sitting there," Demars was saying. "Yes, we bloody well warned them what the consequences would be if they did. . . . Where are we meeting? . . . Yes, the troops up here are top notch, I'll make certain we keep in contact at all times. I don't think they'll try anything. They know we mean business; they've got a dent in the side of one of their buggies to prove it. . . . Yes, I will, commander. Over and out." He attached the walkie-talkie to his belt.

Andy approached him. "I got your telegram, Dr. Demars."

"Archway!" Demars exclaimed, beaming. He pumped Andy's hand. "Delighted to see you. Place hasn't been the same without you."

"What's all this about? It looks like a war zone."

"We're in a bit of a pickle," Demars said, tipping his helmet back. "Those boys out there have it in for old Egyptland, I'm afraid. They showed up one night and started knocking down the perimeter wall. Let me tell you we put a stop to that in a hurry."

"But who are they?"

"No time now," Demars said, checking his watch. "We've got a staff meeting in five minutes down at headquarters. Why don't you come with me and get the lay of the land, so to speak." He turned to a lithe tanned woman nearby. "Jean, I need to run down the hill for about an hour. I'll keep my speaker open. If those blokes move even a millimeter, alert me straightaway, right?"

"Right, Dr. Demars." She raised her binoculars to her eyes.

Demars hopped into a jeep, Andy climbing in on the

passenger side. The tires spun in the sand, and the vehicle leapt forward. As they passed by the bulldozers, Demars glared at them. "They'll never defeat us," he said resolutely. "Our pyramid is built for eternity. Even if they could get those beasts in there, the best they could do is scratch up the surface. Can't be burned, the bricks are fireproof. Could blow the whole enterprise to bits, but it would take a ton of explosives. No, anyone who wants to get rid of the pyramid will have to dismantle it brick by brick, the same way it was put together." He grinned, glancing at Andy. "And you know what that was like, right Archway?"

"It was the best summer of my life," Andy said.

"I knew you'd come back to fight for it. It's a real sign of character, my friend. None of your fellow pyramid-builders answered the call."

"To be honest, Doctor, I didn't have much choice. The pyramid is about the only thing left standing in my life."

"For whatever reason, Archway, I am happy to have you on board."

They pulled up outside the white blockhouse-shaped building that housed the administration offices at Sunnyside and headed inside.

When they stepped into the conference room, Andy was not surprised to see Wake, seated at the table, or P. T. Sunnyside, standing in front of the room. But there was Maria, sitting across the table from Wake. What was she doing here? They both looked at him with angry surprise, and turned as one to P.T.

"I'm afraid this poses a bit of a problem, Dr. Demars," P.T. said. "This meeting is intended to be high security."

"You mean Archway, here?" Demars grinned proudly, placing a hand on Andy's shoulder. "No need to worry about this chap. He's true blue. Came all the way from the Middle West to fight for Time Hill."

"I'm not sure you understand, Doctor. Mr. Archway

was under contract to us at one point. He has since defected to the Drabford side, which I hope you understand is a concern in light of the current situation."

"Drabfords? Those bastards? Andrew?" He looked at his protégé. "Is this true, Archway?"

"Yes, but . . ."

"My god, man, you're a spy!"

"No, it's not like that," Andy said. "I don't belong to them anymore. I quit. I quit everything." He turned to P.T. "The only reason I came back to Sunnyside was out of a sense of personal loyalty to Dr. Demars. When the fight for the pyramid is over, I'll leave. I don't want a job. I don't want to get involved in your petty squabbles. I don't want anything. I've been gone a long time, and I just want to go home when this is finished."

"Where were you?" Wake inquired.

"Soma."

"Oh, my God," Maria said under her breath.

"You didn't get the record," Wake said, and turned to P.T. "They might have dumped him over there just to get rid of him."

"What did you tell the Drabfords about our operation?" asked P.T.

"I didn't tell them anything. I didn't have a chance. I barely saw them. The only time I talked to them face-to-face, they were too busy shooting bottles off a fence post to pay me much attention. Say, what do you mean they dumped me?"

"We can't waste any more time on this," P.T. said. "Dr. Demars, see to it that someone you trust is with Archway at all times. If he even breathes suspiciously, let me know and we'll throw him off the grounds. Now take your seats. We have a long agenda to plow through."

As they seated themselves, Andy kept an eye on P. T. Sunnyside. He had undergone a remarkable transformation, from a genial grandfatherly figure, the Dean of the American

Funeral, to this irascible, war-ready commander. Andy watched wide-eyed while the General laid out the battle plans.

"We've fought the bastards to a standstill," Sunnyside said. "The exhumations have stopped. The bulldozers haven't budged in two days. A fine job, folks, keep it up. Things are a little tougher on the legal end of things, but we're still hopeful. Judge Titterbag says he will keep the restraining order in place until a decision is reached, possibly in a week or two. If we can hang on until then, we'll pull through this. We need to keep the faith, stay disciplined and not spread rumors.

"Any word on a settlement?" someone asked.

"No, and I'm skeptical that there will be one. We've offered the midgets more cash than they could ever use, but I suspect the only settlement that would satisfy them would be one where they would take full possession of Heaven Hill. Of course, that will not happen."

None of this made any sense. Andy stood up. "What the hell's going on here?" he asked. "How could the Drabfords be involved in this? I never heard anything about this before."

"You've been away too long," P.T. replied with a knowing grin. "The goddamn midgets filed a lawsuit against our acquisition of Heaven Hill, and paid off a judge to rule that the state illegally awarded the property to us. The bastard also awarded them damages for their lost revenue, somewhere in the neighborhood of a hundred kazillion dollars, and allowed them to take over our assets in case we couldn't pay the bill, which obviously we can't. It's all bullshit, of course. The appeals court will overturn the ruling, no question. Now, let's move on to other business. As to the rationing program . . ."

When the meeting broke up, Wake came over to Andy and said, "I'm trying to understand what happened with you last year, but it's going to take some doing."

"I don't expect anyone to understand. I don't think I understand it myself, Wake."

"You didn't break the record, then."

"No, and to tell you the truth, I'm not sure I care."

"Son, I know things seem tough now, I know you probably feel like you lost everything. Just remember you're the same innocent kid I came across at the junk pile. Don't forget Uncle Ned there in the garage. Your gift is still inside you, nothing can take that from you. Not me, not the midgets, not even yourself. You got sidetracked, that's all."

Lowering his head, Andy said, "I don't know, Wake. I thought I was destined to break Mordecai's record, every decision I made seemed to be leading toward him. I thought I was put here on Earth to chase him. Even knowing how he wound up, I was willing to take the consequences."

"Listen, Andy, I'm not trying to make you feel better, but you've got a lot more going for yourself than Mordecai ever did. Don't get me wrong, Mordecai had a certain greatness, but it was limited. He had to go for the record because that's all he knew to do. He didn't know the art, had no interest in it. He was a machine. If he hadn't had the pursuit of the record to motivate him, he would have been a booze-swilling bum. It wasn't the record that turned Mordecai into a derelict; that's who he was. He was just fortunate that he had the record to put food on his table after he left the business. Do you understand that, kid?"

Andy looked at the scout. "I'm sorry I crossed you, Wake."

A smile creased Wake's worn face. "Well, look at the mess you would have been mixed up in if you had gotten on that plane with me. I'd probably be standing here apologizing to you."

As Andy left the conference room with Demars, he passed by Maria, who was talking to Commander Sunnyside. She glanced at Andy with an uncertain look in her eyes. He was going to stop and say something to her, but then she turned her head and resumed her conversation.

The next day, Andy took a break from the siege and came down from Time Hill to the workshops. A skeleton embalming crew was still at work, and he continued down the hallway. As he passed by one of the rooms, he heard a rhythmic tapping noise. He stopped in the open doorway. Inside, Maria was seated at a computer terminal, her nimble fingers flying across the keyboard. Andy watched her, fascinated. After a few moments, she said, without taking her eyes from the screen, "What do you want?"

"I . . . nothing. What are you working on?"

"Ah, how I miss these little conversations."

"I'm glad you found a job here."

"So was I, until all this garbage started. These squabbling boys. I'm tired of it." She turned to him. "What do you want from me?"

"I really am interested in what you're working on."

She gave him a short shrug. He moved close enough to see her screen. An image of P. T. Sunnyside dominated the display, along with a set of on-screen buttons.

"I guess you have a right to see this, considering you dreamed it up."

"What do you mean?"

"Very much like you to forget. P.T. said he and you thought it up together. He calls it a video tombstone. It's Sunnyside's response to Drabford's post-need scheme."

Getting another dumbfounded look, Maria explained to Andy the rise of the post-need phenomenon, and said, "I'll show you how this works." She wagged a pencil at the screen. "Relative comes to the cemetery, finds the departed's tombstone, or tomb*screen*, as P.T. likes to call it, and presses a finger to one of these buttons. You can choose from Life History, Living Relatives, Last Words, or Memory Message." She put her finger on the first button on the screen, and held it there. Images appeared on the monitor: a farmhouse, boy on a bicycle, family posing at a train station, a school building, graduation pictures, a modest funeral home, a young P.T. posturing on top of Heaven Hill, faster and faster the images raced by until they were a solid blur.

"Next, you can hit Living Relatives." She did, and a series of unfamiliar mugs paraded across the screen, none of whom bore a resemblance to P.T.

"Or Last Words. Not everyone will have last words, at least any that will be remembered, but it's here if they need it. I just made some up for him." She touched the button, and these words appeared: I HATE THOSE GODDAMN MIDGETS. "Finally," she said, "you can call up a person's epitaph, under Memory Message. Personally, I feel that this should always be displayed on the tombscreen, but P.T. feels we should make the image of the dead person as big as possible, and there isn't enough room on the screen for an epitaph when you do that. I'm working on him, though. I told him the whole thing doesn't have to be on the screen all the time, it could scroll continuously across the bottom. Of course, then you lose some of the artistic effect." She pressed the final button. The following verse appeared, written in elegant script:

**My life's been hard
And all things show it;
I always thought so,
And now I know it.**

"I made that one up, too," she confessed. "P.T. also wants to add an oral history button, where friends and relatives talk about their memories of the deceased, but that would probably be an upper-end option, because you'd need someone to conduct and edit the interviews, although a family member could do most of the job with a little help from us. The number-crunchers are still debating it, I guess."

"This is really something," Andy said. He placed his hand on top of the computer and tried to look her in the eye. "Listen, Maria," he said, "I'm sorry I acted the way I did. I—"

"I don't want to hear it," she broke in. "I told you about the computer because you asked. I just don't want to deal with you on any level other than professional, okay? You walk in the room yesterday like nothing's happened, like everybody's supposed to stand up and cheer that you decided to show up and bless us with your presence. It's not that easy, Andy. It's not going to be that easy."

*   *   *

Andy retreated to the confines of the Egyptville compound. The standoff continued for another week, and then, without warning one morning, Demars called his forces together at the base of the pyramid. The man looks positively ashen, Andy thought. Demars held in his hand a slip of paper, which he smoothed out. "I . . . I've just been informed of some rather tragic news," he said, his voice wavering. Now he read from the paper: "Sunnyside regrets to report the death of its founder and president, P. T. Sunnyside."

The crowd gasped.

"Mr. Sunnyside suffered a fatal stroke at 9:02 this morning in his office. Mr. Sunnyside was believed to have been on the phone receiving word on the outcome of the Drabford Diversified lawsuit when the attack occurred. His body was immediately transferred to the cryogenics center, per his instructions."

Demars took a deep breath, tears spilling down his cheeks as he read on. "In this morning's outcome the appeals court sustained the district court's earlier decision on the Heaven Hill case. Beginning immediately, Heaven Hill is the property of Drabford Diversified.

"Tomorrow morning," Demars continued, "representatives of Drabford Diversified will be arriving on site to begin determining which employees they would like to remain with the company and which employees shall be given their release. All employees should report to work tomorrow as usual."

People began hugging and sobbing.

Now Demars folded the paper and slipped it into his shirt pocket. He looked sadly at his forces and said, "We all lost a great friend in P. T. Sunnyside. P.T. saved me at a time when I could have easily fallen into despair. I never believed I would end up at a place like this, I'm an Oxford professor, for goodness sake, but then I never knew there was an individual as unique as P. T. Sunnyside. He was a genius. I was proud to work for him, and I know, when I cross the same border that P.T. did today, I will remember these days as the happiest days of my life."

The demolition supervisor gave the Time Hill work crews one hour to gather up their possessions and vacate the area, and at that time, roped off the vicinity and signaled the bulldozers to commence with their work. The first attempt, simply to plow over the pyramid, failed. They tried igniting it. They tried blasting it. They tried beating on it with their fists. The pyramid remained standing—brooding, defiant.

The foreman stormed over to the cordoned area where Demars and his forces were watching. "Okay, asshole, what's the deal here? What's it going to take to knock down that goddamn thing?"

"It will take more than you've got," Demars said scornfully.

"We built it to last," added Andy.

"I don't get paid enough for this," the man grumped, and stalked back over to the pyramid.

By nightfall a gang of workers, illuminated by a set of klieg lights, could be seen creeping across the surface of the pyramid, dismantling the ancient edifice brick by brick.

❊   ❊   ❊

Meanwhile, that same night an emergency meeting had been called at Sunnyside, presided over by legal whiz Johnny Goosehaus. Leaderless and afraid, they listened.

"Thanks for coming," he began, "under what I know are rough circumstances for all of us. P.T. always wanted his dreams to be carried on after his death, and he made plans in line with this thinking. During the past year he made a series of videotaped instructions—for those of us who would be carrying on his legacy. The first of these tapes is to be shown at the time of his death. I'd like to show it for you now. Lights, please."

The room darkened, and a moment later the image of P. T. Sunnyside appeared on the screen. He was seated at his desk, hands folded, looking fit. "It's January 1, 2000, folks. Happy Millennium! Don't forget to begin work on the moat at Medievalville this week. You . . ."

"Damn, that's not right," Goosehaus said, going over to the video player. He ejected it, shuffled through a stack of tapes, and inserted another one.

"If you're watching this, then I died today," P.T. began again matter-of-factly. "Don't take it too hard, we all go through this door eventually. Hey, I expect to come back through this door someday, if the doctors can find a cure for whatever put my lights out, so don't have a stroke or think you're seeing a ghost if you run into me on Heaven Hill in a few years. Now, I made these tapes to help guide you over the next ten years, a period of time, a transition, which I think will be vital to the long-term health and well-being of Sunnyside. All future development at Sunnyside has been plotted out on a very specific timetable, so it is crucial that you follow these instructions and keep things rolling. First of all, I want to stress to you how important Time Hill is to the future of Sunnyside."

"Shit," someone muttered.

"Dr. Demars, you're doing a fine job up there in Egyptville. Don't forget to get started on the set of children's pyra-mids and the Egyptian-motif playground. Both of these should be completed within three months after Time Hill opens. I know you didn't want a fast-food stand on the grounds because it wouldn't be historically accurate, but how about if we made the stands pyramid-shaped? It's just a thought."

"Please turn it off," Demars said in the blackness.

The screen went dark, and the lights came on again. "We should probably look at these before we show them to anyone," Goosehaus said. "Particularly in light of the circum-stances surrounding Mr. Sunnyside's passing and the tenu-ous hold that many of us may have on our jobs. He couldn't have known it would be like this."

"The poor guy," somebody said.

"Look at it this way," said Goosehaus, "at least he didn't have to live to see the destruction that has taken place, and will take place, over the next few weeks."

"I know we're sunk," Maria said, standing up, "but there must be something we can do to save Heaven Hill. All the statuary, the murals. I'm afraid Drabford's going to come in here and level everything."

"P.T. worked so hard on Heaven Hill," Wake said sadly. "When we first started here, I'd get restless in the mid-dle of the night and go out walking, two or three in the morn-ing, and the lights would still be on in P.T.'s office. We'd talk for a while, and he'd spin what I thought were these wild fan-tasies about what Heaven Hill would look like in twenty, thirty years. He was so concerned about his customers; he wanted to make the death experience more enjoyable for the survivors and the departed." Wiping at his eyes, Wake said, "This is a goddamn tragedy, that's what this is."

"Well, we could try to get Sunnyside on the National Register of Historic Places," said Goosehaus. "But that takes time, and the Drabfords move fast. Besides, everything here is a copy of something else. I hate to say it, but there's really not much original work here, and I doubt if anyone besides us would be interested in preserving it."

"Maybe if we talked to them," Maria suggested.

"Be my guest," said Wake. He looked over at Andy. "You worked with those goddamn midgets. Any ideas on how to handle them?"

"Don't throw me out for saying this," Andy replied, "but they aren't that much different from P.T. in a lot of ways. They believe in building history from the ground up. They believe in complete control. They don't compromise. They don't take prisoners. If any of you think you're going to be here once they take charge, you better think again. They'll bulldoze your asses right out the door."

Now Demars rose. "We need to present a united front," he said. "Show them we mean business. Bluff them if necessary. Keep them off balance like a champion boxer."

"We need to talk to them," Maria repeated. "We can meet them at the gates when they arrive tomorrow. Who will come with me? Wake? Dr. Demars? Goosehaus? Andy?"

Unenthusiastic nods all around.

❖   ❖   ❖

Early the next morning, the quintet met at the gateway to Heaven Hill. It was a cloudy day, rain clouds boiling over the mountains in the distance. "Any idea when they're supposed to show up?" Demars asked sleepily.

"I don't think we'll have to wait long," Wake said. "The midgets have been planning a long time for this day. This is much more than a business deal to them. The fact that it killed P.T. will only fire their eagerness."

"I was thinking about something last night," Andy said. "P.T.'s body is frozen, right?"

"Yes," said Goosehaus. "He was taken immediately to the cryogenics chamber after he was pronounced dead."

"And that's on the grounds, right?"

"That's right. It's across from the crematorium."

"Then who owns P.T. Sunnyside's body?"

There was silence for a moment, then Wake said, "God damn."

"It's something I hadn't considered," Goosehaus reflected, tapping the side of his thumb against his chin.

"What difference does it make who owns his body?" asked Demars. "He's dead. What possible use could he be to anybody?"

"I'll tell you what difference it makes," said Wake. "The public might think P.T. was just being eccentric when he had his body iced, but the midgets won't see it that way at all. What Andy said about them last night was right. They won't think it's a joke. They'll take him at his word. And what kind of care do you think they'll give to the body of their sworn enemy, knowing that some day he may resurrect himself? They'll pull the goddamn plug and defrost him, that's what they'll do."

"We need to get a relative to take him out of here," said Goosehaus. "I don't see any other way."

"So what happens between now and the time this relative can be located and asked for approval to get him out of here?" Wake asked, his voice rising. "What happens if this relative has no interest in removing P.T. from his resting place?"

"It's a problem," Goosehaus admitted.

"Here comes another one," Andy said.

The group looked to where he was pointing. There, at the gates to Sunnyside, came a thundering herd of horses, the riders outfitted in Western gear. At the front of the pack were a trio of chestnut stallions with the Drabfords riding atop.

"I'll be damned," said Wake.

The lead horses pulled up in front of the Sunnyside holdouts. "I see some familiar faces here," Bob Drabford said casually, looming above them. "Wakefield, Archway. Archway, I'm disappointed in you. Not surprised, but disappointed. Mr. Slade spoke so highly of your loyalty."

"How could you have thrown me into a place like Soma?" Andy spat out.

"You had good odds in Soma," said Preston Drabford, reining in his horse as it tried to move out of line. "We never promised you anything more than a chance."

"It's good to see you fellas here," Wake said suddenly. "Since P. T. Sunnyside wasn't able to join us today for obvious reasons, I would like to be the one to show you the grounds." His lowered lip quivered. "P.T. would have wanted it that way."

"Very sporting of you, Wakefield. Lead the way."

As Wake began walking up the path, he looked back at his comrades and said, "Why doesn't everyone come with? It will be sort of our farewell tour."

They started down the path, Wake and friends walking between the Drabford's steeds, the horses carrying their associates trailing behind. When they reached the turn off that led into the heart of Heaven Hill, Wake glanced at his watch and said, "Tell you what. There's some marvelous statuary in a little valley to our left. You really must see it. Why don't we start there and then we'll make our way into the main part of the grounds?"

"Sounds fine," Drabford agreed.

So they left the path and headed into the valley. Andy was glad they started here; this valley was his initial vision of Heaven Hill, that first morning at Sunnyside when he and Wake bunked down in the cottages at the top of the hill.

"Now this piece here," Wake explained as they came to a statue of a Civil War soldier taking aim with his musket at an unseen target, "was sculpted by Zim Zellmer back in 1924. It's called *Follow Me, Fellas*. Look at his expression, etched with the tragedy of brother fighting brother."

"Very nice," Everett Drabford remarked. One of the horses whinnied.

In the distance, Andy heard a low rumbling noise. He cocked his head, listening intently, and immediately recognized it. It was coming closer, coming from beyond the hill on his left. It was getting very loud, very near. Suddenly, it appeared over the hill, swallowing the sky.

The Drabford Brothers screeched in unison, their horses rearing up and throwing them as the biggest lawn mower in the world roared over the hillside. Pandemonium broke loose. The horses went into a frenzy, tossing their riders, trampling the bodies cowering on the ground, stampeding.

Andy ducked as a hoof from one of the horses swept overhead. It thumped him over his ear and he grunted, falling to his knees.

"Follow me!" Wake cried as a shower of grass clippings rained down on them.

Andy felt cool, probing fingers on his head. "Andy's hurt!" Maria shouted, and she and Demars scooped him up by the arms and got him running. "I'm all right," Andy said, his head buzzing, as they ran over the hill to the administration complex.

"Who's got a vehicle here?" Wake said breathlessly as they passed by the crematorium and headed to the cryogenics lab. "It's got to be bigger than a car."

"I've got a station wagon," Maria said.

"Perfect. Get it over here."

While she ran off to bring her car around, the others went into the cryogenics lab, a small, circular glass-walled structure with cold air blowing out of vents in the ceiling. "This way," Wake said, and led them to a large steel door. He opened it, fingers of fog poking across the floor. They went inside. It was hard to see; the room was bathed in a diffuse purple light. Columns of glass cases were fitted into the walls like bunks. Hooked up to the cases were a variety of tubes and wires, which in turn led to a console with jitterbugging lights. They quickly checked the cases, Goosehaus finally saying, "Here he is!"

Inside the case was the nude body of a man, frost on his mustache and eyebrows. They stood around the case in a circle, gazing silently at him.

Andy leaned over the case, pressing his face close to the glass.

"That's no —"

The room abruptly dissolved before Andy's eyes, swept out his consciousness by a sheet of darkness.

REBIRTH

nineteen

I THINK IT'S time for me to file away my scouting forms for good, Wake Wakefield decided as he rode the jet back to Iowa. It's a corporate game nowadays and I'm not a player. The people who owned funeral businesses these days increasingly operated them purely out of a profit motive. If it wasn't the Drabfords, it would be somebody else. Sure, the old-time funeral owners, the ones who had grown up in funeral parlors watching their parents practice the trade, shafted the customer on occasion, fitting the corpse with a hundred-dollar pair of shoes when a fifty-dollar pair would have served just fine, but at least the funeral business was in their blood. They weren't simply bankers looking at the bottom line.

The sad thing, Wake thought, is that the young kids out there, the future Holmeses and Mordecais, are molding themselves according to the needs of the new order. Can't blame them. It's a tough job market out there and it doesn't pay to develop skills that aren't immediately salable. But what is being lost now? How much talent is being blunted before it even has a chance to develop?

What is making matters worse is the shrinkage of the

funeral business. Many towns that used to have a handful of homes now only possessed one. And in the large cities, conglomerates run the show, buying out the competition whenever there is a perceived threat. In contrast, hordes of new students are flooding into the embalming schools, people who grew up reading *Respectful Casket Tales* and *Shroud,* inspired by the legacies of giants like Holmes from the golden age of embalming. What happens to them when they look for work after completing their education? How many of these careers are in oblivion, or are even unable to begin? What can there be for all of these embalmers?

After Wake arrived at home, he telephoned his daughter Mollybellum in Newton and told her the news.

"Gosh, Dad," she said, "I'm really thrilled for you. I worry about you when you're on the road all the time. You'll finally have time to use the fishing pole I gave you made out of that stuff that went to the moon. You can stop over and see us as often as you like. Little Soosin talks about her grandpa all the time. I'll put her on. Here, dear, Grandpa's on the phone. She just loves the ABC book you bought her. I'll have her read it to you."

"Hi, hi."

"Is this my sweetie pie?"

"Yas."

"Do you like the book Grandpa Wake gave you?" Wake asked her. "Can you read a little for me, angel?"

"Yas. A is . . . is for airtight, what the cas, what the cas . . ."

"Casket, honey."

". . . should be. B is for bur . . . burial, so deep you can't see. C is for cas, cas . . ."

"Casket, darling."

"She's doing great," Wake said. "I can't wait to see her."

Unknown to Wake, after they finished their conversation Mollybellum contacted the ESA, the Embalming Scouts of America, and told them about his retirement plans. They agreed that a testimonial dinner was a fine idea, and made arrangements accordingly.

Wake pretended to be steamed when he got the invitation in the mail, but deep down he was quite pleased by the honor. Finally, the big night came. Wake rented a tuxedo and was waiting for Mollybellum and Soosin to arrive when the phone rang.

"Hello?"

"Hello, Wake."

"Well, you big dummy, it's about time you called."

"I understand this call isn't a surprise."

"Nothing surprises me when it comes to you. Where are you calling from?"

"I'd rather not say, not sure how secure the line is. Wake, how would you like to come back on board?"

"Back on board what? You don't have a boat."

"Well, I've got something in mind. I could use you, Wake. We can build it together, from the ground up."

"You caught me at a bad time. I'm getting ready to go to a retirement dinner."

"For who?"

"Me."

"You're sure?"

"I've thought about it a lot, chief. It's a good time for me to get out. I need to hold some hands that aren't propped up with positioning blocks."

"Congratulations, then. Keep me in mind, though. Next summer those cool, pale hands might be looking pretty good."

"How will I find you?"

"Don't worry, I'll find you. Take care, buddy."

"Good luck, chief. Keep in touch."

twenty

THE RAIN SWEPT over the mountains into the valleys, washing the grime from the sky. It quickly filled the storm sewers, sending torrents of water into the streets. It pounded the desert sand, forming small pools and rivulets where none had existed before. It streamed down the hat of the border guard who came up to the station wagon.

"Heading home?" he asked.

"Yes," said the woman in the car. "I live in Guadomilia."

He checked the interior of the station wagon, glancing first at her front-seat passenger, then at the back seat. "What's wrong with him?" the guard inquired, wagging a thumb at the prone figure in the back with a bandage wrapped around his skull, a spot of blood seeping through the white fabric.

"Fell off a horse," she said. "He'll be okay. I just need to get him home."

"Open the trunk, please."

"Can I give you the keys? I don't want to get soaked."

"Sure."

A short time later, the guard reappeared at her window. "Enjoy your stay, ma'am," he said with a routine smile and waved them through.

*　*　*

Andy woke in a strange place, his temples throbbing wildly. I'm still in Soma, he thought, panicking. He sat up, and peered at the vague, dark shapes in the small, spare room. Dresser, mirror, lamp. No, not the mission, he thought. What happened? He remembered running, chaos, the horses with the crazed look in their dull limpid eyes.

He touched his head, felt the coarse texture of a bandage. I was hurt, he thought. Carefully climbing out of bed, he went to the window, and pulled apart the curtains. A bare-dirt backyard, bathed in pale moonlight. Clothesline, a child's bicycle, what appeared to be a homemade chicken coop.

The door creaked open, sending a shaft of yellow light across the floor. Andy turned and saw a figure in silhouette standing in the doorway. "You really shouldn't be up yet," she said. "The doctor will be here in a few minutes."

"Maria . . ."

Coming over to him, she said, "I'm serious, Andy," and led him back to the bed.

"What happened to me?" he asked her, as she eased his head onto the pillow. "I don't remember what happened. There were horses . . ."

"One of them kicked you in the head. You said you were okay, but then you passed out. Things got crazy then. We had to get out in a hurry."

"Where is this place?"

"It's my home," she said, pressing her warm hand against his cheek. "Now you try to get some rest."

Later, a doctor came and examined Andy. He probed and poked and then told Maria something in Spanish. She nodded. "It's just a mild concussion," Maria said. "He's going to prescribe some pills for you. Otherwise, you should get as much rest as you can."

After a couple of days in bed Andy improved, and at dinnertime instead of the usual tray of tortillas, corn, and fruit, Maria said, "Do you think you're up to eating with the family tonight? They're anxious to meet you."

"I think so. I'm feeling a lot better."

"No one speaks much English," said Maria, "but I know they'll be patient with you."

Maria brought Andy, dressed in a borrowed nightshirt, out to the living area where her family was seated at the dinner table. They watched him curiously as he padded across the scrubbed wood floor.

Maria said something to them in Spanish, Andy recognized his name, then, to him, she said, "Andy, this is my family. My parents, Domingo and Gloria, my sister Linda and her daughter Nona, my grandma Lupi, my brothers Pedro and Fernando, my uncle Don."

They smiled broadly at Andy, who couldn't take his eyes from her uncle. I may have taken a blow to the head, Andy thought, but Uncle Don bears an uncanny resemblance to the late P. T. Sunnyside.

❋ ❋ ❋

Andy retired to his room after dinner, and a short time later there was a knock at the half-open door. A head poked in. "Can I come in?"

"Your English is very good, Uncle Don."

"I've been practicing."

"Pull up a step, as my coach used to say."

"Good to see you, kid," Uncle P.T. said, dragging a wooden chair next to the bed. "You had us worried there for a while. Maria said the doctor thinks you're going to come out of this just fine."

"I feel pretty good, considering," said Andy. "I'm not sure what put me out, the horse or not seeing you on ice. Who was he?"

"A Mrs. Obo, upper bracket all the way, had read about the post-need need in *Palatial* magazine. A new make-up job and box wasn't good enough for dear Thebian, she wanted a more permanent preservation situation. There was a vague resemblance, but a little hypo filled with massage cream here, a little strategically placed putty there, and we're in business. Close enough for those goddamn midgets, anyway. Looks different, Mrs. Obo? Perfectly natural result of the cryogenics process."

"Who did the work?"

"I did," P.T. said, raising his hands and gazing proudly at them. "With these. I wasn't sure I had the touch anymore. You know, I was a pretty fair country embalmer in my day, son."

"There must have been another way," Andy said. "You'll never be able to go back to the States again."

"It was either this or punch a time clock for the midgets, and I would rather trade places with Mr. Obo than be subjected to a fate like that." He shivered. "I don't even want to think about it."

"Boy, this is tough."

"Don't feel sorry for me, kid. It's at least half my fault. I'm not much of a businessman, I'm afraid. We had a real cash flow problem at Sunnyside. If someone couldn't pay their bill, I'd take artwork or have them paint a mural or install a bathroom in the visitor center or sing at a wake, whatever they could offer. You can't live long on barter in a money economy. I could survive losing Heaven Hill, but those punitive damages drove me underground for good."

"So what are you going to do now?"

Just then Maria came into the room. "Oh, Uncle Don,

I'm so happy to see you're getting along with our guest."

"We're amigos," said P.T., looping an arm around Andy's shoulder.

"If Andy's feeling up to it, I thought we could go tour around the town tomorrow. It's All Souls' Day, should be fun. What do you say?"

"I think I'll be able to manage it," Andy said.

"I'd love to," said P.T.

"Great. Don't expect too much, though. Guadomilia isn't exactly Rancho Norman Rockwell, but it's home."

❖ ❖ ❖

The next morning, the trio ate a quick breakfast and wandered out into the streets of Guadomilia. It was All Souls' Day, and the town was in a happy mood. "Let's go to the bakery first," Maria said. They went inside the crowded store, smelling of baked bread and spices. She chose a couple of bread loaves decorated with stylized bones and tears formed out of dough.

"What do you call that?" Andy asked.

"*Pan de muerto,*" she replied. "The bread of the dead. It's traditional."

"Interesting design," said P.T.

Maria paid for the bread, and as they left the store, Andy noticed something odd in the showcase of the store next door. The case was packed with an array of human skulls in a variety of sizes, all decorated with colored paper and labeled with an assortment of names. "What are these?" Andy said.

"*Calaveras de azucar,*" she explained. "It's candy. They only make them for All Souls' Day, you give them to a friend as a gift. I don't think they have any Andys, but maybe I can find an Antonio." She went inside.

"You didn't answer me before," Andy reminded P.T. "What are you going to do now?"

Looking at him with a knowing smile, P.T. said, "We're going to have to have a talk, kid."

A short time later Maria rejoined them, presenting a walnut-sized skull to Andy. Antonio had been crossed out, Andy written above it. "Custom made," she said with a grin. She saw him gazing hesitantly at it. "Go ahead, eat it. It's good."

He bit tentatively into the skull, and smiled. "Candy," he said.

"There's a lot of special foods we eat on All Souls' Day," Maria told them as they walked down the bustling street. "When we left this morning my mother was making *calabaza en tacha,* which is a preserve made by combining small pieces of pumpkin with sticks of sugar cane, haws, spices, and a brown sugar called *piloncillo.* We also use food on our family altar. I'll show you when we get back."

As they meandered up the sidewalk to the house, Andy took hold of Maria's arm while P.T. continued on inside; the screen door clapped shut. "Wait a minute," Andy said. "There's something I want to ask you."

"What is it?"

"Why did you bring me here?"

She hesitated, then said, "You were hurt. I didn't know what else to do with you, where else to take you."

"Come on, Maria. This was P.T.'s idea, wasn't it?"

She looked at him pensively. "Well, yes."

"I knew it."

"But that wasn't the only reason," she said. "You've changed since the last time I saw you. I almost feel like I know you again. I need to see you like I did the first time we met. Maybe we'll find that place sometime. I would like to. But not now. Not yet."

Andy knelt down, picked up a pebble, and flipped it into the street. "P.T. said he wants to have a talk with me. I know what that means. I can see it in his eyes. He's got plans, Maria, big plans." He looked at her. "You knew he was going to fake his death, didn't you? He was preparing for the takeover all along, wasn't he? The tombscreen you were working on wasn't a prototype; it was the real thing."

"You should talk to him, Andy."

"And what am I going to be? The front man for his dreams? He'll have to keep a low profile, even down here. He'll need some sap to keep the spotlight off him. Some hick embalmer from Podunk, Minnesota."

"You're not being fair."

Andy laughed bitterly. "We must have looked pretty ridiculous to him, making our big stand for truth and justice up on Time Hill, holding off the bulldozers with our ideals. And Wake! Get the horses to panic and then go racing across the hills to save the corpse of our frozen leader from the clutches of those goddamn midgets. What a noble thing to do! What a wonderful display of loyalty!"

"Andy, stop . . ."

Still kneeling, Andy buried his head in his hands, rocking back and forth. "When am I going to wise up, Maria?"

Maria cuffed him on the shoulder. "When are you going to stop letting people lead you around?" she said heatedly. "When are you going to stand up for yourself? When are you going to take responsibility for your own life? I don't know where you want to be, I'm not even sure you do, but it's not P.T.'s fault and it's not my fault that you're messed up. What happened to you? What are you afraid of? You were better off when I first met you and you didn't know anything." She gave him a look of disgust and stormed into the house.

Andy glumly sat on the step, watching a skinny dog sniff his way along the street. The screen door creaked open and Andy waited, expecting more angry words, but then a small form sat down on the step beside him. Andy looked over and jumped a little seeing the leering skeleton's face that overwhelmed the tiny brown body. Andy slowly lifted up the mask. It was Linda's daughter, Nona. She looked up at Andy with big dark eyes, a loop of black hair curling on her forehead.

Andy took the mask from her and held it in front of his own face. Nona giggled, and her small fingers pulled down the mask. Andy slipped the mask onto her face again, careful to make sure her ears were not bent back by the elastic band. He took her by the hand and they went into the house.

"This is called an *ofrenda*," Maria was telling P.T. as they stood by a decorated shelf in the living room. "We place pictures of our dead relatives here, then surround them with these garlands of yellow flowers, called *zempazuchitl*. Then, at the foot of the display, we place the food and drink."

"What happens to the food?" P.T. asked.

"We eat it, although many of our people believe that the food, after being offered to the dead, is flavorless, that the dead take the essence of the food." Maria glanced at Andy, then continued. "We also have a tradition of spending the night at the cemetery. Maybe you'd like to try this?"

"I'm game," said P.T. "What about you, Andrew?"

"Sure, why not?"

Just before dark, as they were getting packed for the graveyard, someone knocked at the door. Maria's mother opened it, and after a brief exchange, the visitor handed her an envelope and departed. Smiling, she said, "Domingo."

Her husband came over, his eyes dropping to the envelope she held in her hand, and put a look of mock terror on his face. Everyone laughed, and he took the envelope, opened it, and pulled out a sheet of paper. He began reading.

"Oh my," said Maria, "someone sent papa a *calaveras*."

"What's that?" Andy asked.

"They are verses that celebrate the death of a living person and his or her arrival in heaven or hell. Many times they are sent to politicians or famous people, but anyone can get one."

"I'm glad I'm not an icon here," P.T. said.

"It is a joke, but with good reason. Death is easier to live with if you act with a sense of humor toward it. The dead person should be respected and honored, but death itself should be mocked. It's different in the States. The dead are respected, but death itself is feared, and never talked about. So the fear grows. We fear death, too, and for this reason we make fun of it so that we don't fear it as much."

"Respect and humor," said P.T.

"Just like you, P.T.," Andy told him.

"There's a line from a poem I remember," Maria said. "Not for a second time do we come to earth, Oh princes! rejoice and bring flowers. We are going to the kingdom of death. Only in transit are we."

* * *

Later that evening, Maria's family visited the cemetery and decorated the graves of their relatives with yellow flowers, candles, and dishes of food. Once the task was completed, most of the family departed for home. Maria, Uncle Don, and Cousin Andy remained behind to keep up the vigil. Maria murmured prayers in the midst of the family grave site, her voice drifting into the clear night sky, waiting for the coming of the dead.

Beneath a nearby gnarled tree Andy and P.T. talked softly.

"This is the life, isn't it?" P.T. said, resting against the tree trunk, hands clasped behind his head. "The Day of the Dead. They're talking my language, kid."

"I like it too," said Andy.

"A fellow could find some peace here," P.T. went on. "There's room here, to think, to create. It reminds me of when I first came to California. Virgin territory. Possibilities."

218

"Do you have anything particular in mind?"

"A few notions, a couple of stray thoughts. That's about it."

"I understand you had some role in bringing me across the border. Is it true?"

P.T. sat quietly for a moment, wagging his foot, then said, "I really like you, kid. We don't think alike, but we do complement each other. I always say I'm looking to the future, so that the business will outlast me."

"I've had people tell me there's only one way to do things," said Andy, "and that's P. T. Sunnyside's way, that you want complete control, that you'll choke off anyone who marches to a different coffin drummer. Is it true?"

Chuckling softly, P.T. said, "Depends on which side of the trocar you're on, I guess. I think I'm a pretty easy guy to get along with. The folks who have problems with the way I operate are usually the same ones who are outraged by my undertakings, those who cheer the banal. Listen, Andrew, if you're going to do the high-calling bit, it's a no-compromise situation. I'll work with others and compromise as much as anyone when the ideas are being formed and fused, but once the ground is broken, the dove becomes the falcon."

I had a dream about a falcon once, Andy thought.

"Why don't you stay and work with me, kid?"

Andy sat silently, listening to the undertone of Maria's prayers.

"There was a woman I knew in Soma named Roon," he finally said. "Her dream was a tower. It crumbled beneath her and she couldn't escape. You had a dream, a tower, Heaven Hill. It crumbled beneath you. Yet here you are. Why?"

"Just lucky, I guess."

"I'm serious, P.T. This is important."

"Well, I guess it goes back a long ways, kid. When I first started in this business back in my home town of Corn

Heights, Illinois, I had this idea, see. There was this place in town, Thistle Hill we called it, right by the grade school. It had a great view, I thought I could see the whole world from up there. I wanted to start a cemetery there, my very first. Oh, I had big plans for it, garish yet respectful, you understand. I wanted to make it a place people would want to visit, even if they didn't have any relatives plotted there. But the planning commission wouldn't even consider it. Cemeteries shouldn't be so obvious, they said. Should be stuck away in some dark, forgotten spot. I appealed to the city council, the county board, the local newspaper. I could have stayed on Thistle Hill, I guess, camped out there until they gave me my way. But why? It was *their* problem. There were plenty of hills in the world, plenty of places to start over. Rebirth, Andy. That's what this is all about. You dream, you build, you watch it fall, slowly or too quickly, and then you begin again. Nothing's going to last here in this dismal place. Maybe there's some land where you don't need to re-born things, but I haven't been there."

After contemplating this, as a cloud obscured the half moon, Andy said, "I think I need to move on, P.T."

"I was meaning to talk you into joining me with my little speech," P.T. said, "but I think I achieved the opposite effect."

Andy laughed ironically. "Funny, never thought I'd be turning down an offer to be partners with P. T. Sunnyside."

* * *

Come morning, the sun's rays skimming over the mountain peaks, Maria was curled up asleep by the tombstones, and when she was shaken awake she saw not the visage of a departed relative but Andy.

"Time to go," he said. "All the dead souls have gone back home."

"Don't tell my mother I fell asleep," Maria said with a sleepy grin. Sitting up, she looked around and said, "We have to gather up the food and bring it home, to complete the vigil."

"I'm going to be leaving this morning," Andy told her.

She gazed at him, searching. "You talked to P.T."

Andy nodded.

"Where are you going? Do you have any plans?"

Shrugging, he said, "I'm not sure. I'll probably go home for a while. I feel like I lost something, and that's as good a place as any to start looking."

"Yes."

"Can I visit you sometime?"

"Yes, I hope you will. I will expect it."

He smiled. "Good enough."

She stood up, scanning the graveyard. "Where did P.T. go?"

Turning around, Andy said, "We were right over by that tree. Strange. I'm not sure where he went." Then he looked back at her. "How do I get to the bus station?"

"Three blocks south of the bakery. An old red-brick building." She touched his arm. "You could stay for breakfast, you know. Or even stay until tomorrow morning. There are buses that go to the border all day."

"I'd better leave," he said with a wan grin. "I finally said no to someone, and I don't know if I could do it again if P.T. gets another chance to work on me."

"Yes, it is the best thing," she replied quietly, unable to look at him.

He started walking then, down the grassy slope of the graveyard, weaving among the vigilants packing up their food, heading back into town.

Andy found the bus station without much difficulty. It was already sweltering inside, people sleeping on benches or sitting against the walls. A fan rattled, barely stirring the stale air.

Going up to the counter, Andy told the clerk, an older

man with a white mustache and a green visor, "One-way ticket to Golbyville, please."

The man smiled. "Gringo."

"Los Angeles?"

"Tijuana."

Andy nodded in agreement. "Tijuana it is, then." He pointed at his watch. "What time does it leave?"

The man gestured at the loading gate, through a glass partition, where a bus was in the process of loading. "Tijuana," Andy said, pointing in turn at the bus.

"*Sí, señor.*"

Andy gave the man his credit card and was awarded his ticket. He hurried through the gate, handed the driver his ticket, and climbed on board. The bus was crowded, but he found a seat next to the window near the back. A woman with two children sat down beside him. One of the children, a small girl, was carefully holding an All Souls' Day toy: a skeleton sitting studiously behind a typewriter. Andy smiled at her, and she shyly looked away. A short time later, the bus rocked forward and chugged away from the station, rolling down the quiet early-morning streets.

Andy settled into his seat as the bus left the small midtown area and made its way into the residential section. They passed by the cemetery where the vigil had been held, and all the vigilants appeared to have departed. Three blocks farther down the road a man stood on a vacant hillside, his arms raised to the sky, graced by the morning sun. Alongside him stood a dark-haired woman carrying a basket. Andy watched them as the bus puttered by, craning his neck to see them as long as possible, then the bus made a turn and they were gone.

twenty-one

IT WAS COLD and blustery in Golbyville as the bus took the turn off into town, past Mrs. Zeeny's canning sculpture, draped with toilet-paper streamers that whipped in the wind. Smashed pumpkins dotted the street. A dummy in a hangman's noose swung wildly from an old oak tree. Townsfolk walked down main street hunched over, faces set in grimaces, hands stuck deep in their pockets. The bus stopped outside the Bible and Bait Shop and a handful of the passengers got off.

Andy started walking briskly in the direction of the feed store. He was just wearing a light cotton shirt and pants, and he was freezing. He picked up his pace, and as he passed the feed store and started up the county road that led to the farm, a pickup pulled up alongside him.

"Want a ride?" the white-haired man asked with a fraternal smile. "It's a mighty cold day."

It was their neighbor, Mr. Kopishkee. "Sure," Andy said, and climbed in.

"You're Andy Archway, aren't you?" he said, putting the truck into gear again.

"Yes. How are you doing, Mr. Kopishkee?"

"Fine, fine. Say, we haven't seen you around in a while. What have you been up to?"

"Oh, not much. Trying to get started on a career."

"You still working with the dead?"

"Well, I don't know. Sort of, I guess."

They drove for a bit, then the neighbor said, "My brother Ray over in Houdin is doing poorly, mind cancer, isn't expected to last the week. Some folks from out of town are running the funeral home there, and the family would rather deal with someone who has some local roots. Could you do a job on him, if, God forbid, he should pass into the night?"

"I hadn't planned on working yet, I'm not really sure where I want to go from here."

"Well, think about it anyway, would you? We sure would appreciate it. He's not dead yet, so you've got plenty of time to mull it over."

"What sorts of things does he like to do?"

"That's easy. He's president of the Houdin Model Railroad Club. He lives for his trains. You should see the setup they've got above the old firehouse! Why, they've even got trains running around and around tracks set up like a Möbius strip. It's really something to see."

"Did he work for the railroad before he retired?"

"Naw, he wanted to, but his right arm was knocked off at the elbow by a grain auger when he was a kid. He worked in insurance for a while, then he became assistant county auditor."

"Well, no promises," said Andy. "But I'll consider it."

"Can't ask any more than that. I'll let you know how he fares."

Mr. Kopishkee dropped off Andy at the top of the driveway. The flag was down on the mailbox, so Andy flipped open the latch and scooped up the contents. Walking on down to the farmyard, he absently flipped through the mail, the usual assortment of bills and swine testosterone ads. He stopped short. At the bottom of the pile was a postcard, the front depicting a collie with sad, sad eyes and angel wings. He turned it over.

"All dogs may go to heaven, but what will yours look like when she arrives? Take no chances. Contact Slade Pet Embalming, Houdin. Professional, discreet, spill-free."

Andy grinned and headed to the house.

It was a lonely homecoming, Andy discovering that his parents were not home. They probably were paying their respects at Scarecrow Days in Plankton, he thought.

Andy saw his shed nestled in the trees behind the house, and could not resist reliving some fond memories. He went over to it, leaves crunching under his feet. He slowly opened the door, inhaling the warm pulpy smell, and stepped inside. The shrine was as he remembered it, the image of Mordecai everywhere. He remembered how mad he was when he lost his copy of the Mordecai issue of *Embalmer's Weekly*. He smiled. It seemed like such a silly boyhood infatuation now. He had latched on to Mordecai as the icon of his interest in all things funereal, and now he realized that the funerary world was a much larger, more diverse place than he ever dreamed. Although Andy still respected what the man had accomplished, the giant Mordecai who had once dwelled in Andy's fantasies now seemed to have shrunk to a more human size.

The notion of selling his collection entered his mind, and the idea did not shock him.

Andy left the shed, latching the door, and cut through the grove to the old garage. The smell of formaldehyde lingered, and he found pleasure just touching and holding familiar objects, like his home-brewed embalming fluid, cobwebs now strung between the bottles, and his favorite jury-rigged trocar.

The thought occurred to him that he could move back to the farm for good and set up shop in the garage again. It wouldn't be difficult to refurbish his old equipment. And he already had his first customer lined up, a real tantalizer. Imagine what I could do with a railroad motif, he thought.

But something didn't feel right. Although Andy once had a kingdom here, to keep the world at bay, now the world beyond the farm's castle walls did not seem so large or frightening anymore. Though it was a disappointment seeing the world for what it was, at least he could move freely through it now. The thought of spending all of his time in the twenty yards between the embalming shed and the junk pile made him feel nervous, trapped. They were right, he said to himself, swishing a bottle of forest green embalming fluid back and forth, you can't go home again. He hungered to see different places. California was certainly interesting, if a little strange, and there must be more places like that all over the country.

I don't have to stay here, he told himself, pacing back and forth in the garage, growing excited. *I don't have to stay here.* I've got some money saved up. I've got plenty of talent. I can do anything I want in this world.

Andy took their old blue '57 Donnahoo and drove to Boyland, the trailer and miniature golf place over in Bald Lake.

"Whatcha' looking for, pal?" asked the salesman, a hairless man who obviously spent a lot of time in the heavy-metal lake as a youth. He was wearing bright red polyester slacks and a wide polka-dot tie.

"Something I can pull behind this car," Andy said.

The salesman showed Andy a long gleaming teardrop of a trailer. "This is your '93 Humdinger," he said as they went inside. "It's fully equipped with sauna and billiard room." He took a pool cue from the rack and set the cue ball and nine ball on the table. "See, this table is designed by the same outfit that made several parts of the rocket that went to the moon. It's self-stabilizing. You can drop that nine ball in the corner pocket while going around a hairpin curve at seventy-five miles per hour. Go ahead, try shaking the table while I shoot."

Andy gave the table a small push.

"No, *hard!*"

Andy grabbed hold of the end of the table and rocked it as hard as he could. The salesman lined up his shot, brought back the cue, and gave the ball a poke. It rolled smoothly across the felt and plunked down into the designated pocket.

The salesman grinned. "Ain't that something?"

"Actually," Andy said, "I was looking for something a little more bare. I plan to do a lot of remodeling of the interior."

"A fixer-upper, eh? Got just the thing for you."

The salesman led Andy over to a trailer tucked in the back corner of the lot. It was small and the inside was a wreck—the kitchen table uprooted, the cupboard doors hanging by their hinges.

"This baby's a '64 Woodtick. Used to belong to a polka band that played around here. The Six Angry Dutchmen. They weren't quite my style. I think they're all in jail now."

"Looks perfect," Andy said. "How much?"

"Two grand and I'll throw in a free game of mini golf."

"How about fifteen hundred and skip the golf?"

"I'd like seventeen. There is some historical value to it. It may be worth a lot of dough someday if the boys ever get out on parole and become famous."

"Sixteen and give me a hand hooking it up to my car."

"You got yourself a trailer, buddy. And I'll even throw in that game of mini golf."

After a wobbly trip home, Andy backed up the trailer into the grove by the garage. His parents were home, and they followed him.

"What the hell do you call that?" his dad asked with an amused grin as Andy climbed out of the car.

"How much do you want for the Donnahoo, Pop?"

"Take it."

"Thanks."

"What are you planning to do, Andrew?" asked his mom.

"Well, first I plan to do some major interior decoration. I'll need to use your tools, Dad."

"You can borrow them, but don't expect me to give them to you when you're done. And don't forget to put them back where you found them. And don't use my good hammer. Hell, I'd better help you, that way I can keep an eye on them myself."

"That'd be great, Pop."

Andy and his dad set to work that afternoon. First, Andy stripped the trailer bare while Pops made shelves with holes big enough to fit bottles in. They placed the embalming table where the kitchen table had been, using the same brackets to secure it to the floor. They screwed in hooks and hangers for his tools of the trade and stuck the pumps on the kitchenette counter. Pop nailed together a big bin with a lid for motif items. They pounded and painted and hammered and cursed and two weeks later the reborn trailer was ready for the road. As a final touch, Andy nailed his embalming certificate to the wall.

"She's a beauty," his dad said as they stood back and admired their handiwork.

"You'd never know a polka band had owned it," added Andy.

❀   ❀   ❀

The next day, Andy packed his belongings in the car and trailer and said farewell to his folks.

"Where are you heading first?" his dad asked.

"Not sure. I've got a map and my instincts. I'm going to follow the weather, stay ahead of winter. I'll work my way back up north in the spring. I can't stay away for long, it seems."

"Did you pack enough underwear?" inquired his mom.

"Probably not. I'll have to start buying my own." He grinned. "It will just be one of the many adventures I'm going to have over the next few months."

"You didn't take any of my tools, did you?"

"I think I put them all back, Pop. I can check if you want."

"Naw, you don't need to do that. Just stick them in a box and send them to me."

"It's a deal."

The Archways exchanged hugs and kisses, and then Andy climbed in the Donnahoo and cautiously pulled the trailer out of the grove. He made a circle in the farmyard and started up the driveway, waving to his folks as they walked across the yard and again as they rushed around to the front side of the farmhouse. He took the turn onto the county road, the trailer lurching slightly, then straightened the rig out and headed down the highway.

❅ ❅ ❅

Andy had scattered luck his first couple weeks on the road. For now, he wasn't overly concerned because he was not working too hard at drumming up customers, just enjoying the scenery and the freedom.

He had been crisscrossing between southwestern Minnesota and the southeastern corner of South Dakota, happy to be welcomed to each state again and again, when the first snowfall of the season fell. It was time to drift south, and on his way through Iowa he stopped at a small white house in Flankville.

As Andy started up the walk, the door to the house swung open and its occupant came down the steps.

"Andy!" Wake said, stopping in surprise.

They clasped hands, and Wake squeezed Andy's shoulder. "I wasn't sure I'd ever see you again."

"How are you doing, Wake?"

"Splendidly." He glanced at the trailer parked in front of the house. "Is that your rig?"

"Yes, isn't it great? It's completely outfitted for embalming. I'm going to travel around the country with it, pick up jobs where I can."

"Where are you headed now?"

Andy laughed. "Anywhere south. We had snow last night in Minnesota. I don't want to get caught in a blizzard with this thing. I'll be back up in these parts in the spring, though."

Glancing at his watch, Wake said apologetically, "I hate to do this to you, kid, but I'm on my way to meet my daughter and granddaughter in Newton. We're going to the zoo. They've got a new ant farm that is supposed to be pretty neat. Can you come back tonight? We could have dinner. You can stay over if you'd like."

"Sure," Andy said, "I can hang around town this afternoon. I need to get a spare tire for my trailer. I'll come back around five or so."

"Five o'clock, then." Wake headed over to his car, then turned back. "I won't be late for our dinner," he said, probing his rib area with his fingertips. "I'm really starving."

Andy wasn't able to locate a spare tire for the trailer. The one trailer store in town didn't carry Andy's model, and the clerk expressed some shock that there were any Woodticks still on the road. So, Andy spent the rest of the afternoon down by the pond at the city park, tossing doughnut crumbs to the geese.

Just before five he drove back over to Wake's house. There were two cars in the driveway, neither of them belonging to Wake. He went up to the door and knocked.

An unfamiliar woman answered the door. She looked like she had been crying. Do I have the right house? he wondered.

"Uh, excuse me," Andy said. "Is this Wake Wakefield's house?"

She nodded.

"Is he around? I'm supposed to be meeting him at five for dinner. I'm a friend of his, Andy Archway."

"You saw him . . . today?" the woman said, her voice heaving.

"Yes." Now Andy was growing concerned. "Who are you? Where's Wake?"

"Why don't you come in?" she said.

Andy followed her into the house. There was a young red-haired man wearing a clerical collar sitting on the couch. "My name is Mollybellum Wakefield," said the woman, seating herself beside the man. "This is Pastor Lime. What did you say your name was again?"

"Andy Archway. I'm an embalmer. Wake scouted me. We were in California together a couple weeks ago."

"There's been an accident," Pastor Lime said. "The police believe Mr. Wakefield had a heart attack while he was driving. If anything worthwhile can come out of this it is the fact that Mr. Wakefield was able to hang on and guide his car off the road and into the ditch before he died. He may have saved several lives with that courageous act."

"Wake's dead?" said Andy, stunned.

"It was his time," the pastor replied.

Andy dropped into a chair. "I was just talking to him. He looked fine."

"You were the last person to speak with him, Mr. Archway," Mollybellum said, wiping her nose with a handkerchief. "What did he say?"

"I . . . I don't remember. Wait, yes, I do. He was really looking forward to seeing you and your daughter. I met him as he was coming out of the house and I was afraid he was going to run me down, he was in such a hurry. You were going to the zoo."

"Yes. We waited over an hour for him, and called here and he wasn't here and we went home and the phone was ringing and it was the sheriff and—" She began crying. Pastor Lime comforted her, patting her arm. "He lived a long, fulfilling life," he told her softly. "It was his time to join the Lord."

Andy sat unmoving, the room turning into a blur. He blinked the tears away and rose. "I should go," he said. "I'm a stranger. You need your family here."

"It's all right," she said. "You were the last person to see him." She forced a smile, her eyes red and bleary. "I'm glad he was excited to see us. Makes me feel him again."

Andy started for the door, then hesitated. He turned back to her and said, "Have you made arrangements for him?"

"Not yet," she said. "When he talked about the funeral business he always had such anger in his voice. He said even the undertaker here in town wasn't to be trusted. I'm not really sure what to do."

"I'm afraid I can't help you," Pastor Lime said. "I have expressed my feelings about the business to some of the less respectful members of the profession and word gets around. They won't give me much cooperation, I regret to say. They don't even want to hold services in my church. It's disgraceful. Of course, Mrs. Wakefield, if you wish I will accompany you to the funeral home of your choosing."

"I can take care of Wake," Andy said evenly.

They looked uncertainly at him.

"I'm a licensed embalmer," he said. "I was a friend of Wake's. I was the last person to talk to him."

"I don't know," said Mollybellum. "Where are you located? I don't want to move him very far."

"I can locate wherever you like. I work out of a mobile unit. I want to do it, Mrs. Wakefield."

"How much will it cost?" Pastor Lime asked.

Andy shook his head. "I won't take any money for the job. I owe Wake a lot. This won't even the score, but it's all I can do for him right now."

Mollybellum looked at Pastor Lime. "Do you think it's okay?"

The pastor looked at Andy. "How do we know you're telling us the straight story?"

"I can give you some names of people in Golbyville. That's my hometown. I embalmed quite a few folks in those parts. When I was in school at Holmes . . ." His voice trailed off. He was about to tell them about his exploits on the competitive embalming field, then changed his mind. "I'll give you some people's numbers in Golbyville. You can talk to them."

"You understand our situation," the pastor said.

"Of course." Andy went over to Mollybellum and knelt down in front of her. "It would be an honor to embalm Wake, ma'am. If I check out, will you give me that honor?"

She nodded, smiling tearfully. "Yes."

"It would work out very well," Pastor Lime said. "We can hold the visitation as well as the memorial service in the church, where such things belong."

"I should warn you," Andy said. "I don't do things totally traditionally. I try to be creative, put the essence of the person I'm working on into the tableau."

"The essence?" asked Mollybellum uncertainly.

"The soul, the heart. A portrayal of the departed's individuality. I've had many satisfied customers. It was why Wake signed me to a contract in the first place."

"Then I'm sure it will be fine," Mollybellum said.

Getting the green light, Andy went to work, first calling home and having his mom talk to the pastor and give him the numbers of everyone she could think of that Andy had done embalming for, then he stopped at a thrift store and other establishments around town to find materials for the tableau.

No junk piles for good ol' Wake, Andy thought.

When he had collected the proper materials, he collected Wake's body from the hospital's morgue, parked in the church parking lot, and got down to business.

I miss you already, pal, Andy thought, squeezing his friend's cold hand as he lay on the slab in the trailer. I'm going to make you proud of me, Andy thought, making a small incision in the jugular and expertly inserting the tube. He switched on the pump and the blood rushed out into glass receptacles. When this process was completed, he made another incision, choosing the carotid artery, and pumped in a pale red embalming fluid. As the fluid coursed into the body, Andy readied his trocar. In a short time the fluid had filled the vascular system, and the flesh appeared to warm up, taking a slight sunset glow. Now Andy jabbed the trocar into the abdomen, poked around the entrails and chest cavity, then switched on the pump. The contents were sucked out, then replaced with cavity fluid. Andy sewed up the hole.

While he allowed the restorative to work, Andy prepared the tableau in the church. A great idea had possessed him. He had concocted it when he remembered what Mr. Kopishkee had said about his brother and his Möbius model train. Not exactly Möbius, but in the mind-bending vein. He borrowed several folding chairs from the church's basement and lined them up in a row at the front of the church. He placed a notebook and pen on one of the chairs. Flowers won't be a problem, he thought, because people will be sending plenty of those. The casket arrived, and he had the delivery men put it in place in front of the folding chairs. The home had been reluctant to sell him one on the spot, but the extra three grand over retail made them eager to please.

Andy went to get a hamburger at the local Bun 'N Run, returned to the trailer, and took a nap, and then calculated Wake's body was ready. He dressed Wake in a wrinkled blue sweater and corduroys, the typical outfit Andy recalled Wake wearing, and tugged his worn brown loafers onto his feet. Andy hefted Wake into church. As he was trying to get Wake to sit up in the folding chair, using a cord hidden beneath his clothes to lash him to the back of the chair, he noticed Pastor Lime out of the corner of his eye, standing off to the side, watching silently.

"Hi," Andy said, tilting Wake's shoulders from side to side in an attempt to get his head to stay put. "I didn't hear you come in."

The pastor came closer, slowly.

"I won't be long here. The sitting erect effect can be a little tough to master, especially if you don't have any scenery to hide your wires." Wake's head seemed to hold, and Andy tucked a pair of tongue dispensers under his chin. He stood back with his hands on hips, surveying his work, then placed the notebook on Wake's lap, hooking one hand around it and the other around the pen. He stood back again, and looked at the pastor. "What do you think? Is it too plain?"

"If Wake is here," said Pastor Lime, slowly, "then who's in the casket?"

"It's an empty. You can put him in there after the service. You get it, don't you? Wake's a scout, see, checking up on a new prospect. Have you ever heard of the Möbius strip?"

"Yes, I guess I have."

"It's sort of the same thing. It's like watching somebody on TV watching TV. It's a mind bender. I'm waiting for flowers so things don't look so bare. People will send flowers, won't they?"

"Oh, I'm sure they will." The pastor leaned forward, peering at the body. "What happened to his face? It looks so . . . red."

"That's his natural color. See, Wake was outside a lot, driving all over the place, and he got a lot of sun. So I made him a little rosy just like he had driven eight hours in the middle of summer to check out this prospect."

"Very . . . interesting." Pastor Lime scratched his head. "You do this all the time, you say?"

"It's the only way I know how."

Sighing, the pastor said, "Well, I talked to quite a few people up in Golbyville, and they were all delighted with what you did for their loved ones. It certainly is . . . *unusual.* I just need to figure out what I'm going to tell my congregation."

"It's art, Reverend. Tell them it's art."

*　　*　　*

Andy attended the memorial service held the next day, finding a perch in the choir balcony. There seemed to be some confusion among the people sitting in the back of the church, but those up front, those who knew Wake best, caught on right away, nodding and smiling to each other.

Afterward, Andy greeted Mollybellum on the steps outside the church, as the friends and relatives lined up their cars for the trip to the graveyard. "You have my sympathy," he told her, taking her hand.

"Thank you, Mr. Archway," she said. "Everyone has been remarking on how unique a setting it was for a memorial service. People said Wake looked just like they remembered him."

"I wanted to do it right, for Wake. And for you, ma'am."

"Are you coming out to the cemetery? Would you ride with me?"

"I'd like that."

The procession headed out of town a short distance to the cemetery. The mourners gathered around the grave site and Pastor Lime said a prayer while the casket was lowered into the ground. A cold wind blew through the temporary shelter that had been set up.

"Ashes to ashes, dust to dust," said the pastor.

Good-bye, my friend, Andy thought. I'm gonna miss you.

twenty-two

ANDY CLEANED UP his trailer and deposited the contents of the receptacles at the local dump site. He pulled the trailer to a vacant hill on the outskirts of town. As darkness fell, he flipped on the small lamp at his table. Spreading out a road map, he took a pen and marked his route.

He circled Flankville, then drew a line to Aimless, Kansas. From there to Saddleup, New Mexico. Mid-November, he figured. Then on to Adobe Springs, Arizona. December. He drew a long line across the border into the heart of Mexico, making a circle around Guadomilia. The new year, he thought.

Andy went outside. It had gotten colder, the wind shifting to the north. A few snowflakes fell from the bleak November sky.

From the modest hill where he stood, Andy could see the town lights illuminating the clouds overhead. He turned and looked into the darkness. Yard lights dotted the farmlands. Clumps of brightness in the distance signaled other small towns, the road ahead.

Andy knelt down, sliding his hands into the pockets of his sweatshirt.

I can see the whole world from up here, he thought.

about the author

David Prill grew up in Bloomington, Minnesota. He attended a variety of colleges in Minnesota and California before graduating from the University of Minnesota with a journalism degree. In 1991 he was named Best Columnist by the Minnesota Newspaper Association for a political humor column he wrote for the *Minnesota Daily*. He also spent a year working as an editor and writer on a weekly newspaper in St. James, Minnesota, covering events such as the Watonwan County Fair, Railroad Days, and the Lost City. He currently lives in the Minneapolis–St. Paul area.